THE HOWL

OF KISS AND CLAW

BOOK 1

MELISSA HAAG

ISBN 978-1-943051-75-5 (eBook Edition)

ISBN 978-1-943051-44-1 (Paperback Edition)

Editing by Ulva Eldridge

Cover design by Shattered Glass Publishing LLC

© Depositphotos.com

To the werewolf lovers in the world,
Thank you!

THE HOWL

Most parents want their kids to grow up to be something respectable like a doctor or a lawyer. My mom wants me to become a man-eating ho. I, Eliana Barchim, vow to never follow in my mother's footsteps.

Eliana's determination to never be the succubus her mother wants her to be starts faltering when her mother unexpectedly interferes. It doesn't help that a local shifter with a cute dimple is trying to help cheer Eliana up when her best and only friend leaves town. With her control slipping, Eliana resorts to something drastic to get rid of her mom.

However, Eliana's fear of ruining the one person she can trust to stand by her side might be the thing that brings her carefully composed control to its knees. Nothing can withstand a starving succubus's hunger.

CHAPTER ONE

Fighting tears, I drove away from my best friend's house.

Megan going to New York for a few weeks shouldn't have been grounds for a torrential sobfest. But, Megan wasn't just a friend. She was my only friend. The only person who never judged me because of what I was or my hunger.

Even as I thought of it, the need to feed rose sharp and heavy. Wiping away the tears tracking down my cheeks, I glanced in my rearview mirror and cringed at the sight of my blackening irises.

"You are not hungry, Eliana Magdalene Margarete Howland. You are not a Barchim."

Instead of making me feel better, using my mother's last name as a reminder of why I needed to fight my hunger only made me sadder. And that additional sorrow only made me hungrier, which turned my eyes completely black.

I switched on the radio to a deafening level and sang along with the music, glad the magical barrier that encircled Uttira and the surrounding countryside didn't keep the station out.

My hunger hadn't completely faded by the time I pulled into the oversized garage attached to the Quills' house. While I knew

I'd need to give in and feed eventually, I was determined to put it off for as long as possible.

If only Megan were still here. Her anger did nothing to nourish me, but at least it felt like feeding and tricked my body for a little while.

I smoothed a hand over my blonde hair and checked my eyes in the mirror to ensure they were once again a mellow brown. Not noting any redness from my recent tears, I got out of the car and grabbed the cooler I'd taken from Megan's house.

When I entered the kitchen, Mrs. Quill looked up from her cup of coffee. Her gaze swept over me before landing on the cooler in my arms. Despite my petite size, the jam-packed container didn't burden me. Extra physical strength was one of the few traits I didn't mind inheriting from my mom.

I set the cooler by the fridge and started unpacking the food.

"What's all that?" she asked.

"All the perishables from Megan's place since she will be gone a while."

"That was nice of you to help her. Did she and Oanen get off okay this morning?"

I wanted to groan at her wording when my mind went south. Why did I always have to think dirty thoughts? Why couldn't I just think normal thoughts like normal teens?

"Yes, they're on their way to New York."

"Do you think she'll ever forgive us?" Mrs. Quill asked.

I shrugged and stuck the lettuce in the crisper. It was an honest, noncommittal answer. After the bullcrap the Council had pulled, Megan had every right to hold a grudge. The Council needed to stop meddling in the lives of the youth stuck in Uttira.

"Are you hungry, Eliana?" Mrs. Quill asked, pulling me from my thoughts.

I realized I was just standing there and quickly reached for the bread.

"A sandwich does sound like it would hit the spot. Would you like me to make you one, too? There are plenty of options with what I brought over from Megan's."

"You know that's not what I meant. You can't survive on human food."

"Who said I'm trying to survive on it? I like the taste. Mom eats it all the time." Usually at high class restaurants paid for by her adoring harem of men, but I pushed that thought aside and focused on the food in front of me.

"Look at me, Eliana," Mrs. Quill said.

Don't be black...Don't be black, I chanted to myself as I lifted my gaze.

The woman who'd raised me for the last four years smiled at me kindly.

"You know you only need to ask, and I will gladly feed you."

It took everything I had not to vehemently shake my head.

"I know," I said. "Right now, all I want is a sandwich."

"Very well."

She didn't leave the room, but instead watched me closely as I made my early lunch. Likely, she wasn't fooled. She rarely was, which made my life that much more difficult.

"I think I'm going to eat this while I watch some TV," I said, picking up the plate.

"Enjoy, sweetie. I'll call you when dinner is ready."

I nodded and fled.

Upstairs, the room connecting my bedroom to Oanen's had everything we could possibly want for entertainment. From gaming consoles to high-quality screens, comfortable couches, and our own refrigerator, the room was meant to be a teen's oasis.

And it had been with Oanen here. Now that he was gone, it just seemed empty.

Oanen had been one of the best parts of my time in Uttira until Megan showed up months ago. He was the best almost brother I'd ever had.

Catching myself in a downward emotional spiral, I went to the snack fridge and grabbed a dark chocolate candy bar. The bitter tang of the chocolate distracted me from everything but the flavor I so loved. I didn't need to eat food, not like humans did, but chocolate was one thing I thoroughly enjoyed despite the pointlessness of eating it. Bake it. Freeze it. Melt it. It didn't matter what form the chocolate came in. There was something about it that helped keep my real hunger at bay, which was why I kept an impressive stockpile of it hidden in the snack refrigerator.

Content for the moment, I plopped on the couch and tucked the rest of the chocolate into my sandwich so Mrs. Quill wouldn't see it if she came in to check on me. She'd know right away what was going on if she saw the chocolate. And the last thing I wanted was to worry her, because if she was worried, then she would tell her sister, Adira. Not only was Adira a member of the Council, she was also Girderon Academy's Student Coordinator. If she got involved, I'd be wearing far too little to school tomorrow.

I took another bite of chocolate and turned on the TV to watch an action flick. The bloodier, the better, given my current mood.

An hour later, I was feeling a bit more in control and absently reached for my phone when it buzzed.

Fenris: First security sweep done. Megan's car is still here and unmaimed.

I rolled my eyes as I typed back a quick message.

Me: They just left. Of course her car is still fine.

Fenris had been inadvertently making my life impossible for

months now. It wasn't his fault he smelled like lust all the time, a scent no succubus could seem to ignore. His hormones were due to his wolf genes.

Instead of thinking of genetics, my mind went to his jeans. The dark pair that rode low on his hips and loose on his legs. Oh, the things they did to his backside...

My vision sharpened immediately, and I knew my eyes had gone black.

Using the remote, I turned on some really loud party music in an attempt to corral my thoughts. But, my phone vibrated in my hand to let me know Fenris had replied.

Fenris: It doesn't hurt to be cautious. How's your car?

My insides went hot then cold at the idea of Fenris coming here.

Me: My car is fine. Go home, Fenris.

I threw my phone onto the cushion next to me and got up to dance like I was in a dance-off for the next thirty minutes. By the time I stopped, I was tired and sweaty.

I hated that I wasn't a normal teen. Why did I always need to think about sex and being touched? About being liked by a boy? No, not liked, worshipped. I thought of how my father worshipped my mother, and every ounce of succubus hunger left me.

Calmer, I went to my room for a quick shower then stood inside my closet in indecision.

Adira had given me strict orders that I was to pick clothes from the right side of the closet. Reaching out, I trailed my fingers over one of the many dresses on that side. Low neckline, thigh-high slit, silky material, the dress was what a normal succubus would use to incite lust in those around her.

All of the clothes to the right were beautiful beyond a doubt, and I loved wearing them. But only in the privacy of my own room.

Never in public. A shudder ran through me at the thought of what would happen if I wore those dresses in public like Adira wanted.

Taking a deep breath, I tried to find a compromise. I understood that the adults in my life were worried that my instincts weren't developing appropriately. And their concern was the only reason I was even attempting to meet them halfway with my wardrobe. Well, their concern and my fear that they'd involve my mother if they got too worried.

After selecting a dress that Adira would approve of, I found a lacy bralette and a pair of knee-length biker shorts to wear underneath it. Then, I chose a cute pair of flats that didn't at all go with the gorgeous, shimmery number I'd picked. Spiked heels with thin straps would have set off the length of my legs the best, but setting off any body part was the last thing I wanted to do.

With my cleavage safely hidden by the bralette and the thigh slit thwarted by my shorts, I felt marginally ready for dinner.

Too bad I still had hours to kill.

I debated what to do with my time. I loved the greenhouse on the roof, but it would only make me miss Megan and Oanen more. And, I'd already spent enough time watching movies.

Leaving my room, I took the back stairs out to the gardens instead. The brisk winter wind robbed my arms of any heat the moment I stepped outside. I rubbed a hand over my skin and followed the snow-covered path to the bench in the center of the garden.

I stood there and looked out over the dormant grounds. It was beautiful in summer. Green and lush. Filled with singing birds and other small creatures that made noise. Now, it was silent. Silent and lonely.

Like I'd been before Megan.

Hugging myself, I thought of my life in Uttira and wondered

if I would ever be able to go back to the isolation I'd found so comforting before Megan's arrival. I doubted it.

While I knew her and Oanen's stay in New York was only meant to be for a few weeks, I also knew Megan well enough to understand she'd never be happy spending all of her time in Uttira. Especially given her history with the Council and Adira.

That meant I either needed to make more friends or figure out a way to leave Uttira and join Megan. I wrinkled my nose at the latter. There was only one way out, and I was nowhere near getting my mark of Mantirum. Yet, making friends seemed just as impossible as earning my mark.

Deciding to delay worrying over friendships, I went back inside to wait for dinner in the entertainment room. With a small stash of dark chocolate truffles in my lap, I lost myself to three hours of visual carnage before the faint chime of the doorbell disturbed my peace.

I frowned at the time and stood to check myself in the mirror. Hopefully Adira would find my compromise suitable and leave the left side of my closet alone.

The low murmur of voices reached my ears as soon as I arrived at the top of the steps. None of them sounded like Adira, who usually joined us for dinner. Curious, I descended and went to the dining room.

Mrs. Quill was greeting our dinner guest with a gracious welcome when I entered, and the familiar back of a black head of hair slowed my steps.

"Thank you so much for inviting me, Mrs. Quill. Your house is beautiful," Eugene said.

Mrs. Quill opened her mouth to reply, but I interrupted her.

"Why is he here?" I asked.

The sick feeling in my stomach grew as Eugene turned to look at me with a smile. As the newest human in Uttira, he didn't know to be wary.

"Hey, Eliana."

Ignoring him, I continued to stare at Mrs. Quill.

"He's here because I invited him. With Megan and Oanen gone, I thought you might like company your own age at dinner."

We both knew that wasn't what this was. Her next words proved it.

"I'll let you two talk while I let Mr. Quill know dinner is ready."

Instead of getting angry, another dangerous emotion for me, I looked at Eugene as she left the room.

"I'm sorry if I sounded rude. Very little is as it seems in Uttira."

"Even here?"

"Especially here."

He nodded thoughtfully and seemed to notice my dress for the first time. I hated the look of appreciation that crept into his gaze until his hand smoothed down his own shirt.

"I'm feeling really underdressed right now."

The button-up shirt was neatly pressed and complemented the dark jeans he wore. I knew these clothes were a vast improvement over what he'd been wearing when he'd arrived in Uttira. After all, I'd helped select his wardrobe.

"What you're wearing is completely suitable for a family dinner. My dress is a prop I'm required to wear for dinner."

"Required? If I were a girl, I'd want to wear that all the time. You look killer in it."

His simple words, meant to be high praise, hurt deeply.

"I'd much rather just be me than a killer anything," I said.

Some of the humor left his gaze.

"Right. Sorry. I forgot for a minute."

"Then I guess it's a good thing you're here. I'll keep reminding you. Nothing is safe here, Eugene. We may look human, but we're not. That's something you have to remind yourself of constantly."

He looked around the room uncomfortably.

"I can't believe you grew up here."

"I didn't. The Quills took me in when I was twelve."

"They aren't your parents?"

"No. My mother is currently living in New York, and my human father is in Arkansas, far away from this place."

He watched me for a moment, probably thinking I was going to continue with an explanation of why I wasn't living with my parents. However, since I knew why Mrs. Quill had invited him tonight, even if he didn't, I didn't want to encourage any kind of bonding between us.

"I get that you're all scary monsters who want to feed on humans in some way," he said when I remained quiet. "But that doesn't scare me nearly as much as ending up back on the streets does." His gaze went to the crystal wine glasses and actual gold utensils placed on the table. "This place looks so..."

"Ostentatious?"

"I don't even know what that word means, but sure."

"It means flashy and over-the-top."

"Yep. Ostentatious. You're lucky people with money took you in."

Mr. and Mrs. Quill took that moment to enter.

"I believe Eliana called it a perverse way to flaunt one's money when she first came to live with us," Mr. Quill said.

"There was a lead up to that statement," I said with a rueful smile. "And I've since realized the error in my thinking."

Mrs. Quill chuckled and gestured to the table.

"Dinner is ready. Eugene, you may take the seat beside

Eliana," she said, not even glancing at the empty setting across from us. That could only mean that Adira meant to join us.

As soon as we were seated, Mrs. Quill started serving, using her magic to move whatever she'd cooked in the kitchen to our plates. Eugene was suitably impressed and asked questions until he took his first bite of her beef wellington, a favorite dish of Mr. Quill's.

"I've died and gone to Heaven," Eugene said.

"I hear Valhalla is the place you want to go for riches and endless feasting," Adira said, suddenly appearing in her seat. "How are you enjoying Uttira so far, Eugene?"

He set down the fork which had frozen halfway to his mouth at her abrupt appearance.

"It's great. Thank you for bringing me here."

"Of course. How do you like attending Girderon Academy?"

"I love it."

"Are you certain? It's never too late to go back to your old life."

"It is for me," he said. "There's nothing for me to go back to."

Something about her line of questioning and the way she was studying him made me suspicious.

"Good," she said. "Then I think it's time for you to take Eliana for a walk. She's hungry."

My mouth dropped open as did Eugene's. He looked from me to Adira and back again.

"I thought the goal was to not be eaten by anyone here," he said.

"Correct. However, Eliana won't consume you physically. She's not that type of creature. She consumes energy, but not enough to harm you."

"Oh."

I could feel his eyes on me again, but I didn't look away from Adira.

"No," I said firmly.

"Yes," Adira said. "You're hungry and need to feed. Your continued denial of your nature will not change who you are or what you need to do."

I fought against the panic worming its way under my skin.

"You can't force me to feed."

"Can't I? You will feed on Eugene, or he goes back to the human world tonight."

Eugene swore under his breath and fully turned toward me.

"Hey, I really don't mind, Eliana. Just do what you got to do. As long as it won't kill me, I'm fine with it."

His naivety reminded me of Megan. Instead of giving in to panic, I set my napkin on the table and smiled at Adira. Her normally bland expression flickered with a hint of surprise.

"Do you think I'm joking?" she asked.

"No. I think you're entirely serious. But, I also think you're forgetting something very important. Megan warned you what would happen if you continued to mistreat the humans in Uttira. And I promise you that if you return Eugene to the human world as a means to coerce me, Megan will turn the full wrath of her fury on you. Choose your blackmail wisely, Adira, because Megan still hasn't forgotten how all of you manipulated her."

Mrs. Quill paled at the reminder, and I felt a fair amount of guilt for it. However, I refused to back down.

"So be it," Adira said. "Remember you made this choice, Eliana. I am not giving up on you."

With those ominous words, she disappeared. I had no doubt Adira would attempt to make me regret my choice not to feed from Eugene. Even after all these years, she still didn't understand my aversion to feeding. Yet, I would never regret my choice tonight.

"Mrs. Quill, will you please wrap Eugene's dinner so he can enjoy it at home?"

"Of course."

With a wave of her hand, his food left his plate and a white paper bag containing his dinner appeared. I grabbed the bag and stood.

"I'll follow Eugene home. Don't wait up for me."

Eugene stood quickly and followed me out of the room. Neither of us spoke as we left the house and walked toward the car in the driveway.

"You don't need to follow me home," Eugene said. "I'll be fine."

I wrinkled my nose at him.

"They almost fed you to me, and you were willing. You're not fine, Eugene. You're in over your head. Get in the car, and lock your door. The car's warded and will keep you safe unless something tricks you into getting out of it. I'll follow you home to make sure that doesn't happen. And next time, be sure to decline any dinner invitations that will keep you out after dark."

"Okay." He started to get in then hesitated. "I really hope you're going to explain what just happened in there."

"I will, but not tonight. Tomorrow, okay? I'm freezing." I really was cold, but mostly I just didn't want to talk about how I'd likely just made my situation worse in some new and unimaginable way.

As soon as he locked his car door, I picked up my skirt and jogged to my car, grateful I'd gone with the flats. The ride to Eugene's house was uneventful, and I waited in his driveway until he waved to me from his kitchen window.

With Uttira's newest human relatively safe, I turned my car around and drove back home. Despite my comment to the Quills about not waiting up, there wasn't anywhere else in town for me to go. Hanging out with Eugene was definitely not an option. As much as I would like to think he would be safe with me, I couldn't trust myself when I was this hungry. I wasn't willing to risk him just to avoid Adira and the Quills.

However, I cringed at the thought of facing Mrs. Quill so soon after reminding her and Mr. Quill that the mate of their only son probably never wanted to see them again. It'd been a poopy move on my part, but Adira had left me little choice. I would not feed on humans. Ever. If I had a choice, I wouldn't even feed on Mrs. Quill.

Hating my line of thinking, I turned on the radio and sang along to some music. By the time I pulled up to the garage, it was only half past six, and every light was still on in the house. I debated what to do as I turned off the engine. There really wasn't much of a choice; I'd need to sneak into the house.

In the quiet, the snow crunched loudly under my flats as I walked around to the back gardens. The long line of privacy hedges posed a slight problem as I wedged my way through their barren branches. But every scrape I received was worth it to avoid the disappointment I was sure I'd see in Mrs. Quill's eyes if I walked in through the front door.

Picking twigs from my hair, I scanned the darkness for the path to the house. I could just walk forward until the security lights turned on, but I knew there were rose bushes somewhere close by. I didn't want to damage my dress any more than I already had.

A low growl rumbled from the other side of the hedgerow. I slowly turned.

My mom told me over and over that all the monsters in Uttira had nothing over a succubus. But, she was biased, and I'd seen enough during my four years here to make my hair white.

Whatever was on the other side of that bush sounded as mean as heck.

"Go find someone else to bother," I said bravely while retreating a step.

There was a rustling then –

"Eliana?"

"Fenris? What are you doing here? I told you my car is fine. Go home."

I took another step back and started breathing through my mouth, hoping it would be enough to save me.

"I'm not here because of the car. Why do I smell your blood?"

The branches started to crackle, and I realized Fenris was probably very naked on the other side of the hedge since clothes didn't shift. In my panic at the thought of him pushing his way through to me, I inhaled through my nose.

The scent of his lust hit me hard, and my vision sharpened on his hand as he reached through the hedge. My gaze locked on his strong fingers, and I shivered. I could feel them on my skin. One thought, one command, and he would be mine.

I whirled and ran for the house.

Fenris called my name, and just as the door slammed shut behind me, a howl rose.

CHAPTER TWO

Setting my head against the door, I took a deep, calming breath. The distance I'd put between Fenris and me did nothing to alleviate the hunger that started in my middle and radiated right into my bones. The hunger didn't care that I liked Fenris as a person. My hunger didn't discriminate. It didn't think of the consequences. It only wanted to be fed. Anyone would do.

The sudden pounding from the other side of the door made me jump.

"Eliana?" Fenris called. "I need to know you're okay."

There was honest concern in his voice, and I felt terrible for causing it. Of course he had been worried that he'd smelled blood. Any nice person would be.

"I'm fine," I said, my mouth close to the wood panel. "Go home."

There was a thump on the door, followed by the muffled sound of his voice, but I couldn't make out what he was saying.

"It works better if you open the door," Mrs. Quill said from behind me.

I startled for the second time but didn't turn to face her. How had sneaking into the house gone so wrong?

"I'm sorry I disturbed you, Mrs. Quill," I said. "Everything's fine here."

There was a moment of silence before she spoke.

"Eliana, turn around."

I wrinkled my nose and turned to face her. Her sad gaze locked with mine.

"Sweetie, it breaks my heart to see you like this."

I smiled and glanced down at my arms, purposely misunderstanding her.

"The scrapes aren't that deep," I said. "I promise I'm fine. Fenris is fine, too. He just smelled my blood and was worried. I should really clean this up. I'll see you in the morning."

I fled before she could stop me.

Back in my room, I avoided my reflection and stripped from the dress to take care of all the scrapes. If I were well-fed, they probably would have healed already. But I wasn't. So I dabbed the cuts and tried not to pay attention to my heightened eyesight. It wasn't easy when every pore and fine line in my skin stood out so vividly.

Thankfully, Mrs. Quill didn't come to my room to press me further, and I changed into my pajamas in peace. I was grateful for the home she and Mr. Quill opened to me, but I didn't need another well-intentioned lecture on feeding myself. I needed understanding. I needed Megan.

Glancing at the clock, I debated. She'd only left this morning, and I didn't want to be the needy type of friend who would bug her hours after leaving. Talking to her could wait until tomorrow.

Knowing it would be a long time before I fell asleep, I cautiously opened the door to the entertainment room and went to the refrigerator.

With a bowl of double-chocolate brownie chunk ice cream in my lap, I did my best to drown my sorrows and soothe my hunger. However, the horribly unrealistic vampire movies filled with the blood and action that I usually loved did nothing to distract me, and my hunger continued to plague me.

By midnight, I had a stomach ache from too much ice cream and a heavy heart. Setting the empty container aside, I reached for my phone and dialed Megan. She picked up after a few rings.

"You officially broke your promise," I said. "It's after midnight. You said you would check in daily, and I didn't get a call yesterday."

"The day I left doesn't count," she said with a laugh in her voice.

"Sure, start bending the rules already. So, what's it like having freedom?"

I heard a rustle on the other end of the phone.

"Knock it off," she said, slightly muffled.

"Do I even want to know what Oanen's doing?" I asked.

"Not Oanen. A brownie named Piepen is messing around with some guy's eye."

I sat up.

"A brownie?"

"Yeah, long story."

"I've got time."

"I let him out of a cage, and now he's following me."

In the background, I heard a high-pitched voice claim he wasn't following her but helping her. Then a lower voice argued about who got to take care of Megan's house. I started to snicker.

Less than twenty-four hours out of Uttira and Megan already had creatures fighting over her.

"Two of them?" I asked. "What are you going to do with two?"

"One's a brownie, and one's a goblin. And I have no idea."

"They're not going to like the hotel or the car. They're much happier in real homes," I said.

"She sounds nice," the high-pitched voice said. "I like her."

"Aw! Isn't he sweet," I said.

"Stop," Megan said. "He can hear you, and I think you're going to give him a heart attack. What's wrong with hotels?"

I listened to the outrage from the goblin and grinned wider.

"Tell them to come to Uttira. You'll be happier, and so will they. I'll feed them both for you," I offered, liking the idea of having something to do outside of schoolwork and boredom.

"Are you sure?" she asked.

"Yep. It'll be fine. Tell the goblin I'll have a bowl of honey-soaked oats waiting for him at your house," I said.

She gave them directions, and I listened to her tell the goblin that he needed to protect the brownie and not eat his wings. I cringed at that. Brownie wings were a delicacy I would never understand.

"It sounds like you've had an eventful first day," I said.

"You have no idea. I just woke up in an abandoned warehouse after eating a janky burger at a questionable bar. And the goblin I just sent your way knows who did it, but he's bound by a spell that won't let him speak. Like the library. However, according to the brownie, the goblin will be able to talk in a few days because I'm his new master."

I thought of the secrecy spell that bound the people who read anything in the library they were referencing. But, all spells had limits and loopholes, especially the secrecy one.

"I'll call you if he says anything about who his previous master was," I said.

"Thank you. And watch yourself around them. Oanen said they wouldn't hurt me, but Elbner, the goblin, seems sketchy."

"Did he make you mad?" I asked, knowing her fury sense was on point for spotting wickedness.

"Surprisingly, no."

"Then I'm sure he'll be fine."

In the background, an eagle's cry split the air.

"I better go," Megan said. "Oanen's coming, and I need to check on the guy Elbner knocked out."

"What guy?"

"I'll tell you later."

The line went dead, and I tossed my phone aside. While Megan was obviously dealing with her own issues, I couldn't help but feel disappointed that she hadn't asked how I was doing. But, what would I have really said? That I was doing awful because she'd left and I had no one to talk to about how hungry I was? That it felt like the hunger was eating me from the inside?

Sighing, I turned toward the balcony windows and blindly stared out at the darkness.

No, there was no need to involve Megan in my misery when there wasn't anything she could do about it.

I STIFLED a yawn and studied my makeup. Although I'd kept it natural, the cosmetics still enhanced my features far more than I was comfortable. Makeup always attracted attention I didn't want. Yet, it was a necessary evil. Especially today. It helped hide the dark circles under my eyes so I didn't look as tired as I felt.

As I stared at myself, my eyes flooded with black then back to brown again. I wrinkled my nose and turned away from my reflection. Why couldn't my body just cooperate with my brain? I didn't want to feed. Ever. End of story. My hunger needed to get on board with my life plan of normalcy.

Hoping to distract my body, I went downstairs for some real food. However, instead of finding a deliciously toasted bagel waiting for me, I found Adira.

I paused at the sight of both her and Mrs. Quill sitting at the dining room table. They wore twin, serious expressions that I knew had nothing to do with them being siblings.

Oanen had called me after Megan, last night, and explained that their investigation into the dying trolls was dangerous to Megan. She wasn't acting like her normal, angry self, and he needed me to get the goblin to talk as soon as he got here.

I'd never asked if he'd told the Council, but based on the solemn expressions of the two women before me, I was guessing he had. Adira's next words confirmed it.

"We'd like to discuss what happened last night," she said.

"Did Megan get drugged again?" I asked, hurrying to sit.

"Again?" Mrs. Quill asked. "When was Megan drugged?"

"Last night." With a sinking feeling, I looked from her to Adira.

"We were unaware of that," Adira said. "But I will be sure to contact Oanen for the details. For now, I'd like to discuss why you entered this house with visible signs of hunger you refused to acknowledge when Anwen confronted you."

Annoyed, I fisted my hands under the table.

"Mrs. Quill didn't confront me. She asked me to turn around; then she showed concern. I hear that's a typical reaction when you care about someone who's been hurt. And, I was when pushing my way through the bushes. As for my eyes, you know as well as I do that a succubus's eyes change for more than hunger. Fenris wasn't leaving, and I'm a teenager prone to mood swings. For as old as you are, none of this is new to you."

Adira said nothing for a moment as she studied me, and I fought not to fidget under her scrutiny.

Since coming to Uttira, I'd followed the rules and done what I'd been told. Until Megan came. She'd changed things, not just for me but for the other creatures in Uttira. Now, Adira's feelings about those changes were plain to see in the slight crease between her brows.

"Megan's influence continues to spread," she said finally.

"A good thing, I should think," I said. "No one wants a meek succubus running around. It's not part of our inherent nature."

Adira gave me a slight nod.

"Very true. Your mother will be happy to hear you're standing up for yourself."

I almost cringed at the mention of my mom.

"To help you embrace this burgeoning boldness, I've updated the left side of your closet. Please go upstairs and change before you leave for the Academy. I'll check in on you later today."

She disappeared abruptly.

"I'll fix you something to eat," Mrs. Quill said gently before leaving as well.

Alone, I leaned forward and let my forehead thump to the table.

Today was going to be a new level of hell, thanks to my big mouth. I didn't have the pebbles that Megan had to stand up to Adira. Why had I even tried?

The phone in the pocket of my skirt chirped, and I pulled it out to see a text from Fenris.

The car's still fine. Not Megan's house, though. Still looks like it should be burned to the ground.

I rolled my eyes and pocketed my phone again. Megan's family home was the complete opposite of the Quills'. In the wrong light, it looked two seasons away from condemnation. In the right light, it didn't look much better. It wasn't nice for Fenris to say so, though.

Knowing there was no point in putting it off, I went back to my room and looked at my closet. Gone were the cute, knee-length dresses I favored. In their place were tops and jeans. I closed my eyes before looking again, confused at the extremely non-sexy clothing options.

Grateful it wasn't filled with a bunch of barely-there dresses, like the right side, I grabbed a pair of jeans with a white blouse and went to change. I realized the mistake in my thinking as soon as I tugged the jeans up. They were clingy. Every slight curve I had was on display. The top, while flowy, was see-through. I went to grab a cami to layer under it but found the drawer filled with lacy bralettes. Adira had left me nothing to use as layers for modesty.

After searching the closet for several minutes, my only solution was a bralette under two shirts. Doubling the material made it mostly opaque. Satisfied, I went for my shoes and groaned at the options. All I now owned were hooker heels.

I seethed for a moment then strapped a red pair on. A glance in the mirror told me I looked amazing. Hot as heck, even.

"Worst day ever," I said to myself before grabbing my jacket and heading downstairs.

A chocolate chip bagel with chocolate hazelnut spread waited for me in the dining room. I devoured it, grateful to Mrs. Quill, then hurried out the door before she could see my two shirts. If I got to school quickly enough, maybe I could avoid being spotted by the majority of my peers, too.

While hiding in the first session's classroom would help my morning, I knew I'd need to leave it eventually. I hated that I'd be seen like this. Well, hate was a strong word. I loved the clothes; I just didn't love what would happen when I wore them around other people.

My phone chirped again.

I looked at the new message from Fenris.

We should repaint for Megan. You in?

And spend days with Fenris in the process? The answer was easy.

No. She likes her house the way it is.

Checking my mirror, I backed out of the garage while ignoring my once again black eyes. I didn't make it far before I knew I had to pull over to remove my shoes. Wriggling my toes and using my blinker, I shook my head at what my mom's reaction would be if she ever found out I couldn't drive in heels. Hooker heels were a succubus's standard accessory. They made a person's backside look amazing. And, that was exactly why I avoided wearing them.

I pulled through the Girderon Academy gates ten minutes ahead of my usual time and found the parking lot still fairly empty. Relieved, I hurried to park then opened my door so I had more room to put my heels back on.

The glossy red toe stood out starkly against the snow. Adira was insane for making me go to school in these. My feet would freeze just getting into the building because no one had shoveled the parking lot yet.

"Those are new."

The nearby, abrupt words made me jump.

"Sweet baby Jesus in a strawless manger, Fenris, you scared me," I said, scowling up at him. "You need a bell."

He wore his usual crooked smile that made all the girls go crazy. When he added a chuckle to it, my stomach dipped and heat flooded my middle. I knew he was in danger before my vision even sharpened.

I looked away quickly and shoved the strap of my heel through the clasp before standing.

"I better get inside." I moved to step past him, but he

shadowed me. Despite the heels, he was still a good four inches taller than me, bringing my nose to his throat.

Another car pulled into the parking lot, and Fenris's name was called by three different she-wolves. Having grown up together in his pack, they knew him well and were always clinging to him, each hoping to be the one whose scent he caught when he succumbed to his mate run. Megan referred to them as his her-herd. I knew she thought their devotion to him was pathetic, but I pitied them. And him. They were all slaves to their instincts.

He waved at them but didn't move away from me. Gaze locked on his shirt, I waited.

His scent, always so flooded with lust, changed subtly. He had to be getting close to his mate run. The way he smelled now was positively mouthwatering.

I started mouth breathing in an attempt to calm down, but I knew it was already too late for that.

"Seriously, Fenris, I need to go."

"I know. You always seem to be rushing somewhere, which is why I came over here. I wanted to make sure you were okay after last night. I didn't like smelling all that blood."

I almost snorted. He made it sound like I'd been bleeding out.

"I had a few scratches. It probably smelled like more to you than it was. Sensitive nose and all. Can I go now?"

In the silence that followed, I was tempted to peek up at him to see why he wasn't answering. But if I did that, he'd see my eyes and know what was happening to me. And I really didn't want him to know. It would be beyond embarrassing for the most alpha wolf in this school to think I was hungry for him. Heck, it would be embarrassing for any of the students to think I was hungry for them.

"Fenris?" I asked, growing a little panicked and desperate.

I heard him breathe in deeply and wanted to cringe. Great, now he probably knew he was making me nervous, too. Stupid werewolf nose.

"I really wanted to talk to Lucas before class," I added.

"Yeah. Sure. I'll see you at lunch."

He stepped aside, and I made a beeline for the door, not even slipping once. While I knew I had insane skills when it came to heels, I didn't want other people to know. So, I slowed to a power walk once I was inside and headed to Human Studies.

Lucas Flavian, the teacher, looked up from his papers.

"Good morning, Eliana. You're early today."

"Yep." I settled into my desk with a sigh.

"Anything wrong?"

"I'm just absorbing the peace until chaos descends," I said.

He smiled and nodded.

"It does get a little crazy in here at times. If you ever need to step out, you know you can."

I nodded and turned my gaze to the clock.

"Hey, Eliana," Eugene said, sliding into the desk beside mine a few minutes later.

"Since when do you need to take Human Studies?" I asked with a frown.

"Since this morning. Adira said she'd be changing up my schedule so that I can get to know the students and faculty before settling me into a human schedule."

"Ah." I doubted very much that Adira was changing his schedule for his benefit. After rejecting the opportunity to feed from him last night then coming home hungry afterward, Eugene was likely here to tempt me.

"Would you happen to have Self-paced Science and Algebra after this?" I asked.

"Nope. I aced out of both of those. I'm in Self-Discovery next. Sounds fun, right?"

I sighed and leaned toward him as more students entered the room.

"No, Eugene. Nothing here is fun. It's dangerous."

"Adira said that while I'm on school grounds, nothing can kill me."

"She's right about that, but there are things worse than death, Eugene. Don't forget that."

He paled a little and nodded as Belemina, two desks up, laughed and flashed her fangs back at us.

"Worse than death? Don't be dramatic, Eliana. Your little human would exist in a constant state of bliss with some of us."

"And without any thoughts of his own. A slave to compulsions he wouldn't be able to fight."

"He wouldn't want to fight them." Her gaze shifted to Eugene. "I'll give you a taste if you want."

"Uh...no, thanks," Eugene said, looking right at her.

I pinched his arm.

"Ow!" He scowled at me. "I thought you were the nice one."

"First rule to ensuring you're not being compelled is to avoid eye-contact," I reminded him. "You need to spend more time with Ashlyn."

"We're hanging out after school."

"Can I come?" Belemina asked.

I frowned at her.

"No."

She pouted and turned toward Lucas as he closed the door.

For the remainder of class, Eugene called attention to himself by asking every question imaginable. He'd insulted or annoyed at least half the class by the time the bell rang.

"I better walk you to your next class," I said, standing.

As soon as I did, his gaze swept down my length.

"Wow. You look really nice today."

While I knew he meant his words as a sincere compliment, my hunger took them as an invitation. My vision sharpened, and I quickly looked at the floor while trying my best not to notice how amazing Eugene smelled.

"It's safer if you don't compliment anyone here. And by here, I mean the Academy and Uttira. We all have different natural lures to pull humans in. Appearances, our voices, scents...you name it, and one of us can probably do it."

"Sorry. I didn't mean anything by it."

"I know. How about you lead the way to your class, and I'll follow you. Remember, eyes on the floor."

"How am I going to know where I'm going?"

"Just do your best. If you're late to class, the teachers won't yell at you. They won't look for you either. So try not to be late."

"You're making me nervous."

"Don't be nervous. That's a smell too many people here will like. Be cautious. It'll keep you alive."

I didn't look up until he turned toward the door. When I did, my gaze caught on how his jeans clung to his backside. The hunger gripped me harder, and for a fraction of a second, I hesitated to follow him. But, there were too many like Belemina in the hallway to let him go alone.

Hurrying to catch up, I started for the door and noticed Lucas watching me. He nodded at me but said nothing. He didn't need to. I knew he'd witnessed the change in my eyes, and Adira would know about all of this before the day was done.

Stupid hunger.

Out in the hallway, I kept my head down and trailed Eugene. The catcalls grated at me as did the comments. But, at least I was keeping most of the other students from focusing on Eugene.

I glanced up at the room numbers to see if we were getting close.

"Looks like someone put on her big-girl pants," Eras said from nearby.

I blushed and refused to acknowledge the incubus who'd caused Megan so much trouble.

"She doesn't just have her hot pants on," another incubus said. "She's got her feed on. That human doesn't stand a chance. My eyes have never gotten that black. Have yours?"

Heat and panic flooded me. My eyes weren't normal? Adira had told me that all succubi and incubi's eyes turn black. Had she lied to me?

I quickly averted my gaze again and nudged Eugene to walk faster.

As soon as he was safely in his class, I hurried to the nearest restroom, needing a mirror. Staring at myself, I looked at the black voids that were my eyes. It wasn't just the irises; it was the whites, too. They'd done this since the moment I hit puberty, though. How else were they supposed to look? I thought back to all of my peers who were like me and realized I'd never once witnessed another succubus's or incubus's eyes change. Was this not normal? What was wrong with me? Why was I the only one getting hit right between the eyes with the horny hunger stick?

"You're pretty today, little bit."

For a change, I didn't startle at the unexpected sound of someone else's voice. It might have been because of the smooth, low rumble in Emory's tone. More likely, it was because I knew the gentle giant who'd once almost face flicked Megan.

Smiling at the memory, I watched some of the black fade and looked up at Emory.

"Thank you," I said before realizing the wrongness of our conversation.

I looked around the bathroom and spotted all the urinals of varying height.

"Mother Mary's biscuits," I muttered.

Turning for the door, I face-planted into a spectacularly muscled chest that smelled like Grandma's spice cake. My mouth watered, and I breathed in deeper without thinking.

"It's best to avoid the blue biscuits if you're hungry, right, Emory?" Fenris said, his hands steadying me.

I jerked back from his chest and stared up at him with wide-eyed shock. Of all the people I would run into, why him?

He smiled down at me.

"Not that I'm complaining about bumping into you, but what's a girl like you doing in a place like this?"

CHAPTER THREE

No matter how hard I tried, I couldn't focus on human biology. My mind kept going back to werewolf biology and how good Fenris had smelled. Spice cake wasn't right. His scent was so much more. A combination of every human food I'd ever loved times ten. And, that heady aroma had only grown more potent as I'd stood there frozen in his arms. Even now, I could catch hints of his scent in my hair, which was pressed to my nose in an effort to inhale every last bit of him.

I dropped my hair and struggled to read the words on my tablet. With only a handful of lessons left in my independent studies, I should have been racing to finish so I could use the second session as a free period. Yet, there I was sniffing my hair like a new succubus. Idiot.

Shifting in my seat, I looked around the room to see if anyone had noticed my momentary slip. It was unlikely, given that there were only a handful of students present. Most of our kind didn't go far into human education since they had no desire to go to college. Some of us, usually those who'd grown up in the real world, still clung to the idea that college was a good thing. I wasn't so sure anymore because I feared what I might turn into in a college setting.

Ashlyn, a human who'd been in Uttira her whole life, glanced up from her book and caught me looking around. Her role as tutor was still fairly new, but I'd hung out with her a few times before she'd decided to come to school. While I considered her a friend, we definitely weren't as close as Megan and I were. It was hard to let myself get too close to someone my biology wanted me to use as a food source.

"Having trouble?" Ashlyn asked.

"Not with the material," I said.

Someone in the room snickered, but I couldn't be sure who.

Sympathy filled Ashlyn's gaze.

"You should hang out with us at lunch," she said. "We can talk more then."

Having lost my usual lunch companions, Oanen and Megan, yesterday, I was grateful for the offer until someone said, "Hell, yeah. Succubus snacktime."

Dropping my gaze before my hunger could react, I focused on my tablet for the rest of the session. When I would have escaped at the bell, Ashlyn caught my arm.

"Seriously, Eliana. Don't eat alone. I know what that kind of seclusion can do. Join us. You don't have to talk or even eat. Just don't be alone."

Ashlyn, more than anyone else, understood true loneliness. The concern in her eyes had me nodding even as I questioned the wisdom of hanging out with the humans on a day when I was so hungry.

She smiled at my agreement and dropped her hand.

"Meet us by the pool after the bell."

"The pool? Are you sure that's smart?"

"Yeah. It's good practice for the new humans. We'll be there to keep an eye on them."

I knew she was only trying to help the other humans who'd arrived at Uttira a short time ago, but I hated the idea of placing them so close to something so dangerous.

Ashlyn caught my hesitancy.

"It'll be fine, Eliana. I've invited a few other people I think we can trust to help keep an eye on them. And remember, no one can die in school."

I kept my mouth shut and nodded. Why did everyone think the worst thing to happen to them would be death?

With a heavy heart, I left the self-study room and went to my next session. Self-discovery was as woo-woo as it seemed. Instead of providing us with real information about what we were and why we had the instincts we had and how to curb them, we were taught how to "look inside" and to "embrace our differences" and a bunch of other nonsense that made me want to run screaming from the room.

The next class was marginally better, but only because I had to endure it every other day instead of every day. At best, General Living Studies was a mind-numbing experience since I'd grown up in the human world. However, it was required curriculum. So, for the next hour, I listened to a troll complain about the limitations on food diversity—he wanted human bone dust on his pizza—and a mermaid ask if eating human toes would be okay if the human lived.

My stomach was squeamish by the time the bell rang, and my doubts about having lunch near the pool had grown. Still, I grabbed my lunch and made my way toward the indoor pool.

The sirens' songs teased my ears as I drew closer. The melody wasn't bad. It just didn't do anything for me, not like it would for the humans. While I knew I was immune, I also knew that not all creatures were. Though I wasn't positive, I was pretty sure their songs had gotten to Oanen and Megan once. I hoped Ashlyn had selected her help wisely.

Through the windows to the pool room, I watched the mermaids and sirens swim and dive in the myriad of connecting pools. There were freshwater swimming areas, waterfall features, pretend boats, and rocky outcroppings for preening. Several of the females were topless.

If Eugene thought my jeans and heels looked good, he wouldn't stand a chance in there.

I opened the door and breathed in the scent of the minerals in the water. It was the only redeeming quality for the enormous space. With the irony scent clogging my nose, I didn't smell much else.

"Over here," Ashlyn called. She had moved a table near the edge of one of the pools. Eugene, Kelsey, and Zoe were already sitting and unpacking their food.

Eugene gave me a quick smile and made room for me while Ashlyn explained the risks of the pool.

"The most dangerous types of creatures you will encounter near the water are mermaids and sirens. However, there are many, many more that might also pose a threat. Be sure you read the books I've recommended to become familiar with all of them and their lures. For now, we'll focus on resisting siren song and mermaid trickery."

"Trickery?" a mermaid said, giggling near the edge of the pool. "You're making me blush, Ashlyn. Come here and give me a hug."

A siren rose from the water beside her and started singing.

Ashlyn poked her ear and looked at me. It wasn't until then that I noticed they all wore earbuds and had their phones out.

"We're on a group call and have earbuds that reduce background noise. Reduces, not mutes. Keep an eye on us."

I nodded and started unpacking my lunch. My stomach rumbled when I pulled out the sandwich, but I knew the food I'd packed wouldn't touch my real hunger. Despite the mineral smell, the faint scent of lust tickled my nose. I glanced at Eugene and found him staring at a pair of mermaid boobs.

Elbowing his side to get his attention, I shook my head.

"They use their bodies as lures," I said loudly. "Then they'll talk to you, either nicely or tauntingly, to try to get you close enough to the water's edge where they can grab you and pull you under."

"Hear that, Stacey?" one mermaid said. "The succubus is saying we use our bodies to lure men when she's sitting there in her painted-on jeans and hooker heels. Kettle-pot, much?"

Laughter rose from the water.

I flushed but didn't acknowledge her words.

"The key is ignoring them," I said to Eugene.

His gaze kept flicking to my mouth. My brain knew he was trying to understand what I was saying...that he was probably subconsciously reading my lips, but my hunger went another direction. It whispered that he wanted me. That he would kiss me and his lust would satisfy my hunger. His touch would soothe my aches and fill me. He would be mine. All I needed to do was—

"Sorry I'm late," Fenris said, sitting at the table across from me.

I jerked back, realizing I'd been leaning toward Eugene, who was staring at me wide-eyed.

"Sorry," I mumbled before dropping my gaze to my sandwich. With startling clarity, I could see each tiny air pocket in the bread.

Embarrassment consumed me, flushing my face and spreading heat right to my toes. I hadn't even noticed the change happen. I'd just turned into a monster right in front of my friends.

Locked in self-loathing, I didn't hear what was being said until someone kicked me under the table.

"You okay?" Ashlyn asked.

"Yep. Fine," I said without looking up. I took a quick bite of my sandwich so I wouldn't need to say anything else.

Beside me, Eugene shifted in his seat and bumped against me. I kept my eyes on my sandwich.

"Your real eyes are pretty cool," he said, leaning toward my ear. "You didn't scare me. I trust you."

His words were meant as a comfort. Instead, his exhale was tickling my neck and making my hunger worse. That and Fenris's constant aroma of spiced cake lust were enough to drive any sane succubus crazy.

"Let's focus on the mermaids," Ashlyn said, saving me.

"Yes! Focus on us," one of the girls in the water called. "Eliana's skin and bones. I have curves that will fill your hand. Take a peek."

I rolled my eyes, tired of the constant judgment regarding my weight, and took another bite of my sandwich.

Eugene shifted beside me again as Ashlyn continued her lesson.

"Like Eliana said, the best way to deal with mermaids is ignoring them and keeping your distance when they're in the water. They use their natural environment to confuse and subdue their prey."

"Prey? That's such a harsh word," one of the mermaids said. "I prefer the phrase short-term lover."

"When they are on land, they aren't much of a threat because they're weaker and less agile with legs," Ashlyn said without pause, causing a flurry of hisses and curses from the water.

"I'll show you weaker, mouth breather. Come say that to my face."

"They like to act angry to goad their prey into arguments or play on your other emotions to induce pity. No matter what they say or do, keep away from the water. Got it?"

The trio of new humans was silent so long that I glanced up. Kelsey and Zoe, orphaned sisters from New York, were about my age. Neither of the brunettes looked up, but I caught Kelsey's nod beside Fenris as his gaze locked with mine.

"You okay?" he mouthed.

I gave a small smile and nod and told myself I was lucky to have such an amazing group of friends. Even if none of them actually knew the real me. That thought just brought back Eugene's comment about my real eyes.

I nudged him to catch his attention and leaned closer.

"They aren't my real eyes," I said.

"What?" Eugene asked, turning his head to look at me.

"My real eyes are my brown ones."

He frowned, and before I could stop him, he pulled the earplug from his ear. Several sirens immediately started to sing. I watched his eyes glaze over.

I grabbed for his earbud to shove it back in his ear but missed when he turned his head toward the water. He leaned in his seat, teetering toward the pool. I grabbed for his shirt, my hold barely there as three mermaids surged up from the water and grabbed him.

He was gone in seconds.

I dove in after him. The water churned with the number of mermaids and sirens that surrounded us. Eugene was pulled away from me. I fought to get to him, but they tugged my hair and clawed my face, trying to keep me from him.

Something inside me snapped. My vision sharpened,

showing me a galaxy of tiny bubbles reflecting light within the water. The beauty didn't distract me from my purpose, though.

The next mermaid to reach for me got my full attention.

"Kneel before me, mermaid," I mouthed underwater.

Her eyes went wide as her fins disappeared, replaced by feet. She started to sink even as her arms flailed to bring her to the surface.

My gaze swung to the cluster of mermaids and sirens fighting for Eugene.

"You will all kneel before me," I mouthed.

They shifted from fins to feet and began to sink the same as the first one had, leaving Eugene floating unconscious in the water. I swam to him and wrapped my arms around him to bring him to the surface.

He didn't gasp for air when our heads cleared the water.

"Eugene?" I said, tapping his face. He couldn't die. Not like this. Not in the pool.

I barely had that thought when he gave a watery cough. Water gushed from his mouth, and he started treading water. His eyes met mine.

"Are you okay?" I asked.

"Yep. Stay away from the water. Got it."

I grinned.

His eyes dipped to my mouth.

Before I could think, I had my legs wrapped around his waist. He continued to tread water for both of us as my hand pressed against his chest just over his rapidly beating heart. The way he looked at me, full of need and desire, and the way the sweet scent of his lust filled my nose made my head swim with giddy anticipation. He was almost mine. I could feel it.

"Tell me you want me," I said, my mouth an inch from his.

His shaky exhale warmed my lips. I could already taste him.

"I want you, Eliana. I want you so much it hurts to breathe."

His words smothered my raging hunger. Detangling myself from him, I pointed toward the edge of the pool where the others were waiting.

"Go, Eugene. Before the mermaids get their tails back."

"But…" He looked at me with a longing that made me sick with regret and shame.

"I'm dangerous, too, Eugene," I said softly. "And I'm trying to save you. Please. Get out of the water."

"Come on, Eugene," Fenris called. "Swim or I'm going to need to jump in there, too, and no one wants to smell wet dog for the rest of the day."

Some of the remaining daze left Eugene's eyes, and he gave Fenris a quick smile before starting toward the edge of the pool.

I treaded water until he was out then self-consciously swam to the edge. When I glanced back, the mermaids and sirens had their fins once more but didn't make a move toward me. I could see plenty of hate in their eyes, though. Hate for me because I'd forced my will on them. I'd coerced them like they'd coerced Eugene.

"It doesn't feel good being manipulated, does it?" I said softly.

A siren flipped me off before swimming to the other side of the pool.

Ignoring the rest, I went to the ladder and climbed out. Fenris was there to offer me a hand.

"Like the shirt," he said with a wink.

I glanced down, flushed at the sight of my clearly visible bralette, and bolted for the rarely used changing rooms connected to the pool. It wasn't the secluded haven I'd hoped it would be, though.

In the center of the tiled room, a group of three girls sat around a candle on the floor. One wore large dangling crystal earrings and rings on her fingers inset with different stones. Another had curly dark hair pulled back into a thick ponytail. And the other had the most amazing sparkling eye makeup. They all looked up at my entrance.

"Do you mind?" the one wearing jewelry asked, arching a brow. "We're in the middle of something here."

"Sorry," I mumbled. Still too panicked to think clearly, I grabbed the paper toweling and tried blotting my shirt.

"Pretty sure that's not going to fix your problem," the girl with the ponytail said. "Want us to try a drying spell?"

I glanced at the group again and the pink flame of their candle. It finally registered that they were in the middle of practicing magic.

"Thank you for the offer. But, it might be better if I go home for new clothes. I wouldn't want to get you in trouble."

"Suit yourself," the third girl said with a shrug. They joined hands again, and I hurried from the bathroom, almost running into Fenris again.

He held up a white towel.

"Thought you might want this."

I grabbed the towel and clutched it to my chest.

"Um, can you let Adira know that I needed to run home and change?" I said, backing away. My gaze shifted to Eugene. "And can you keep an eye on them?"

"Sure thing. I'll keep your lunch for you, too."

I was in the hall before he said the last word.

Forgetting I was wearing heels, I held the towel to my chest and ran for the exit. Students stepped aside for me, smirking or laughing as they watched my escape.

The heat of my mortification prevented my hair from freezing as I burst outside and fled to my car. The tremble in my hands didn't make starting the car very easy, and before I put it into reverse, I tried to calm down by looking at things objectively.

Nothing bad had happened. Eugene would shake off the effects of my influence in a few days. The mermaids had gotten what they'd deserved. And Fenris seeing my bralette wasn't the end of the world. His kind stripped down in front of each other all the time. He'd probably seen a million bras by now.

Yet, knowing all that did nothing to ease my humiliation. I'd almost fed on Eugene. In public. He was supposed to be my friend, not food.

What would my father think of me?

My mom's words echoed in my mind. "Off limits always tastes best."

Backing out of my spot, I blasted my music and did my best to forget all of it. However, by the time I reached the Quills' house, my frame of mind wasn't any calmer. What had happened hadn't just upset me. It terrified me. I'd never come so close to unwittingly feeding on someone before. Well, not since the last time I went home to see my dad.

The gaping hole of guilt and regret that had opened inside of me in the pool grew larger at the memory. No one could hate herself as much as I did.

Parking the car in front of the door, I slipped inside the house, removed my shoes, and quietly made my way upstairs. The moment I stepped into my room, I knew that Adira had gotten my message because a new outfit was laid out on my bed. I should have felt relief that it was jeans and a top. Instead, all I felt was dread that I needed to go back to school.

I stripped from the wet clothes and hung them in the bathroom to deal with later. Once I finished toweling off, I dressed in what Adira had set out for me, after adding another shirt, then left my room.

Mrs. Quill was coming up the stairs as I was heading down. From the study on the floor above, I could hear the low murmur of Mr. Quill's voice.

"You're home early," Mrs. Quill said.

"I fell into the pool and needed to change."

Her gaze swept over me, noting my still wet hair.

"Perhaps you should take another minute to blow dry your hair. I don't want you to catch a chill."

I smiled at her. Mrs. Quill cared. Really cared. And I loved her for it even when she went to Adira with her concerns when I wished she wouldn't.

"I'll turn up the heat in the car and be fine. I'll see you at dinner." I gave a small wave and jogged down the steps in my newly acquired, dry heels. This time, they were black instead of red.

Once I was in the car, though, I paused. I didn't want to rush back to school and face my fresh humiliation. Yet, I couldn't stay home or Mrs. Quill would notice. Where could I go? I immediately thought of Megan's house and remembered my promise to watch for her goblin and brownie. Relieved I had something to distract me, I started the car and headed toward the store for some supplies.

Taking my time, I browsed the aisles as if Uttira's sole food retailer actually had mouth watering, shove-them-in-my-face items instead of boring healthy options. Once I had the oats, milk, and honey, I reluctantly paid for my items and hauled them back to my car.

Like a good citizen, I drove the exact speed limit, or maybe a little under, to Megan's rundown, two-story house. Though I'd only known her for a few months, seeing her vacant house dredged up a new pang of loneliness. How could I so deeply miss someone as new to my life as Megan was?

I knew the answer before I had even finished the thought. Megan was the type of person I wished my dad would have been. She didn't cower to anyone, not even the Council. She certainly wouldn't have succumbed to my mom.

Shaking those thoughts from my head, I got out of the car and looked at the house's peeling white paint. The goblin would love this place so long as I remembered to feed him. I wondered if Megan realized what she was about to unleash on her home. Probably not. But, she wouldn't care what the goblin fixed, either. Like me, she'd lived in Uttira because she'd had to.

Inside, I grabbed a bowl and filled it with the oats and milk, then topped it with honey. I left the mixture on the table along with a note with my address so the brownie and goblin could let me know when they arrived.

Making myself at home, I turned on the TV and stayed there until twenty minutes before the end of the day. I knew Megan wouldn't mind. Heck, she would have encouraged me to skip the rest of the day. But I couldn't. I needed to check on Eugene to make sure he was okay.

When I walked back into the Academy, I had just enough time to slip into my last session to be seen. I was surprised to see Eugene at the back of the room, sitting next to my usual spot.

He gave me a quick smile, and I ignored the looks and whispers as I took my seat. I was used to them by now. The weird succubus who wouldn't feed. The reject. Let them think what they wanted. I'd never be like them. Humans would never be food to me.

As soon as the bell rang, I turned to Eugene.

"You okay?" I asked.

"I'm fine. A little damp, but I didn't want to go home and miss anything. You okay?"

Guilt hit me hard.

"I almost fed on you, Eugene. Don't worry for me. Fear me."

He sighed and shook his head.

"I get what you're saying and know you're trying to keep me safe, but you're not seeing things from my side. You almost fed on me, but you didn't. You stopped. And, you stopped the mermaids. As far as I'm concerned, you're not a creature I need to fear. You're one I need as a friend." He gave me a questioning look. "So are we good?"

"We're good. Just don't be alone with me. Ever. Okay?"

"Sure."

I knew by that answer he wasn't taking me seriously.

"I better go," I said.

Head down, I left the room and started for the parking lot.

"Eliana!"

I recognized the voice and wanted to groan. Fenris was the last person I wanted to see at the moment.

Picking up my pace, I hurried down the hall.

He called my name again, sounding closer. I wrinkled my nose and elbowed a dryad out of my way. Her indignant huff barely registered as I focused on the distant door. I was so close.

A hand settled on my shoulder at the same time Fenris's scent filled my senses. My vision started to sharpen, and saliva pooled in my mouth.

I needed to feed. Badly.

Afraid for Fenris, I shook free of his hold and ran, bowling people over in my need to get to my car.

As I backed out of my spot, I saw Fenris standing just outside the door, a look of hurt on his face. Far above him, Adira stood at the edge of the Academy's roof, her gaze shifting from Fenris to me.

For the first time in my life, I spun gravel.

CHAPTER FOUR

I wiped my damp palm against my skirt. While I hoped the provocative dress and scarlet red lipstick I wore would be seen as a peace offering, I doubted it would be enough for Adira.

Taking a calming breath, I stepped into the dining room.

Mr. and Mrs. Quill, who were speaking softly by the sideboard, quieted and turned toward me. Mrs. Quill's concerned expression melted to one filled with joy.

"Eliana, you look stunning."

It took every ounce of self-control I possessed not to tug at the hemline of my extremely short skirt.

"Thank you."

I glanced at Mr. Quill to gauge his reaction and found his gaze completely clear of any infatuation.

"It suits you, Eliana," he said with a kind smile.

"Adira said she might be late. Let's start without her," Mrs. Quill said, already moving to her seat, which Mr. Quill pulled out for her.

"The mashed potatoes look delicious," I said, sitting.

"Thank you. I tried a new green beans recipe tonight, too."

I smiled and held out my plate, grateful for the normalcy of the conversation and the Quills' lack of reaction to my clothes and makeup.

"How are the new humans doing at Girderon?" Mrs. Quill asked.

"Eugene, Kelsey, and Zoe seem to be liking it so far," I said, purposely using their names.

"Any trouble from the other students?" Mr. Quill asked.

I was saved from answering what felt like a staged question by a knock on the door.

"I'll get it," I said, quickly leaving my chair.

The moment I opened the door, I regretted leaving the table. Fenris stood on the front stoop, wearing the same clothes he'd worn to school and looking just as delicious. His scent teased my hunger, and I quickly started mouth breathing.

"Hey, Fenris. We're actually eating dinner right now. Sorry." I started closing the door, and he put a hand against it, his smile unwavering.

"I won't keep you long." He held up my pink insulated lunch bag with his free hand. "I tried catching you after school, but I don't think you heard me."

We both knew that was a lie.

"Thanks," I said, taking the bag.

He didn't release the door.

"Kelsey and Zoe are taking a shift at the Roost tonight. Want to meet me there to help keep an eye on them?"

Taking a shift meant that they would be sitting at a table in Uttira's only teen club so all the underage creatures in this town could practice their hunting skills. It wasn't safe for the humans and was something that Megan was against. So was I. But, going anywhere with Fenris that involved him mingling with the opposite sex would be a colossal mistake.

Even with my mouth breathing, I could taste the change in his scent at the mention of the Roost.

"Kelsey and Zoe will be safe enough with you around. I should really spend tonight going over what I missed today. Thanks for the invite, though."

"That reminds me," he said, reaching into his back pocket and producing a piece of paper. "I got some notes for you."

He handed the paper over, and a zing of heat coursed through me at the brush of his fingers against mine.

"Thanks," I said, stepping back and pushing the door against his hold.

He exhaled heavily and dropped his hand.

"I'll see you tomorrow."

His gaze didn't flinch from mine even as I slammed the door in his face.

"That was a bit rude," Adira said from behind me. "You should meet him at the Roost tonight to apologize."

I wanted to stomp my foot in irritation at her ill-timed appearance. Instead, I turned toward her with a bright smile and thankfully clear eyes.

I didn't know when I'd gained a backbone or how long it'd last, but I took advantage of it while I had it and held her gaze.

"Is that an order or a suggestion?" I asked. "It's sometimes hard to tell."

Like Fenris, Adira exhaled deeply and stepped aside.

"Only a suggestion."

My new defiant attitude faltered for a moment, and I almost thanked her. Instead, I moved to rejoin the Quills in the dining room.

"Was that Fenris?" Mr. Quill asked.

"Yes. He brought my lunch bag and notes for the classes I missed," I said, setting both on the table as I resumed my seat.

"You missed more than one class?" Mrs. Quill said, obviously doing her best to sound surprised.

Did they honestly think I didn't know that Adira kept them apprised of every move I made or that they likewise kept Adira informed? I wasn't simple. My weekly calls with Mom made it very clear how watched I was.

"Yes. After I pulled Eugene from the pool, I left to change."

"You were gone a long time," Adira said, watching me closely.

"Yep. I hung out at Megan's for a while to let my embarrassment fade."

"Embarrassment?" Adira asked. "Over what?"

"Maybe the fact that the aquatic loving student majority saw my bra, thanks to the inadequate clothes in my closet," I said in a calm and even tone.

"Hardly inadequate. It did its job. Had you lingered, you would have had your pick from your classmates. Any number of them would have happily had sex with you and fed you."

I fisted my hands in my lap, furious beyond speech that everything came back to sex and feeding. There had to be more to life than sex and food. Passions outside of...well, passion. Books. Movies. Music. Art. There were so many other things out there. Things I hadn't even explored because they were busy trying to force-feed me their agenda.

"I'm sixteen. I don't know what I want. I especially don't know *who* I want. And I resent that all the adults in my life are pushing me to make a decision I'm not yet ready to make. If my lifespan is as long as my mother's, why does everyone insist on rushing me? I will take things at my own speed. If my welcome here has an expiration date because of that, please just say so. It won't offend me. I realize how much all of you've already sacrificed for me, and I'm very grateful for it."

Mrs. Quill's expression turned to concern.

"You're welcome here for as long as you'd like, sweetheart. No one is pushing you to leave our home, only to find a steady source of food. We just want you to know that we understand your needs and that you're welcome to bring a boy or girl or both home with you any time you'd like."

I wanted to hit my head against the table. If they truly understood my needs, we wouldn't be having this conversation.

"If I'm truly welcome here, stop pushing me. Please. You're only making things worse."

Mrs. Quill flinched like I'd slapped her, and Adira's expression hardened.

"I would hardly attribute our concern as a damaging factor to the situation in which you find yourself," she said.

Mr. Quill's phone buzzed.

"You're right. Your concern isn't damaging. Your meddling is. It didn't help the situation with Megan. Why do you think it will help me? I didn't appreciate you inviting Eugene for dinner yesterday, and I don't appreciate you purposefully putting him in my classes. Classes that will not benefit him in any way."

Adira opened her mouth to respond, but Mr. Quill interrupted.

"Adira, I could use your counsel on a matter of importance."

She closed her mouth and nodded serenely. I watched them both leave the room. Whatever message he'd received had to be important to pull him and Adira away from dinner.

Picking up my fork, I took a bite of the now cold potatoes and looked at Mrs. Quill.

"They really are delicious."

She smiled sadly at me.

Adira and Mr. Quill never returned to the table. I helped Mrs. Quill clean up then went to the entertainment room where I paced and watched the door. It wasn't like Adira to forget about a conversation that involved my lack of feeding. That she hadn't yet tracked me down to resume her lecture was beyond odd. It was unsettling. As was the way Mrs. Quill had disappeared into Mr. Quill's office the moment we'd finished cleaning up.

I thought of Oanen and Megan and what they were doing in New York then started to worry. Adira and the Quills were always trying to shield me from anything that might impede my progress toward becoming a full feeding succubus. What if something had happened to Megan and Oanen in their mission to find who was killing the trolls, and everyone was keeping it from me?

The temptation to sneak to Mr. Quill's office and listen at the door coaxed my feet into the hallway. I knew it was wrong, but I couldn't ignore the feeling that they were keeping something important from me.

Fear curled into a ball inside of me, its weight settling in my stomach as I hurried down the hall. The low murmur of concerned voices coming from Mr. Quill's office drew me to the door. I couldn't hear what they were saying, but the tones of their voices sounded like they were disagreeing.

Barely breathing, I pressed my ear to the wood.

"You risk angering her mother," Mrs. Quill said. "Are you prepared for the consequences?"

"I'm confident that Megan will be able to control the situation," Adira said.

I frowned. Since when were they more concerned about Megan's mom than Megan?

"And if we push too far and anger Megan again in the process?" Mrs. Quill asked.

"I agree with Anwen, Adira," Mr. Quill said. "We are fortunate Megan is still willing to help with the investigation in New York. With the latest report from the Flagstaff Council, we need to understand the purpose behind these deaths. Three Nemean lions isn't coincidence; it's ritualistic."

"An assessment of which I fully agree. Which is exactly why Megan and Oanen need to move quickly. The troll death may be the continuation of the same ritual," Adira said. "And while it is our obligation to watch for and stop these threats to humanity and our kind alike, we cannot forget our obligations here."

Her voice grew louder as if she was moving closer to the door. Torn between hearing more and not being caught, I hesitated just long enough to hear her next words before hurrying away.

"I worry for Eliana."

My heart raced as I paced the entertainment room and tried to make sense of what I'd heard. What was the Council planning to do that would tick off Megan? And who would be crazy enough to kill not one but three Nemean lions? That Adira and Mr. Quill thought something dangerous was happening in New York was obvious, but why would Adira say she was worried for me and not Megan? Add to that the fact that they were worried about Megan's Mom's reaction, and I couldn't help but come to one conclusion. They thought Megan was going to die.

I needed chocolate.

My phone rang before I made it more than a few steps toward the fridge. When I glanced at the screen and saw Megan's name, I immediately answered.

"Any sign of the brownie or goblin yet?" Megan asked.

"Not yet," I said, the idea of her dying coloring my tone.

"What's wrong?"

"Nothing."

"Are you trying to lie to me?"

"Yes. Because I want you to focus on getting the job done so you can get home sooner."

"Talk, succubus."

I sighed.

"I didn't know how lonely I was until I made a friend, and she left. And then, I find out someone is trying to kill her, and my only friend might not come back."

"I miss you, too. And that poisoned burger wasn't meant for me. Oanen overreacted because of the whole bird bond thing. As for the smiling dead trolls, we have a few leads. It shouldn't be too much longer. I'm coming back. I promise. How did it go at the Academy today?"

Her words didn't erase my concern, but I tried to pretend they had.

"Good. Eugene is loving classes and asking a ton of questions. It rubbed a few people wrong, but by the end of the day, I think they were catching on that Eugene is impressed and curious and not a threat. Oh, a siren almost got him into the pool at lunch, but Ashlyn was there to block him," I said, not mentioning the second, successful attempt where he had actually gone in. "And, Fenris was being pretty good about keeping an eye on the humans, too."

"Oh? So you and Fenris were hanging out?"

I snorted.

"No way. He keeps texting me annoying updates. I think he misses you."

"Then, I think you should be a friend and keep him company."

"Not me. I think the new girls are stirring his wolfie hormones or something because he's getting worse."

"Worse? You mean he's flirting with you now?"

"No. He hasn't changed at all in that way." Fenris had always flirted with other girls, especially Megan, but never really with me. Thankfully. "It's his lust. I can barely be in the same room with him."

"How's your succubus training going? Adira still dressing you?" Megan asked, skillfully changing the conversation to a topic I found less upsetting. But only marginally.

"She set out clothes for me this morning. I got creative with them while still following the rules. I wish everyone around here would just leave me alone. I might be a little on the small side, but I don't think I'm unhealthy. Nothing to warrant this much unwanted attention.

"So how is it staying in New York? Are you missing your backpack with all the wicked you're running into? Did you kill anyone yet without me?" I asked.

While only sexual energy fed me, it wasn't the only energy I could take. Draining Megan's anger had saved her more than once. The fact that I'd had to tackle her from behind a few times, in order to help her, brought a small smile to my lips.

"Not yet. It's weird here. Most of the time, it's not as provoking as I thought it would be. People I would have thought I'd want to beat the hell out of, like the goblin, Elbner, don't bug me. Yet today, regular people were starting to get under my skin. I'm just glad it's not like it was the night I came here with Adira. That would have been hell. As it is, I think New York would be more fun if we weren't having to deal with dying trolls."

The reminder made my stomach sour.

"I heard Adira and the Quills talking. While you're checking out the deaths in New York, the council near Flagstaff is investigating the deaths of three Nemean lions."

"What's a Nemean lion; and did they die with smiles, too?"

I nervously laughed.

"No. Nemean lions are a lot like regular lions. They're animals but a lot harder to kill. Their coats are impenetrable by mortal blades. Since they're a protected species by our laws, word is going out, asking for information about their deaths."

"I'm not sure how this is supposed to make me feel better about dealing with troll deaths."

"It's not. I told you so you'd know the Council isn't giving Oanen all the poopy jobs. An enforcer has to look into any death that's questionable."

"Poopy? Adira should forget the succubus clothes and work on your language skills."

"Swearing isn't a language skill."

"Says the person who doesn't know how."

"I know how; I just choose not to."

She snorted.

"I better go. Oanen just walked in with our pizza, and I'm starving."

"I'll talk to you tomorrow."

I stared at the phone after I hung up and briefly wondered if I'd done the right thing by not repeating what I'd overheard or my suspicions that she was in danger. Megan's disregard for authority had caused her problems in the past. If she thought for a moment that Adira was up to something again, Megan's attention would be on Adira instead of the case. And given the seriousness with which Adira spoke about the deaths, the last thing I wanted to do was distract Megan.

No, keeping silent about what I'd overheard was for the best. I only wished coming to that conclusion would have given me some ease of mind. Instead, all I could do was worry that Megan was still in danger. I needed to find out what was really going on.

My phone chirped. Thinking it might be something more from Megan, I hurried to look at the message.

How's the studying going? Done yet and ready for some fun?

I wrinkled my nose in irritation.

While Megan might think Fenris was lonely, I knew better. He had far too many girls clinging to him already, and I had no desire to become another member of his all blonde girl pack. I was definitely the wrong species.

Walking toward the refrigerator, I quickly typed out a reply.

Thank you for the notes today and the invite, but I'm staying home.

A knock on the open entertainment door had me looking up from my phone. Mrs. Quill smiled at me.

"Lander and I are going out for a flight. Do you have enough chocolate?"

The normal question seemed so out of place after what I'd overheard that my return smile was weak at best.

"I have enough for now. Thank you, and enjoy your flight."

"If you decide to take Fenris up on his invitation to the Roost, please leave a note so I don't worry."

She left me in a stunned state of confusion. It took a moment to realize she wasn't somehow reading my texts but that Adira had likely overheard Fenris when he'd been at the door.

Tired and filled with too much worry for Megan, I helped myself to a dark chocolate candy bar. Although chocolate wasn't readily available in Uttira because it had been deemed too unhealthy for the young stuck here, Mrs. Quill knew how much it calmed me and always offered to pick some up when she and Mr. Quill went out. If she knew just how dependent I was on the stuff or how much I had stashed in the house, she probably wouldn't be so willing.

My phone rang instead of chirping. Annoyed, I answered without looking at the screen.

"Hello?"

"Hey, Eliana," Eugene said. He was almost drowned out by

the sultry notes of music in the background. "Fenris mentioned that you aren't coming tonight, and I was wondering if I could stop over by your place instead."

My vision shifted at the thought of Eugene here, alone, with me.

"That's not a good idea," I said. "Especially after the way I behaved in the pool."

"I was kind of hoping we could talk about that. And about what happened at dinner last night. Ashlyn is great about sharing information, but she doesn't know much about succubi, and I'm over my head with what's safe and not safe. Not just with you," he added quickly. "In general."

"I'm humbled by your faith in me, Eugene, and hope that you'll trust me when I say I'm dangerous. I don't mean to be, but like many of the other creatures in Uttira, my instincts rule me. Especially my need to feed. Like Adira said, I feed on energy. And while that might seem like a non-threatening thing, I promise it's not. What I accidentally did today is what Adira wanted me to do at dinner last night."

"Swim with me?"

"No. She wanted me to use my abilities on you to make you want to feed me. To make you more interested in being with me than you should be. It'd be better if you stayed away from me for the next few days."

"Because you think you put some kind of spell on me?"

What I could do wasn't some kind of magic, but I didn't try to correct him.

"Yes."

"I don't feel any different."

"Don't you? Why else would you call me immediately after hearing you wouldn't see me?"

"Because, according to you and Ashlyn, I'm currently

surrounded by creatures who want to consume me in some way." There was a smattering of laughter. "And don't forget that I wanted to talk to you before the whole pool thing happened. So see? Not different."

"I hope you're right."

CHAPTER FIVE

As I pulled into the student parking lot, I groaned at the sight of Eugene leaning against his car.

He smiled and lifted one of the cups he was holding. The gesture just made me want to shift my car into reverse and get out of there. But I couldn't. I needed to deal with the mess I'd created.

While he'd probably told himself it was nothing more than a friendly cup of coffee, I knew better. It was a test gift. If I accepted it, he would show up with something else tomorrow. The gifts would slowly escalate in importance until he was kneeling before me with a ring.

I parked my car and got out, trying my best to look pleasant instead of upset.

"Morning," he said. "I brought a—"

"Never give a gift to a succubus," I said.

His welcome smile faded to confusion.

"Why?"

"Because she'll be that much closer to owning you. If you find yourself thinking about getting a gift for one, run, Eugene. Run far. Run fast. Lock yourself away for a few days until the urge passes. But whatever you do, don't give a succubus a gift."

He smiled and lifted the cup to me.

"Good thing this is only coffee. The girl at the shop swore that double chocolate with extra foam was the way to go."

"It's not just coffee, Eugene. It's a gift for me. If it wasn't meant to be special, you would have gotten one for Ashlyn, too, to thank her."

"I bought her a soda last night. See? Not just you."

I wished I could believe that, but the hint of earnest desperation in his eyes told me otherwise.

"Eugene, I—"

"I'll take that," Fenris said, reaching around me. "Eliana hates chocolate."

My mouth dropped open, and I turned to stare at a grinning Fenris.

"Oh. Sorry about that, Eliana. I'll bring a caramel one tomorrow if you want."

Ignoring Fenris for a moment, I shook my head at Eugene.

"No, I don't want any drink. I want you to see what's happening. You have an urge to bring me something because of the pool. That's all. You need to fight it, Eugene, or you'll be my lapdog before you can say 'arf.'"

Fenris started choking on his stolen drink, and I absently reached around him to whack him on the back.

"And if Adira tries sticking you in any of my classes today, refuse."

He looked ready to object.

"You said you trusted me. Trust me now. I'm trying to keep you safe."

Eugene nodded and started for the door.

"Arf," Fenris said under his breath with a low chuckle that had me inhaling his scent hungrily.

As soon as Eugene reached the door, I whirled on Fenris and yanked the drink from his hand.

"You know I like chocolate."

He grinned at me.

"No, you love chocolate. You'd probably bathe in it if you could. But, did you really want him to know that?"

I hated that Fenris was right.

"I don't like lying."

"You didn't. I did. And I'm completely comfortable with embellishing the truth."

I rolled my eyes at him and tipped the cup back. The explosion of chocolate and cream had me guzzling the contents in seconds.

"Impressive," Fenris said. "Remind me never to get between you and chocolate again."

"Again? You were nothing but a bystander who willingly surrendered the goods."

A carful of his groupies pulled into the parking lot behind him, and the sudden surge of his lust hit me hard.

"I gotta go."

I hustled for the door and kept my head down, hoping that no one would notice my eyes.

A hand closed around my arm, and I found myself spun around. Shocked, I stared up at Fenris. His normally playful gaze grew serious, and the texture of his irises claimed my attention, along with the way his pupils contracted and expanded in a quick, pulsing rhythm.

"I'm starting to feel a little paranoid," he said.

"Huh?" My confusion robbed my hunger of its edge, and my heightened focus on his eyes vanished.

"You're barely near me for more than a few minutes, and you run. Why?"

"I just wanted to get to class before the hallways crowd."

"I thought you didn't like lying, Eliana. This isn't the first time you've run from me. Did I do something wrong? Kill your pet rabbit or something?"

"What? No. It's not anything you did. It's me. It's always me."

"I don't understand."

"I know. And I'm sorry for that, but I really need to go."

He released my arm.

"Run then. I won't chase you." His cocky grin reemerged. "This time."

Not amused by his wolf humor, I hurried away before I went full succubus on him.

In the first session, I should have been okay with his scent absent. However, I wasn't any better. Even though there were no humans present to tempt me, I was still inhaling lungfuls of lust emanating off the troll in front of me. It didn't taste good, but I couldn't stop.

Second hour was worse. A giant was crushing on a druid hard. The potency and unnatural taste of her lust told me it was spell induced. My hunger didn't care. It wanted to be fed.

Fine trembles coursed through me from head to toe. A girl to my right noticed and giggled. Jenna, one of Fenris's devoted females, leaned forward in her seat behind me.

"You okay?" she asked softly,

I wanted to be, but I knew I wasn't. My time was up. I'd held out as long as I could. I needed to feed.

Instead of answering her, I walked out of the room.

The ability to leave whenever we wanted was one of the few perks of Girderon Academy. That and being able to make up any missed work online. Not that many of my classmates chose to leave once they decided to attend.

Graduating Girderon was our ticket out of Uttira. And it wasn't just passing grades that were required in order to graduate. Each and every one of us would need the Council's approval, which was heavily based on Adira's assessment. I would be at Girderon until I was fifty at the rate I was going.

As soon as I opened the kitchen door to the Quills' house, I paused and tried to calm my shaking. One breath after another, I focused on my dad. The memory of his smiling face. The memory of his laugh. The haunted look that crept into his eyes at any reminder of my mother. The way he would cry in his sleep.

It took about five minutes to get myself under control. I pressed the button on the intercom in the kitchen.

"Mrs. Quill, would you meet me in the living room?"

My voice echoed throughout the house. Without waiting for an answer, I headed for the seldom-used room.

Mrs. Quill was just turning on the television when I entered. Her concerned gaze swept over me, and she held out her hand.

Reluctantly, I took it. I didn't need to touch to feed. In fact, I preferred not to. However, Mrs. Quill insisted. She said she didn't want me to ever think what she did was with any detachment. She did what she did because she loved me as much as she would love a daughter, and she wanted me to feel that love every moment we spent in this dumb room.

I sat beside her as the image of her and Mr. Quill appeared on the screen. The first time we'd done this, I'd been terrified that she was going to show me a bedroom home video. It wasn't ever anything like that, thankfully. This time, it was a video from her perspective, flying on Mr. Quill's back. I could hear the joy in her laughter as he dipped suddenly then launched upward again to soar through some clouds.

"I love you, Lander," she said in the video. "You are my everything."

He cried out sharply then dived again.

The video looped back to where it started and played again. Mrs. Quill's lust, a subtle, steady energy, called to me. Without turning toward her, I opened my mouth and pulled it into me. My shaking eased with the first swallow. The hunger demanded so much more. I only allowed myself five pulls, though. The sweetness of what she felt for Mr. Quill settled into my belly. With their love filling me, I closed my mouth and released her hand.

"Thank you," I said.

"Eliana, that wasn't enough," she said with concern.

"For me, it is."

I left the room quickly. She didn't try to stop me.

Locked in my bathroom, I stripped and got into the shower, not bothering to let it warm. There, I curled into a ball and quietly cried, cursing the gods for making me into the monster I was. It didn't matter that Mrs. Quill was immune to my abilities because of what she was and her bond with Mr. Quill. What did matter was the fact that I would ruin anyone else I fed on.

Like my mom had ruined my dad. My heart ached for him and all that he had suffered. All that he still suffered. I remembered the day Mom showed up at our door to take me back. Dad had taken one look at her and had fallen to his knees. The things he'd said...begged to do to her...still made me flush. The deeply religious man who'd raised me had vanished between one heartbeat and the next.

Mom had laid a gentle hand on his head and told me to pack my bags quickly. I could still picture them like that. Her standing over him as he slumped forward on his knees, his hands clutching her glittery skirt. But mostly, I remembered how my mom had so calmly told me that the longer we lingered, the more he would suffer.

She'd been wrong. It hadn't been the time I'd taken to pack that caused his suffering but how long she'd stayed with him in the first place.

I wiped the tears from my eyes and turned off the water. I couldn't change the past or what I was. But I could choose how to live, and I refused to be like my mother.

I SMOOTHED my hands over my dress. The T-shirt under the strappy dress made me look like an ill-dressed orphan. I hated looking that way but refused to wear anything more revealing on a feeding day.

Adira wouldn't like it, but hopefully, whatever had distracted her enough today to keep her from appearing and teleporting me back to school would also keep her equally preoccupied during dinner so she wouldn't notice.

My phone rang just as I started for the bedroom door, and I paused to answer it.

"Where's the seventies porn background music?" Megan asked.

"What? Ew! Why would you say that?"

She laughed.

"I figured Adira would have converted you by now."

"She's been surprisingly quiet today."

Megan made a non-committal noise.

"So, I have some interesting news," she said.

"You solved the case?"

"No, I saw my mom today," she said.

Megan's estranged mother had left Megan in Uttira with no

information about who or what she was. While Megan had found her mom's phone number just before leaving for New York, her mom had been less than helpful, yet again. She hadn't cared that Megan's powers were going haywire. She'd refused to talk to her about any of it when Megan had called.

"No way. Did she tell you what's going on?" I asked.

"Yep. Apparently, Oanen and I can't be together because griffins have boy baby chickens and furies have girls with anger issues. According to her, we won't mix."

My mouth dropped open for a second, and I felt so angry on Megan's behalf. Her mom wasn't very nice. Couldn't she see her daughter needed her?

"While she might be right about the past," I said, "who's to say what will happen with you and Oanen? I don't think a griffin and fury pairing has ever been done before. At least not in written history."

"I just wish she didn't try so hard to be a pain in my ass, you know?"

I did know, and I wished my friend was close enough for a hug so I could relieve her of the negative emotions she carried.

"I'm sorry it wasn't a pleasant reunion," I said instead.

"It wasn't as bad as it could have been, I guess. She looked exactly the same. But, this time when I saw her, I realized just how much I didn't know about her, other than her taste in men. Back then, I thought she was just a regular, human gold digger, you know?"

Her impression hit a little too close to home.

"My mom's motto is usually the richer, the better," I said.

"Usually?"

"Apparently, my dad was an exception." My old resentment resurfaced. "His devotion tasted sweeter because it had never been given to any mortal before. Only to one of the gods."

"Hey. I didn't mean to bring you down. Let's talk about something else. Anything interesting happen at the Academy today?"

"Not really. I better go. It's just about dinner time. If I get to the dining room first, I can be sitting before Adira arrives."

"Um?"

"She won't notice my dress enough to make me change."

"Ah. Okay. I'll talk to you tomorrow."

I hung up, feeling guilty that I hadn't been more of a consoling friend. It was hard, though. In a way, I wished my mom was more like Megan's. Instead, she called often and always wanted to talk about how my skills were progressing. She would have loved to have a house in Uttira where she could have guided me herself.

Thank the gods for Oanen, though. He'd taken one look at twelve-year-old me, dressed in hooker heels, side slit dress, and with enough makeup to paint a trio of circus clowns, and invited us to dinner. Mom had accepted, thinking he'd be a perfect conquest for me. Instead, she left me in the Quills' care that night.

I shuddered to think what I would have become without Oanen's brotherly protection that day and every day for the subsequent four years. I would have been a destroyer of men—and women—just like my mom.

Staring at my phone, I thought of my dad again. Before I could stop myself, I was scrolling through my short list of contacts and calling him.

"Hello? Eliana?" he answered almost right away.

"Hi, Daddy."

"Baby, is your mom there? I need to talk to her."

My eyes began to water.

"She's not here, Daddy, remember? I live with another family in Maine."

"That's not right. You should come home to me. I miss you. There's room for your mom, too. You should tell her. We can be a family again. I'd lick her until—"

"Daddy, I have to go. I just wanted to let you know that I will never stop loving you, and I think of you every day."

I hung up before he could say anything else. Mom warned me not to call him. My voice was just a reminder of what he wanted most. Her. But I couldn't just cut him out of my life as easily as she had.

I would never be that heartless and cold. I'd rather die of starvation than to accidentally make a sex slave.

Feeling sick at the thought, I went downstairs and sat at the dining room table. I knew I'd timed it well when dishes started appearing on the polished surface. Mrs. Quill emerged from the kitchen a moment later and smiled when she saw me.

"How are you feeling?" she asked.

"Rested. I'd like to say content, too, but I miss Megan too much for that. Are they getting any closer to solving the mysterious troll deaths?"

"They're following some leads. Hopefully, we'll know more soon."

"I know you miss Megan and Oanen, but don't forget you have other friends," Adira said, appearing suddenly. "I think it's time you make an appearance at the Roost, don't you? There's no reason not to practice now that you're well-fed."

Why did we have to play the same game every night? I was so tired of the constant attack. Why couldn't she just let me be who I wanted to be instead of trying to get me to admit to this all-consuming hunger that continually gripped me by my backbone?

"The Roost sounds great," I said with a sweet smile. "Music

and frivolous conversation are just what I need after missing almost a whole day at school. Human guardians have their priorities so backward."

Adira studied me for a moment.

"You seem upset."

The urge to bang my head on the table was almost superseded by my desire to snap at her that I was tired of being told what to do and when to do it. Instead of doing either, I stood.

"I think I'll skip dinner and go straight to the Roost. How long should I stay there to sufficiently ease your worried mind?"

"How long you spend there doesn't matter, Eliana," Adira said smoothly. "It's how you spend your time that matters."

"Right. Socializing, because you're concerned that I've formed too much of an attachment to Megan and Oanen."

We both knew that wasn't her primary concern. She wanted me to be a man-eating ho that fed on anything with three "legs." I flushed with embarrassment and anger at the thought.

Without waiting for her reply, I went to change then left the house. The drive to the Roost took longer than necessary because I went to Megan's house first and replaced the bowl of milk, oats, and honey with a fresh batch.

I was more than a little tempted to just sit there and watch TV instead of doing as I said I would. But, I knew that word would get back to Adira if I didn't show up at the Roost. So, to keep the fragile peace I clung to in my life, I left.

The Roost's neon sign on the roof lit the sidewalk in a wash of color. As soon as I shimmied from my car, the heavy beat of music reached my ears. I secretly loved the Roost, the only gathering spot for Uttira teens. I loved the music. The atmosphere. Watching all the people. If it weren't for what I was, I would have been there all the time to dance the night away.

However, as a succubus, there were too many elements at the Roost to stir my hunger.

Pushing open the red double doors, I took in the large crowd. The cold, winter air from outside drew the notice of more than a few of the outlying dancers. I tried not to pay attention to their stares or tug at the hemline of my mini sheath with a scooped neckline.

As usual, the humans were gathered at a back table. Thankfully, Eugene wasn't amongst them. Skirting the crowd, I started for Ashlyn, Zoey, and Kelsey.

"Hey, girls," I said, sliding onto the bench seat next to Kelsey.

Ashlyn looked up from her book to smile at me, but the other two remained focused on their pages.

"How's it going?" I asked.

"Good. Eras came over and tried to influence Zoey again, but it didn't work. They're almost ready to do this solo."

"The Council isn't still making you work shifts here, are they? This is just supposed to be for learning. Megan—"

Ashlyn's hand covered mine. A jolt ran through me, and I quickly withdrew my hand.

"Sorry," she said.

"It's okay."

"The Council isn't forcing shifts. Coming here and going to the Academy isn't just something for us to do. It's a way for us to integrate. To change mindsets. Hiding in our houses won't do that."

She had a point.

"Is it dangerous to touch you?" Zoey asked.

"Zoey!" Kelsey said, scolding her sister.

"What? I didn't look up or make eye contact, and we've talked to her before."

"To be safe, you should always consider it dangerous to touch anyone who's not human," Ashlyn said with an apologetic smile to me.

"Ashlyn's right. While I wouldn't want to hurt you, if I'm hungry enough I might not be able to stop myself," I admitted.

"And touching would trigger your hunger?" Zoey asked.

"No," I said. "Touching is a way for me to get to you. Like eye contact."

"Oh."

Poor Zoey had learned the hard way that she could fall under an incubus's influence because of eye contact. The unwanted make out session that had ensued had left her feeling shaken and violated. It didn't matter that it hadn't progressed further than public kissing, something my kind wouldn't even bat an eye at. Except, it was for me, which was why it was one of the many items on Adira's checklist for me that I'd yet to accomplish.

"Any word from Megan?" Ashlyn asked, changing the subject.

"Nothing significant. Just that she and Oanen are still in New York and on the case. I'm worried about them."

Ashlyn nodded.

"My uncle told me he'd once witnessed a troll smile. He told me to run if I ever saw the same because whatever made a troll happy wouldn't make me happy."

She looked down at her book again. This time, I was the one to reach out. I could feel the dark energy of her pain. She still grieved for her uncle and the loss of the only family she'd known. Hating to see her suffer, I parted my lips slightly and pulled the darkness into me. Non-sexual energy wouldn't nourish me, but removing it would help her.

She sighed and squeezed my hand.

"Thank you for being a friend," she said. "You don't know how much that means to me."

I thought of Megan and what she meant to me and returned Ashlyn's squeeze.

"I think I might. Now, if you'll excuse me, I need to dance for two seconds so I can go home."

"Two seconds?" Eugene said from beside me. "We can do better than that."

I gave Ashlyn a pointed look.

"It was the pool," I said.

"I've got him. You go." She looked at Eugene as I fled my seat. "Sit down, lover boy. We need to talk."

I hoped she'd be able to get through to him.

Hurrying away, I joined the fringe of the dancers in the center space, making sure to stay out of Eugene's direct line of sight and let myself sway to the music. Megan had once teased me that I had killer moves. She couldn't have been more right. My grace was part of who I was, a lure to pull in prey, which is why I didn't let the music consume me. But I wished I could. As strong as the way I moved called to others, the music called to me. It wasn't because of the Siren's hypnotic song. It was the joy I felt when dancing.

I lifted my arms and turned slowly, swaying as I moved.

A hand closed over mine. Another touched my side.

The scent of lust hit me hard, and I knew my eyes had gone black the moment I opened them.

"Hey, beautiful, I've been dreaming of doing this all day."

The mutt dipped me low, his body arching over mine so close I could feel his breath on my neck.

I trembled in Fenris's arms, torn between the need to slap the smile from his face and the need to devour him whole.

CHAPTER SIX

"Play along," Fenris said, close to my ear. "Eugene is watching."

I wrinkled my nose but kept focused on Fenris as he straightened us then pressed close to me.

"While I appreciate what you're trying to do," I said softly, knowing Fenris would hear me over the music, "I don't think this will help. It will only show him I'm open to having a partner."

Fenris spun me around while his hand molded to the small of my back.

"Not if I get you out the door first."

His hips brushed against mine. I trembled harder, feeling like I was dying. The hunger demanded to be fed. It demanded Fenris. A taste. A touch. Him over me, panting in—

"Fenris, let me go," I begged, panicking.

Suddenly, I was outside and alone. I looked at the door as it closed and almost cried.

Fenris had actually listened.

I kicked off my shoes and slogged through the sidewalk slush to my car. My toes stung with the cold by the time I got in. It was a good distraction, but it didn't subdue my burning need to turn around and feed from every single person in the Roost.

I drove around for an hour before I stopped shaking. It was another hour before my eyes began to flicker back to brown.

Pulling over to the shoulder, I rested my head against my steering wheel in defeat. I'd thought I'd fed from Mrs. Quill enough to take the edge off my hunger. But I couldn't have been more wrong. I needed more. Yet, if I went to her so soon after the last feeding, she'd tell Adira I wasn't consuming enough.

I slapped my hand against the steering wheel in frustrated anger then started home.

Trying to ignore the hunger was out of the question. I would need to find Mrs. Quill as soon as I got home, hopefully without attracting any attention. Using the intercom wasn't an option, just in case Adira was still in the house. I hadn't yet decided how to approach Mrs. Quill when I walked through the kitchen door.

Hesitating near the kitchen island provided my answer when Mrs. Quill entered the kitchen moments after me. She took one look at my face and rushed to hug me. The contact only made my hunger stronger.

"What happened?" she asked, smoothing a hand over my hair.

"I danced at the Roost. I didn't know I'd get so hungry so fast."

She pulled back and looked into my eyes, which I knew were still flickering.

"Was your partner unwilling?"

I knew she didn't mean an unwilling dance partner. She was asking if my partner hadn't wanted to feed me.

"I didn't ask."

She smiled slightly.

"I think your mother would be pleased to hear you didn't ask for permission."

I nodded, glad she wasn't going to ask the big question. If my partner hadn't been openly unwilling, why hadn't I fed?

"Take what you need, Eliana," Mrs. Quill said without releasing me.

I opened my mouth and fed four times. It was more than I'd ever needed so closely together. Yet, the hunger still wormed impatiently in my belly.

"Better?" she asked when I stopped.

I couldn't answer because what she wanted was a lie. Instead, I hugged her tightly.

"Thank you for allowing me to stay here and for taking care of me."

"Always," she whispered.

FOR THE FIRST time in a long time, I didn't want to go to school. I dreaded running into Eugene after Fenris's "help" almost as much as I dreaded seeing Fenris himself. On top of that, I knew I'd need to face an Adira lecture, or worse, for not feeding well enough the day before yesterday. And, as if I wasn't anxious enough, my hunger was still twisting restlessly inside of me. No doubt it had something to do with the single outfit I'd found in my closet when I was getting ready for school.

The Academy gates swung open for my car, and I slowly eased down the drive, trying not to think about what I wore. My outfit was the reason I knew I'd crossed a line in Adira's goal to see me feed on someone other than Mrs. Quill. It didn't matter that I'd already technically done just that at the harvest feast. I shuddered at the memory of that man's taste.

Adira wanted me feeding regularly from my peers, and that wasn't going to happen.

Pulling into my usual spot, I turned off the car and zipped up my jacket. I'd sweat like crazy wearing it all day, but there was no way I'd take it off. It was the only safety I had and the only reason I'd even left the house.

However, the moment I opened my car door, Eugene emerged from the building and held up a note.

"It's not a love letter," he said hastily, "unless you have a thing for Adira."

I made a face, and he chuckled.

"I'm sorry about the last few days," he said, handing me the note. "Ashlyn helped me out last night, and I think I'm good now. You're nice, but I'm not feeling any urge to find a way to get you to like me. Even as a friend."

I exhaled in relief.

"How'd she help you?"

Eugene flushed and sheepishly ducked his head. The hint of lust that drifted from him was answer enough.

"Never mind, I really don't want to know," I said even as my mind started conjuring images of tangled sheets and sweaty bodies.

"It was just a kiss," Eugene said, holding up his hands and taking a healthy step back from me.

I closed my eyes quickly.

"I'm sorry. I didn't mean to scare you."

He chuckled again.

"You didn't. I just didn't want to be an accidental target you'd need to avoid again for days." When I didn't open my eyes, he added, "Seriously, Eliana, your eyes are pretty when they go black. With everything I've seen and learned since coming here, your eyes are at the bottom of the scary-Uttira-sights-to-see list."

I peeked at him and saw him standing several feet away, hands in his pockets. He nodded at the letter.

"Adira told me to stick around until you read it. I'm guessing it won't be good news for either of us, but I want you to know I'm not too worried. If it's a note saying you need to feed on me, you can tell her I refused. I have Megan on speed dial."

I smiled at him in relief and unfolded the letter.

Give your jacket to Eugene. No shortcuts.

There wasn't anything else to the note. Just that. It was enough. No threat was necessary to know I'd pushed her too far.

"I'm supposed to give you my jacket," I said. "But I need you to close your eyes and hold out your hand. Don't open them after I hand it over. Just stand here for a few minutes, okay?"

"You got it."

He closed his eyes and held out his hand. Just to make sure, I walked around him before removing the jacket and handing it over.

"Thanks, Eugene."

I fled inside before anyone else saw me even though I knew I couldn't hide forever. The first person I saw, a troll boy just barely old enough to attend the Academy, stopped in his tracks at the sight of my shirt.

"My brother is nuts. This school is great."

I hurried past him, hoping I wouldn't accidentally taste his brief infatuation.

The next person, a siren, wolf-whistled at me as her eyes devoured the view.

"Eliana, you need to wear that top every day. The boys are going to be tripping over themselves. Girls, too. And I don't mind succubus leftovers. No, not at all. Knock 'em dead, girl."

I hurried to the first session room and quickly slid into my seat. Belemina was the next person to arrive. She took one look at my misery and took the seat next to mine.

"Did a tampon come with that resting bitch face expression,

or is there another occasion you're celebrating with your braless bad self?"

Not only was I braless, but I was also missing the central part of my shirt. In place of solid material, I had three one-inch bands holding the sides of my silk shirt together. I sunk lower in my chair but refused to cross my arms over my chest.

"Go away, Mina."

"Not a chance. In fact, I think I have every class with you today."

I sighed. Thankfully, Belemina's fascination was only for the spectacle I'd likely make and not because she wanted to worship me. I mentally cringed at the thought and at how many more would be like her.

Adira's edict was going to mess with a lot of schedules today.

My prediction proved very true when three of my Human Studies classmates followed me to my self-paced studies. Thankfully, Ashlyn turned them away at the door.

"Because of my fragile humanity, only students enrolled in this class are allowed to enter. If you don't like the rule, take it up with Adira. If you don't follow the rule and leave, I'll take it up with Adira and Megan."

Megan was like Uttira's very own boogie man with the way her name cleared the room.

Being rid of my excess baggage from the first session didn't mean I was free from consequence, however. One of the dwarves sat next to me and wouldn't stop staring at the meager valley between my breasts.

"Yanet, that's not the first pair of boobs you've seen. You have your own," Ashlyn said.

"Mine aren't nearly as pretty or soft looking. By Zeus, I want to touch you, Eliana."

I leaned away from the dwarf teen.

"It would help if you stop staring at them," I said.

"And, if you wipe the drool from your chin," Ashlyn added.

Yanet absently wiped at her chin but didn't look away.

"Sorry, Eliana," Ashlyn said. "I'm not kissing this one."

I was more than a little relieved when the bell rang and I could escape to self-discovery. That relief vanished the moment I walked into the crowded hallway. People were waiting for me. Some heckled. Some stared. Some cheered. I didn't care how they reacted, only that they'd been out there to wait for me.

The succubus side of me preened at the attention of my classmates, and my hunger slithered in my belly. Pushing my way through their number, I made my way to my third-hour session only to stop cold just outside the room as a familiar lustful scent hit me between the eyes.

I looked around for Fenris, trying to decide which way to run, but I didn't see him. With the crowd growing, I bolted into the room and hoped the majority of students wouldn't follow me. A few tried, but there was only one open seat in the room. Right next to Fenris.

I momentarily debated running.

"This is an interesting switch up, isn't it, Eliana?" LuAnn said. "Adira will be so pleased with these results."

Of course, the teachers knew.

I looked at the empty chair and Fenris's group of followers, who sat around him in a cluster. Their lust combined with his made my head swim, but it explained why his was so much more potent.

With little choice, I took the only open seat available to me.

Fenris leaned toward me right away. My mouth watered.

"I came as soon as I heard."

Why did my mind go to dirty things when he said that?

"I thought people you knew would be better than people you didn't. You okay?"

His simple concern helped me keep a tight hold on my control.

"Not really. I know I'm not supposed to hate anyone, but she's really making it hard not to."

He chuckled, not even asking who I meant. There was only one adult who liked making every Uttirian teen miserable. Adira.

"Don't let her see she's made you sweat. You've got this, Eliana."

Did his voice just go husky at the end, there? My stomach pitched with delight, and I found myself leaning in. His gaze dipped to my shirt.

"I see why so many people are talking. It's quite a sight. Do you like the shirt?"

"I like it if you like it."

I flinched. Why had I said that?

His grin widened.

"Don't worry, Eliana. I know the real you. You can't offend me or shock me."

I snorted.

"How can you know the real me when I don't even know the real me?" I waved a hand to indicate the room. "If I did, I wouldn't be here."

"An astute observation," LuAnn said. "Perhaps Fenris could use a bit of self-discovery, too. I hear you're a little late coming into your mate run."

Fenris flushed, an unusual sight.

I didn't see what the big deal was about his mate run. Who wanted to be saddled with a wife as a teen? Sure, he'd just turned eighteen, but that was still pretty young in the lifespan of a wolf.

In that moment, I realized both our species were pushed at an early age to be more than we were ready to be.

"Do you want to be my study partner?" I asked him.

One of the girls around us made a whining noise.

"As a friend," I added quickly.

He looked at each of his girls. One by one, they reluctantly nodded.

"Sure," he said. "I'd love to."

I heard that statement for the truth it was. He was desperate for an escape. That was something I understood all too well. It had only taken one mildly attracted Eugene to make me want to hide. I couldn't imagine constantly being surrounded by people who wanted me to pick them as a partner. And Fenris had been dealing with it for years.

"Perfect," LuAnn said. "Since both of your issues stem from mating, let's start with kissing without killing."

"What?"

While I wasn't the only one to say it, my voice was the most desperate.

My phone took that moment to ring. I scrambled to grab it out of my purse.

"I gotta get this," I said, looking at the screen. "It's Megan."

I ran from the room before anyone could stop me. Thankfully, the halls were empty as I answered Megan's call.

"Hey, Megan," I said breathlessly.

"Hey. Are you okay?"

"Yeah, I just ran out of General Living Skills." I couldn't believe I'd just lied. It hadn't been a conscious decision, just a desperate one. I did not want to tell Megan I'd been paired up with Fenris for kissing practice.

"You didn't need to leave class," she said. "I could have left a voicemail."

"Are you kidding? It's General Living Skills. I know how to live with humans. The class is a waste of my time. What's up? Why'd you call?"

"I'm hoping you can help me pick out a dress. It's supposed to be for a super fancy restaurant. Think high class, not hooker."

I sniggered as I headed for my car. Megan's call was the perfect excuse to escape.

"Turn on video chat and show me the options."

She did as I asked and panned the dresses.

"Try the red one, the gold one, and that lavender one. Those colors will look good on you."

She turned the phone around and shook her head at me.

"Those won't work. I have a bruise and need something with a higher neckline."

"Okay. Show me again."

I picked three different dresses that would cover her neckline and back. When she went to grab them from the racks, I stopped her. I could tell with a glance that those weren't department store dresses.

"No, you don't touch the dresses. You wave one of the attendants over. They handle the dresses while showing you to a fitting room. Send me pics of each one, front and back, so I can tell you which works. I better get back to class."

I'd reached the exit door to the parking lot.

"Thank you," she said before disconnecting.

I hurried out the door and got in my car, shivering at the chill in the air. I hated lying. It went against everything my father taught me. And the shame I felt at lying to my best friend was even greater. Yet, with everything that Megan was dealing with, I couldn't tell her my problems. At least, not yet. When she solved the mystery of the troll deaths and came home, then I'd come clean. Deciding that made me feel marginally better.

The first picture from Megan came through before I reached her house. I waited until I pulled into the driveway to look at the dresses. Each one was beautiful on her, just as I'd known they would be. However, of the three she sent me, the rose gold one was the most stunning,

Be sure to pair it with large diamond stud earrings and a soft updo because of the high neckline, I sent.

It didn't take long for her response.

What exactly does an up do?

You're hopeless. When you get home, we're going shopping for a week so I can be assured you'll not go out looking like a frump.

Frump? When did my grandma get here?

I'm texting Oanen that I need a picture before you walk out the door.

She sent back a laughing face.

With a smile, I got out of my car and let myself into her house. The milk, oats, and honey weren't that old, but I still changed the concoction out with a fresh batch before making myself comfortable in her living room.

I didn't feel an ounce of guilt as I wasted away several hours watching TV. I knew in my heart Megan would have cheered me on if I'd told her I'd ditched school and hung out on her couch. When it was close to the time I normally returned to the Quills', I closed up Megan's house again and made my way home.

The Quills' house was unusually quiet when I let myself in through the kitchen. Thanking my luck, I hurried upstairs to my room. My first priority was to check my closet for my cute dresses. If those hadn't returned, then I would change into some jeans and a new shirt.

Instead of doing either, I stopped just inside my bedroom door and watched Adira turn from the window to face me.

"I'm glad you're finally home. I hope you used your time wisely and practiced the art of seduction as LuAnn suggested."

I struggled to form a response that wasn't a lie.

"You'll be able to put that practice to use now." She held out her hand. "Come with me."

A portal appeared behind her just as her hand closed over mine. With a sickening twist in my stomach, my reality shifted, and I was pulled from my bedroom in Uttira to a bathroom in some club.

I grabbed onto a sink to steady myself. In the mirror, I met Adira's gaze.

"Take a moment to freshen up," she said over the thump of music. "I'll be in the bar area to observe your progress."

She left me there, disoriented and still clinging to the sink.

It took a moment for my surroundings to really sink in. The faint odor of smoke and alcohol, along with the generic row of sinks and mirrors and floor to ceiling tile with dirty grout lines, told a story of too much partying and very little concern about quality. What kind of place had she brought me to?

I saw the answer when the door opened and three women staggered in, laughing and leaning on each other. Their sparkly tops, light dusting of body glitter, and ample display of cleavage were standard club attire. However, the smeared makeup and drugs they openly traded were not.

I left them to their private party and braved the crowded main room. The scent of lust called to me, leading me to several men who idly watched the dancers on the floor from their places at the bar. Their gazes shifted to me, but I ignored them on my hunt for Adira.

A man stepped in front of me. At over thirty-years-old, his gaze had no business shifting down my top.

"Darling, you're the stuff my dreams are made of. Tell me

what you're looking for in life, and I'll make your dreams come true, too."

"I'm looking for a frost giant currently wearing her human form. She looks normal under regular lighting, but if you can talk to whoever's in charge and get the black lights turned on, you'll see something that will blow your mind."

"It's not my mind I want blown," he said, leaning in. "You're a special kind of crazy, but the pretty ones usually are." He lifted a hand to touch me.

"The black lights," I said firmly. "Those come first."

He grinned.

"You got it, darling."

He'd barely stepped away from me when Adira appeared from the depths of the crowd.

"What do you think you're doing?"

"Giving you a choice," I said calmly. "You can take me home now, before the black lights come on and everyone sees you for what you are, or you can continue to try to force me to feed." Her expression hardened. "Pseudo-choices aren't very fun, are they?"

She took my hand, and with a nausea-inducing stomach twist, I found myself once more in my bedroom. Alone.

With a sigh, I sat on my bed. I'd played mean with Adira at the club, meaner even than the night I'd threatened her with Megan because of Eugene. I dreaded what Adira would do in retaliation now.

That dread stayed with me as I watched TV then changed for dinner.

As I slowly made my way downstairs, I caught a hint of raised voices coming from Mr. Quill's office. Changing direction, I went to listen at the open door again.

"Her increasing defiance is a result of Megan's influence. With

Megan's mother focused on her, we're free to focus on Eliana. We're making the right choice, Anwen. Never doubt that."

I stepped into the room.

"And what choice is that?" I asked.

Mrs. Quill's expression started to crumble, and Mr. Quill quickly hugged her close. My stomach churned with fear. Adira's gaze flicked to her distraught sister than settled on me.

"You've been coddled too long. As of now, you will no longer feed from Mrs. Quill. Like other succubi your age, you will need to find your own food source. And since you don't like leaving to hunt for human prey, you'll need to make do with your peers."

I stared at her, unable to process what had just happened.

"Perhaps we should discuss this further after dinner," Mr. Quill said, looking from Adira to me. "Anwen picked up the pizza you love from Chicago."

"Dinner?" I echoed numbly. They wanted me to eat after telling me I couldn't eat. I struggled with the irony while reminding myself I wanted to be a good person no matter how others treated me. I didn't manage to curb all my anger when I spoke, though.

"A succubus doesn't need human food. I'm going to my room unless I'm no longer welcome there, either."

Mrs. Quill's tears cut me as deeply as her abandonment. Hardening my heart to both, I left the room.

CHAPTER SEVEN

I knew I was dreaming the moment my tranquil forest walk turned into a skunk riddled sex fest. Everywhere I looked, they were paired up and humping like crazy. I always dreamed about sex in some way, but this was a new level of awful for me. The scent of skunk lust was as rancid as their spray, and it filled my nose with an intensity that made it hard to breathe. However, despite the smell and the taste, my hunger demanded their lust.

I shook and fought against the urge to feed. One of the skunks looked at me, mid-humping.

"You're like a sleeping princess," it said.

"What?"

The moment I opened my mouth, the skunk-lust filled me. I swallowed it hungrily even as I gagged, and I was about to inhale more when I woke to a small mouth frantically licking my earlobe.

I squealed and scrambled from the bed while wiping at my ear.

"Don't go, princess," a tiny voice said from the darkness. "Let me try again. I can do better."

I hit the light switch and stared at the brownie sprawled out naked on my pillow. The six-inch youth twitched as he frantically tugged on his little stick, his toes curling as he lifted his head to greet me with a smile.

"Hi, I'm Piepen. Thank you for inviting me."

His knees bent a little with a particularly vigorous tug, and his eyes rolled back in his head. His current activity explained why the sour lust taste from my dream still clogged the air.

"Please stop touching yourself."

"Can't. I'm so close. Just a few more—"

"Get off my pillow!"

The scent intensified.

Gagging, I covered my eyes with my hand and felt my way to the bathroom just as he squealed in rapture.

The taste lingered in my mouth, no matter how many times I rinsed. It reminded me of the stuff Dad had put on my nails when I was little in an attempt to get me to stop biting them. I gagged, rinsed again, then brushed my teeth thoroughly. It didn't help. The air was tainted with the smell, which recoated the back of my tongue every time I breathed in.

I turned on the bathroom fan then opened every window in my room before looking at the brownie. He lay stomach down now, thankfully. Still on my pillow, though, stroking the material gently.

"You smell so good," he said, his little voice muffled.

"There's been a misunderstanding," I said. "When I told you to let me know you'd arrived, I should have specified during the day. You need to go back to Megan's house. Now."

His little head jerked up from my pillow, and I stared into his tiny, sad brown eyes.

"Please don't make me stay with Elbner."

"It's too dangerous for you to stay here. Especially after what just happened."

He jumped up from the pillow, his iridescent wings fluttering rapidly as he zoomed toward my face, all six millimeters of his tiny, hard staff aimed right at my eye.

I squealed and ducked only to feel him clinging to my hair.

"I can't go back. Please don't make me. I'll do anything."

Each statement was punctuated by a hip thrust to my head. Without thinking, I swatted him from my hair.

He squealed and flew across the room to land on the carpet where he lay without moving. Fear and guilt speared me.

"Please don't be dead," I said, rushing to him.

"Not dead," he rasped. "In ecstasy. That was the fastest I've milked my acorns yet. Your hand is so soft."

I lifted my hand, gagged at the pale white smear on my skin, and rushed to the bathroom.

After I finished washing, I tried to once more reason with the little creature, who'd relocated to my bed again.

"I don't think you understand the danger you're in here," I said. "I'm a succubus."

He sat up, mid-roll on my pillow.

"Really? Does that mean we can have sex?"

"What? No, it means I'm a danger to you."

His hand was already sliding down between his legs.

"Stop touching yourself."

He lifted both hands high.

"If I promise not to touch myself, can I stay? I hate when Elbner gives my wings tongue baths. They're never clean enough for him."

My mouth dropped open. I knew very well the goblin wasn't bathing him; he was tasting the brownie's wings. The number of wingless brownies in existence was astounding. It really was a miracle that Piepen still had his.

And because of that, I knew I couldn't send him back to Megan's. It would only be a matter of time before Piepen was as wingless as the majority of his race. I sighed in defeat, knowing I couldn't condemn him to that existence.

"I'll let you stay, but only if you swear to follow several rules for your safety."

"Anything," he said, nodding eagerly.

"First, you need to wear clothes around me at all times. Second, you can't touch yourself in my room. Third, you sleep in this drawer," I said, pulling open a drawer in a dresser I never used.

He bowed his head, his mop of shaggy brown hair falling into his eyes as he started to sniffle.

"You want to close me in a drawer?" he asked, hurt pouring from him.

"Of course not. The drawer will stay open while you sleep. It will be your bed, complete with a pillow and a blanket."

"Truly?" he asked, looking up with hope. "You don't want to lock me away?"

"Never," I said, wondering what kind of past the poor creature had already endured in his short life. "If you can follow my rules, you'll be my guest."

He was already nodding excitedly. I grabbed the lust coated pillow from my bed and placed it in the drawer, along with a shawl from my closet, while he zipped across the room to his discarded pants.

Shivering, I started to close windows. The scent of his lust still strongly lingered in the air, though. In the reflection of the mirror, I caught him tugging his pants back on with frequent and unnecessary readjustments of his little package.

He saw me watching and immediately stopped.

Sighing, I pointed at his bed.

"Go to sleep, and no more touching yourself. I mean it."

He flew to his bed and settled under the soft shawl I'd provided, petting it with a contented sigh, before closing his eyes. I crawled back into my bed and exhaled slowly, not sure if I'd be able to sleep while breathing in his nastiness.

After a few minutes, I got out of bed and turned on the ceiling fan. It helped along with the fact that Piepen was softly snoring and no longer touching himself.

With a sigh, I closed my eyes and drifted off.

This time, when the skunk dream invaded my mind, I knew what was happening and woke shaking my head.

My cheek touched a wet spot on my pillowcase. I lifted my head, wondering if I'd been drooling because of hunger. The tiny circle, about the size of a dime, glistened with a non-saliva iridescence.

"Ugh! Ew!"

I sat up and brushed my cheek, which only smeared the nastiness.

"Piepen," I hissed, looking around the room. "I said no touching yourself."

His head peeked up from the edge of his bed drawer.

"I didn't. I swear."

Even as he said it, he started twitching as if the lower half of him, currently hidden from view, was moving. The scent of his lust grew.

"How old are you, Piepen?"

"I just turned fourteen."

I knew he meant fourteen months because brownies weren't as long-lived as most races. Likely because they bred like crazy as soon as they hit puberty, which started after one year of age. So, what he was doing wasn't really his fault. It was his nature for the given stage of his life.

"I need to shower and get ready for school. While I'm gone today, I want you to stay in this room for your safety. You still have your wings, and a lot of creatures in this town will want to change that."

"Thank you for keeping me safe."

Guilt stabbed at me as I stripped my pillow, threw the case into the laundry, then closed myself in the bathroom.

While I would do just about anything to help Megan solve her case so she could get home faster, keeping the brownie in my room wasn't going to work for long. Especially after I'd accidentally fed from him. He was far from safe with me.

I started the shower and stripped out of my pajamas. As much as I wanted to avoid eye contact with the mirror so I wouldn't see what was currently drying to my cheek, I turned to place my pj's on the counter.

I stopped short at the sight of myself. Not because of the smear on my cheek but because of the reflection of my body.

My rib bones shone in startling prominence. The hollow of my stomach was ghastly as were my protruding hip bones. I touched them, not believing what I was seeing. But I didn't feel as wasted as I looked. I felt thin, sure, but not bony.

I frowned and looked down at myself. I was normal. Looking up at the mirror again, I saw the same thing that I felt and shook my head at what I'd thought I'd seen. I was just tired and stressed. My mind was playing tricks on me.

As soon as the water warmed, I stepped into the wet room and stood under the rainfall spray. Soaping my face twice only made me feel marginally better. Breathing in the scent of my floral shampoo, I lathered my hair and tried to find my happy place for the day.

With the brownie and goblin in Uttira, Megan wouldn't be gone for much longer. That happy thought deflated when I realized that Megan had her mark now and would likely leave again for some other case just as soon as she returned. The Council wouldn't want a full-fledged fury in town for long.

Buried under the weight of my depressing thoughts, I didn't immediately notice the splash of water against my legs. However, I definitely felt the splash against my inner thigh since it was accompanied by the brush of tiny fingers.

I squealed and scrambled back a step, looking down to see Piepen, the naked little horndog, bathing in my pubic hair runoff.

His wet, upturned face was filled with joy as he "washed" himself with a vigor that threatened to detach his prized possession.

Without thinking, I lifted my leg to kick him. I wasn't thinking of how it might hurt him or how I was exposing myself. I just wanted him out. However, the moment his eyes widened and his gaze locked on my privates, I knew my mistake. Instead of flying away in terror, he dipped lower. I missed and almost fell.

"The glory of a real woman!" he said in his high-pitched voice.

He twitched and groaned, and his familiar skunk smell clogged the air.

"Oh, what a gift! Thank you for showing me your flower and glistening petals. You've made a man out of me," he said on a sigh and continued to stare. "Your breasts are magnificent, too. Would you like me to wash them for you?"

I sputtered for a moment before my brain formed a coherent thought.

"Get out of this bathroom before I rip your wings off myself."

All trace of color vanished from his exposed flesh, and he zipped from the bathroom.

Shaking and disgusted—mostly at myself for threatening him in such a horrible way—I stood in the water for another minute before rinsing and drying off.

Wrapped in a towel, I peeked into my room and noticed a shaking lump under my blankets.

I opened my mouth to apologize then stopped. If he was afraid of me, maybe he'd keep his distance. And distance would keep him safer.

Leaving him be, I went to my closest and found yet another revealing top waiting for me. I seethed for a moment before ripping it off the hanger and dressing. Piepen remained quietly hidden when I reemerged, but the trembling ball had flattened out.

"We need better rules," I said. "You're not allowed on, in, or near my bed at any time, day or night."

His rhythmic humping of my sheets immediately stopped.

"When I'm in the bathroom, you're not allowed to enter under any circumstances. If you break any of those rules, you'll need to leave. Do you understand?"

He crawled out from under my sheets, his tear-streaked face peering at me before he nodded and fled to his drawer.

"I'll see you after school."

I left my room and went straight for my chocolate stash, tucking two bars into my purse before heading downstairs.

I briefly considered taking a bite of one just to rid my mouth of the lingering taste of brownie lust then decided against it. The last thing I needed was Mrs. Quill telling Adira that I was eating chocolate for breakfast. I didn't want to lose my stash. My steps slowed right outside the dining room as I realized just how important the chocolate would be to me now.

With Piepen's arrival, I'd momentarily forgotten what had happened last night. Mrs. Quill's abandonment stung all over again. I thought of our morning routine of her fixing me human food I didn't really need. Why keep the pretense?

"Don't hover in the hallway, Eliana. Get in here and give your mom a hug."

The sound of my mom's voice propelled me forward. She sat at the table with Mrs. Quill. Both had cups before them.

Mom smiled at me, her blonde hair perfectly lying over one shoulder.

"Baby, you have no idea how good it is to see you. Come sit by me. Tell me about school. Friends. Your life. Anything."

"What are you doing here?" I asked instead.

She waved her hand negligently.

"Just a Council misunderstanding that I'm sure they'll clear up in a few days. Though, I wouldn't mind if it took longer. Just look at you. You're getting so big. Not much in the way of curves, but if that's working for you, embrace it."

She patted the chair beside her.

"Sit. I made you a fun breakfast that I think you'll enjoy."

"Council misunderstanding?" I looked at Mrs. Quill. She knew why my mom couldn't be here. What could the Council possibly—

"They think I've been killing trolls," Mom said with a laugh. "Can you imagine?"

"No. I can't imagine how the Council would possibly jump to that conclusion." I continued to stare at Mrs. Quill. "What game is Adira playing now?"

My mom's gaze shifted between Mrs. Quill and me.

"What games has Adira been playing?" Mom asked, her tone turning dangerously serious.

I looked at my mom, torn. If I admitted everything, she would never trust me in the Quills' and Adira's care again. Yet, if I said nothing, I would continue to suffer Adira's manipulations, which after last night, were getting worse.

"Eliana?" Mom prompted.

"When you brought me here, I was naive to so many aspects of our world."

"Which is why it was time to bring you here."

I nodded.

"And you allowed me to stay so I could learn at my own pace."

"Because you asked."

I could see her growing curiosity as to where this conversation was leading.

"Why does this preluding explanation feel like you're trying to protect Adira?" she asked, a hint of humor returning to her tone.

I couldn't help but smile a little. Though we'd only spent a small amount of time in each other's company since she'd left me here, we'd talked often. Because of that, she knew me well.

"I am. Until recently, I've been allowed to set the pace."

Mom's eyes darkened.

"Until recently? What happened?"

"Adira's forcing me to wear what she thinks is appropriate for a succubus my age. She has also attempted to select who I should feed on and has tried to coerce my compliance."

"I see. And did she give you a reason why?"

"We're worried Eliana is starving herself because she hasn't fully embraced who she is. Until yesterday, she's solely been feeding on me."

My mother stared at Mrs. Quill for a long moment.

"I would like to speak with my daughter alone, please."

Mrs. Quill promptly vanished, and Mom looked at me again, patting the chair.

I took the seat and saw she'd made me chocolate chip

pancakes smothered in chocolate syrup and topped with a death-by-chocolate ball of ice cream that was slowly melting. Her understanding of me almost brought me to tears.

"Thanks, Mom."

She smiled and watched me take my first bite. It was disgustingly good.

"You know that doesn't nourish you, right?" she asked.

"I know. It's a good thing, too, or I'd be fat. How can something that doesn't provide any significant nourishment taste so good?"

"You told me you were feeding, baby."

"I was. Mrs. Quill was perfectly acceptable and willing."

She watched me eat for a moment.

"Are they right? Do you have an eating disorder?"

I stopped with my fork partially to my mouth. The absurdity of her question startled a laugh from me.

"It's not funny, Eliana. I know you've been through a lot and just want to make sure—"

"I'm fine, Mom. I fed off a nasty pedophile this summer. I'm not starving, I'm selective."

She frowned.

"You like pedophiles? I suppose that explains your trim figure."

"Ew, Mom, no! What I like is choosing my own meals. You don't let anyone tell you who to eat or what to wear or when to kiss. Why should I?"

I couldn't believe that just came out of my mouth.

"Oh, baby, I'm so glad I'm here, no matter what the reason. I wish you wouldn't have kept all this from me. Why did you?"

Her gaze turned sad as I tried to come up with a truthful reason that wouldn't hurt her feelings.

"You thought I would try to force you, too, didn't you?"

I nodded, hating the disappointment in her expression.

"Never, baby. All I'm going to do...all I ever want to do...is to encourage you to become the best version of you, whatever that version may be. While I think Adira was trying to do that in her own backward way, you don't have to worry about her anymore. I'm here, and I'm not leaving you again until everyone sees you like I see you.

"Now, tell me all about school, your friends, or anything you want. I'm ready for all the juicy Uttira gossip."

The weight of her motherly affection stifled me.

"Well, I'm not any further in my self-paced studies. Mostly because I'm having a hard time focusing on them with Megan gone. I'm worried about her."

Mom reached out and smoothed a hand over my hair.

"There's nothing to worry about. Megan looked fine. So did Oanen, by the way. I don't know how you lived with that temptation under the same roof. That boy is just delicious."

"Mom, Oanen is off-limits. His dad, too. You know that, right? They're my family."

"Of course I know that. It doesn't mean I can't look and drool a little."

It was in her nature—every succubus's nature, really—to look and drool a lot. And to tempt and lure. As much as I missed my mom and loved her, the Council needed to get their information straight and send Mom home before something bad happened.

"I better get to school. I don't want to be late, looking like this."

Mom's gaze flicked to my clothes as I stood.

"It's definitely not your usual school-girl style."

"No, it's not. I miss my dresses."

"So don't go to school. Stay home with me." Her gaze lit. "I might not be able to take you shopping, but we could go out for a bite to eat."

She didn't mean one of Uttira's restaurants. She meant hunting. And that was the last thing I wanted to do with her. Ever.

"I can't. I missed some stuff yesterday that I need to catch up on."

"I don't know why you bother with the Academy. You could easily test out of the human education classes, and Adira obviously has no clue about guiding a powerful succubus such as yourself."

"Mom, I'm not powerful."

"Nonsense. That misguided thinking only proves my point. The Academy isn't helping you. I should homeschool you."

My heartbeat stuttered for a panicked moment.

"I like school, Mom. I like seeing my friends, and I like being around all the people. Please don't take that from me."

Love and worry glinted in her eyes.

"Never. If you want to keep going, then, of course you'll go. I just wanted you to know that I'm here for you, however you need me."

I smiled, gave her a quick hug, then fled. My mind raced as I drove to school. How could the Council make such a dumb mistake? It was fairly common knowledge that my kind preferred to feed off of humans with the exception of a few other creatures. Definitely not trolls. Or brownies. A full-body shiver wracked through me at the thought of the latter.

And Mr. Quill had said that the killings seemed ritualistic, which meant magic. Succubi didn't have magic. Nothing was adding up.

When I pulled through the gates just behind another car, I knew I was much later than usual. There were far too many vehicles in the parking lot. Heads turned as I got out of the car and hurried toward the building. There was no jacket to hide me this time.

Yanet saw me in the hall, and a wistfulness crossed her expression. Like yesterday's top, today's exposed a good portion of my sternum and cleavage. However, it also dipped far too low on my back. The lack of material combined with the missing undergarment meant that I was a little cold, and everyone could tell.

Crossing my arms, I hurried to the first session's room and slid into my seat. Belemina turned in her chair to give me a knowing look before Lucas's lecture started. The scent of lust slowly built as the minutes ticked by. I felt twitchy with hunger even though the combined lust smelled like cake rolled in chocolate then dropped in a sludge-filled pond.

As soon as the bell rang, I was out of my seat.

"Can I carry your books for you?" the boy next to me asked.

"I don't have any books."

He laughed.

"I said boobs."

With my face heating to molten-core level, I rushed from the room. Mom's words came back to me. Why was I even here? I couldn't remember any of the lecture I'd just sat through. And even if I could remember, was it anything I didn't already know? Yet, going home and agreeing to homeschool would mean that Mom would never leave. Or, at least, not until I was the best version of myself she thought I should be.

My self-paced study with Ashlyn wasn't much better than the day before, thanks to Yanet's very focused attention.

"I can't believe I didn't notice how pretty you were before now."

Her eyes were on my chest, again, not my face.

"Please, Yanet, I really need to finish my work today," I said for the third time.

"Yanet, if you're not here to study, you need to leave," Ashlyn said.

Yanet heaved a sigh.

"I better leave. There'll be no studying with that much treasure begging to be unearthed."

She leaned forward.

"If you ever need my help with that, let me know." She winked an earthy brown eye at me and sashayed out of the room. She didn't smell bad. In fact, I itched to follow her and discover exactly what—

I blinked, my vision flickering between hyper-focused and normal.

Someone sat in the chair beside me, and I made an impatient sound.

"Everything okay?" Ashlyn asked.

"Sorry, I thought it was another..." I glanced around the room and caught the kid with the great smile watching me. He winked and blew me a kiss.

"Never mind," I mumbled to Ashlyn as I focused on my tablet.

"You know, you do look really pretty."

The way she said it gave me an immediate uh-oh feeling. The sweet scent of her budding lust drove my hunger through the roof.

"You know better, Ashlyn," I said without looking up. "What you're feeling is an illusion brought on by my pheromones and body language that I'm trying really, really hard to control right now. But I need your help. Go back to your seat and think about everything your family has suffered because of creatures like me. Don't become the next victim."

There was a moment of silence, then the chair scraped against the floor. I exhaled slowly as she returned to her place in the front corner of the room. While her scent gradually returned to normal, I imagined what it would taste like if I'd helped it bloom. The itch to look at her clawed at me as the remaining time ticked away. I all but ran from the room when the bell rang.

I made it to the bathroom before the halls got too crowded and splashed some cold water on my face. Staring at my reflection, I watched my eyes flicker between brown and black and wondered what would happen next. Without Mrs. Quill, I'd need to feed or die. And as much as I told myself I'd rather die than feed on a human, I wasn't sure I'd be able to stop myself. No matter what Adira and Mrs. Quill thought, I wasn't starving yet. But I would be soon, and let the gods help whomever my hunger chose as my victim because I wouldn't be able to.

"Hey, sucu-babe," Belemina said, walking into the bathroom. "Wanna make out?"

"Now isn't a good time," I said, gripping the sink.

"I'm serious. It might take the edge off."

I lifted my gaze to hers, knowing I'd gone full black.

"The edge and everything else you have. Are you willing to give it?"

She lifted her hands and backed up a step.

"Just trying to be a friend and help out."

"I don't need help."

"Sure. Whatever you say."

She didn't move as I left the bathroom. Students in the hall whispered and laughed as I hurried past them. I didn't care. I just needed to reach the next session room. Then I'd be fine.

However, when I walked into Self-Discovery, I was anything but fine. All the desks were full except one.

Fenris flashed his easy grin at me and patted the empty seat beside him.

"My schedule was changed," he said. "Apparently, we're both late bloomers and need to work that out. Wanna be my study buddy?"

Standing in the doorway, I seethed, knowing exactly what was happening.

The Academy was Adira's very own science experiment, and I was currently a test subject.

CHAPTER EIGHT

"Come in and sit down, Eliana," LuAnn said. "We have a lot of work to do today."

Woodenly, I walked to the empty seat beside Fenris. I could feel everyone's eyes on me. Some were curious—those immune to my special brand of messed up. Some were jealous—mostly Fenris's girls. And the rest were interested. Very interested.

Breathing through my mouth, I tried to listen to what LuAnn was saying. But, it was hard. The iron hold I usually had on my hunger was failing me. As much as I wanted to blame it on what I was wearing, I knew it was more than that. I was lonely without Megan around and on edge because I knew my mom was waiting for me at home. And if that wasn't bad enough, I still had a horny brownie to deal with.

"You okay?" Fenris asked, leaning close to me and tapping my fisted hand.

I suppressed a shiver at the skin to skin contact and glared at him. He knew better.

He cocked his head at me.

"You seem a little on edge."

LuAnn saved me from answering.

"Fenris. Eliana. Since you two are already talking, why don't you pair up for this next exercise?"

"Sure thing, LuAnn," Fenris said with a grin. "What's the exercise again? I wasn't listening."

The shameless way he admitted his disregard almost made me smile.

"Help each other discover what's missing in your lives. What element or elements are holding you back from realizing your full potential?"

"Got it."

"Since this can be a sensitive area, I've appropriated study rooms three through seven in addition to this room. That should enable each pair of you a private space to work. I expect a report tomorrow regarding what you've learned."

I didn't move from my chair. I couldn't. Alone in a room with Fenris? My hunger leeched away more of my control at the mere thought of what could happen.

Before I could blink, the room emptied until only LuAnn remained with us.

"I'll be back to check on you in a few minutes." The door shut behind her.

Fenris inhaled deeply. I wondered what he smelled because all I could smell was his delicious lust. I wanted to lick it off his skin. Rub against his—

"You're angry. And afraid," he said softly. "Why?"

"I'm angry that Adira is toying with my life and afraid I'll give in to my hunger."

He shifted in his seat.

"You know you can't hurt me, right?"

I turned to look at him.

"Can't I? I can make you love me so deeply, so thoroughly, that when I leave you, you'll be nothing more than an empty shell dwelling on what you once had. You'll forget to eat. Forget to wash. You will be broken in ways that will never be fixed. You'll slowly waste away in your desperate and all-consuming desire to find me and win me back."

While I spoke, his normally easy-going personality vanished, replaced by sympathy.

"I get it," he said. "Our situations aren't the same but similar enough that I get it."

His understanding helped me regain a measure of control.

"How are they similar?" I asked.

"All the pack girls are obsessed with being around me. And I don't use that word lightly. Look at what happened to Aubrey."

Aubrey had been the head of his fangirl club and bullied the rest of the girls to the point of submission. Her obsession had ultimately led to her removal from Uttira. She'd been insane with her infatuation with Fenris. And why? That was one piece I'd never understood. Was Fenris more like me than I thought?

"Why are they so obsessed with you? There are other males in the pack, right?" I thought I remembered one a grade ahead of us and two a grade behind. They were quiet and didn't garner nearly as much attention as Fenris.

Fenris shrugged.

"Dad and I have talked about it. He thinks it might be something in my scent. But I don't smell any different from Walden."

"Who's Walden?"

"He's the only other unmated male in my pack."

"Wait. I thought there were three in the school."

Fenris shook his head.

"They're already mated. I'm late with my run. I wasn't kidding when I said we're both behind."

That just made me feel bad for both of us.

"I don't understand what sitting here and talking about it is going to do to help us," I said.

"It probably won't, but it's nice not being surrounded by a bunch of admirers, isn't it?"

He put his feet up on the chair in front of him and grinned at me. And I realized right then that while Fenris always smelled like lust, he'd never seemed overly interested in me.

"Do I attract you?" I asked before I could stop myself.

His humor slipped then returned doubled.

"I'm a male with eyes. Of course you attract me."

I considered him for a moment, feeling a bit of hope and companionship because, despite his assurance that he found me attractive, I knew better. If I'd really attracted him, he would have been compelled to hit on me, just now, in order to find a way to bring us both a bit closer on an emotional level. But he hadn't.

I smiled.

"Thanks, Fenris. So what do you think is missing from your life? What's holding you back from realizing your full potential?"

"That's easy. My mate. Everyone's so worried about me not going on my run yet. But, when the time's right, it'll happen."

As he spoke, the scent of his lust increased, coating my taste buds. I itched to lean toward him and inhale, to take what he had in plenty.

I stood abruptly.

"Tell LuAnn I needed to go."

Before I could run, he grabbed my wrist.

"If you keep running, Adira will keep pushing. It's what she does. Instead of running, tell me what's wrong. We can work through it together."

I trembled, my entire focus on the contact of his skin against mine. My heart thundered in my chest as I struggled not to turn on him. Not to straddle his chair and bury my fingers in his thick, dark hair.

"No touching," I managed.

He immediately released me.

"Okay. But I wasn't touching you when you decided to leave."

I took a slow and steady breath, weighing his words and my options. Fenris had made a valid point. The more I ran or fought Adira's plans, the harder she seemed to push.

Instead of leaving, I moved to a chair on the far side of the room and took a seat. He changed his relaxed position to one of intent study as he waited for me to speak.

"Your dad's wrong," I said after a moment. "You don't smell the same as the rest of your kind. You always smell like lust. You have since the first time I saw you four years ago. It's only gotten stronger. It's hard to be around you. The scent is...overwhelming."

"You're going to need to be a little more specific in what you mean by overwhelming. Are you saying I need to start wearing car fresheners?"

I snorted.

"No. I'm saying you're your own brand of car freshener. Times seven."

"So I smell good in small doses, but too much gives you a headache?"

There was no way I was going to tell him exactly what his scent did to me. It was too embarrassing.

"Something like that."

"Okay. Now that I know, I'll try to keep it in check," he said.

I doubted it was anything he could control but didn't say anything.

"Since we've covered what's missing from my life," he said,

"and why you're running away all the time, let's talk about what's missing from your life."

"Nothing I want is missing."

"Then what's holding you back from realizing your full potential?"

"Who's to say I haven't already realized it?"

He chuckled, the sound doing funny things to my insides.

"If you'd attained your full potential, you wouldn't be sitting in Self-Discovery for the third year in a row."

"Ouch. That's hurtful."

"No, it's not." He tapped the side of his nose. "I'd know if it hurt."

"What's keeping me here is Adira's idea of what I should be versus who I want to be."

"Who do you want to be?"

"Me. Just me. Why can't that be enough?"

"It's enough for me," he said.

His complete acceptance made me want to hug him. Obviously, I couldn't. But I wanted to, and that was enough to get my hunger going again. I looked up at the ceiling.

"Can we talk about something else?" I asked.

"Sure. Let's talk about why you're upset."

I heaved a sigh.

"I'm not upset. I'm hungry." I glanced at the clock and saw only ten minutes had passed. I'd never last a full hour with Fenris.

"Can you throw me my purse?"

"Your purse or the two chocolate bars you have hidden away?" he asked, his voice laced with amusement.

I stopped staring at the ceiling to wrinkle my nose at him.

"Just throw the purse."

He grinned and tossed it to me. I dug out a bar, grateful he didn't tease me about it. The first bite helped distract me from his mouthwatering scent. But only a little.

"Do you want some?" I asked when I saw he was watching me.

"Yep. I do." As he said it, the scent of his lust kicked up a notch.

"I thought you were going to try to keep yourself under control," I said, breaking off a square and throwing it his way.

"I am trying. It's not easy."

I couldn't fault him, not when I was struggling with my own control.

"Sorry. I didn't mean to criticize."

He gave me an easy grin.

"Don't worry about it. Now that I understand it's not me driving you away but my smell, I'd rather have you say something instead of just running." He popped his square of chocolate into his mouth and closed his eyes like it was the best thing ever. I could relate.

When he swallowed and looked at me, there was a mischievous glint in his eyes.

"It's nice being around someone who's not trying to get into my pants. We should hang out more."

I almost choked on my chocolate.

"It's easier on me if I don't hang out with anyone," I said, feeling more than just a little dejected at the thought because it was nice being with Fenris.

"That sounds lonely," he said.

I shrugged.

"What about Megan?" he asked. "You hang out with her."

"She's different. She doesn't seem affected by me. And she needs me."

"Maybe I need you, too."

A small laugh escaped me, and I shook my head.

"I highly doubt that."

He put his hand over his heart.

"Now who's being hurtful?"

"Fine. Why do you need to hang out with me?"

"Freedom."

I knew he meant from his girls, and some of my humor faded. Fenris had come to this class yesterday because he'd heard about my harassment by the other students and had wanted to help me out. Why couldn't I return the favor?

"I'll think about it."

"Fair enough."

LIKE FENRIS HAD SAID, I needed to stop running from Adira's manipulations and face them. And I was, starting immediately. The calming chocolate effect from the two bars I'd eaten had been enough to last the remainder of Self-Discovery with Fenris. Though I'd enjoyed talking to him, his scent had continually provoked me to the point I'd been relieved to escape.

However, leaving Self-Discovery and the tempting shifter didn't settle my hunger. It continued to plague me as lust wafted from my fellow students, thanks to my revealing top.

I managed to make it to lunch without feeding from anyone, but only barely.

Now, I desperately wanted to go home and help myself to more of my chocolate to soothe the gnawing hunger writhing inside of me. Fortunately, I had the perfect reason to leave. My mom. I wasn't running; I was checking on the parent I rarely had a chance to see.

There was no sign of Adira as I left the school grounds and

little traffic on the way to Quills'. I couldn't help but feel a sense of anticipation when I walked into the kitchen. It wasn't just for the soul-soothing chocolate stash I planned to raid, either. While every other adult in my life was there to push me, I knew I could count on Mom to support me in her own, sometimes unhelpful, way.

"Mom?" I called.

No one answered, but I wasn't surprised. It was a big house, which is why we usually used the intercom system. I'd need to show it to Mom.

Leaving the kitchen, I went to look for her. The sound of the TV led me to the teen entertainment space where I found Mom watching an action show.

"Hey, Mom," I said just as the scent of chocolate tickled my nose.

"Oh, hey, baby. I wasn't expecting you home for a few hours yet." She gracefully rose at the same time I rounded the couch. Chocolate wrappers fell to the floor around her. Dozens of them.

My gaze shifted to the fridge.

Oblivious to how she was ruining my life, she wrapped me in a hug. She smelled like the chocolate was coming out of her pores.

"Why are you eating all the chocolate?" I asked.

Mom pulled back and grinned at me.

"I'm starving, and there wasn't anything else even mildly appealing. I see why it's your favorite. But don't worry, I doubt I'll eat it all before Anwen gets back. She went with Lander to find something else for me to eat. That man is positively tempting."

She took an untouched bar from the couch.

"Did you want some? I'm more than willing to share."

She was willing to share my chocolate? Mine?

I counted backward from five before answering.

"No, thank you. I just came home to make sure you're settling in okay. I still have a few classes left before the day's done."

"You're such a good girl," Mom said, smiling at me proudly.

If I were really a good person, I wouldn't be visualizing smothering my mother in her sleep.

"Thanks, Mom. I better get going."

I left her with my chocolate and closed myself in my room. What was I going to do? I'd been counting on my chocolate to sustain me until I figured out how I was going to feed myself without Mrs. Quill. There was a shop I could go to for more chocolate. However, if I brought it here, Mom would likely sniff it out and eat that, too.

My anger at the Council increased. What were they thinking, bringing Mom here and then not having anyone to feed her?

A low whimper broke my thoughts. It took a moment for the pitch of it to register and to recall my small guest.

"Piepen?" I looked around the room for him and found him wilted on his pillow in the drawer. He looked pale, and his eyes moved listlessly.

"Oh my gosh! What's wrong?"

My mind immediately went to the horrible, accidental feeding last night. It'd only been a mouthful, but he was so small. What if it had been too much. He'd been fine this morning, though, when he'd been showering in my runoff.

"Hungry," he rasped.

I couldn't believe I'd forgotten to feed him.

"I'll be right back."

Almost falling on the steps because of my stupid heels, I raced to the kitchen for some food. It was easy to find enough to feed Piepen, thanks to Megan's supplies. I threw together a large salad, drizzled it with honey and granola for extra calories, and hurried back upstairs.

The noise from the entertainment room had changed from gunfire with intermittent talking to a whole lot of groaning. I didn't want to know what Mom was watching now, and I sure didn't want to hear it.

Closing my door, I hustled over to Piepen and offered him a honey-dipped spinach leaf.

"Here. Try this."

He opened his mouth and flicked his tongue out, licking the honey. I had to look away. I was too hungry for hand-feeding a brownie and did not want to give the little guy any wrong ideas if he saw my eyes change.

When I'd offered to help Megan, I'd thought the brownie would be staying at her house. This wasn't what I'd signed up for. Piepen needed to go. The sooner, the better.

"Any chance you've remembered anything useful about the guy who kidnapped Megan?" I asked him while studying the ceiling.

"Useful?" he said, still not sounding like himself.

"What he looked like? The color of his hair? His eyes? How tall he was? His name? Anything?"

"No. He always wore his hood when he talked to my grandparents. They liked him. He helped them find peace."

The leaf was tugged from my fingers a second later, and I looked down to see him chewing with stuffed cheeks.

"So good!" he said around the food.

Already I could see some color returning to his cheeks. It wouldn't take him long to be back to his old self. The thought was equally relieving and depressing since a horny brownie in my bedroom was only one of my many problems. I still had a chocolate-devouring Mom in my only other sanctuary. Then, there was Adira manipulating my schedule and throwing me with Fenris, the one boy who had a scent strong enough to break my will once I ran out of chocolate. Which, at the rate Mom was eating it, wouldn't be long.

I set the bowl down on Piepen's pillow and blindly watched him eat some more before grabbing my phone. My life was falling apart, and I needed help. Badly.

I tried Megan's phone, but it went to voicemail. Desperate, I called Oanen. He picked up after the second ring.

"Please tell me Megan's there. I need to talk to her," I said.

"Hold on."

"Hey, Eliana," Megan said after a moment.

"My mom's here, Megan." Some of my panic and desperation laced my words.

"I know. And, I'm sorry for my part in that. Oanen and I have been telling the Council that we don't think she has anything to do with what's going on."

I snorted.

"Of course she doesn't. She doesn't kill; she just destroys lives."

A tiny squeal drew my attention to Piepen, who was no longer a wilted brownie in his drawer. He zipped around the room and landed spread eagle on my pillow. He immediately grabbed himself.

"Stop touching yourself when you're on my bed. I saw that smear on my pillow this morning, and you're lucky I didn't kill you in my sleep."

"Uh...Eliana?" Megan said.

"Sorry. Piepen and Elbner arrived last night. Elbner's at your place with his honey-milk. Piepen's here."

"That's great."

"No. It's not."

I crossed the room and closed myself in the bathroom so Piepen wouldn't hear me.

"He's in a horny, adolescent phase and keeps touching himself. Brownie lust does not taste like you'd think. You need to get your butt home as soon as possible. The brownie and my mom both need to go."

Just the thought of my mom in the other room upset me all over again.

"She's staying here, Megan. At the Quills'. She's already found my stash of chocolate and eaten half of it. Once the chocolate's gone, she's going to turn her attention on me. She already commented that I look underfed."

Piepen knocked on the bathroom door, and I covered the phone.

"I told you, I need privacy while I'm in the bathroom," I said. "If you can't respect that, we'll need to find you somewhere else to stay while Megan's away."

"I knocked. I didn't come in!" he said, his voice fading as he flew away.

I removed my hand from the phone and spoke softly, needing Megan to understand the seriousness of my situation.

"I caught him showering in the runoff from my pubic hairs this morning. When I went to kick him, he thanked me for the view of my flower."

Megan laughed in my ear.

"This isn't funny, Megan. It's traumatizing. Help me. No one sees my flower. Ever!"

"I am helping. I swear. We're going to follow up on a lead we have that links someone else to the trolls' deaths."

"Who?"

"We don't know his name. He's just a hooded man who talked to the victims at the Goose and Gizzard before they died."

"Piepen mentioned that a nice man, who helped his grandparents find peace, wore a cloak. Maybe it's the same guy."

"Maybe. Talk to Piepen and see if you can get anything useful out of him. A name. An address. What the hell the guy looks like."

"I will. Just hurry."

I opened the door to check on Piepen and saw him holding a ball of material to his face. I frowned, realizing he was licking the crotch of my underwear from the dirty laundry bin.

"Put down my underwear!"

Not giving up his prize, he flew to his drawer and started humping the material like crazy.

Forgetting Megan, I dropped the phone and hurried across the room.

"Do you have to be so gross?" I demanded, pulling the underwear from his hold.

He looked up at me with an indignant expression.

"The scent of your flower isn't gross. It's magnificent. It's magical."

"It's going in the washing machine."

I stormed from the room, taking all my dirty laundry with me.

Could my world get any more insane?

"Sweetie? Is that you?" Mom called as I passed the door.

"Yeah, Mom." I set the hamper to the side and looked in at her. She was eating yet another chocolate bar.

"Would you like to go out to dinner with me tonight? We can't leave Uttira, though. So we'd need to find a restaurant here that makes a passable quality human food."

"Sure, I'd love to have dinner with you."

I'd do anything to get her to stop eating my chocolate and to get me out of the house.

However, four hours later, I was questioning my life choices as Mom sat next to me in the passenger seat of my car.

"For all I know, they've tainted your palate." Mom shivered delicately.

Had I been a human man, the move would have brought about the instant need to comfort her. Instead, I rolled my eyes.

"That brownie lust emanating from your room had me heaving for thirty minutes. I don't know how you could stand being in there with that creature."

"He's a friend of Megan's," I said yet again. "Not a midnight snack for me. I promise I don't find the scent of his lust even slightly appealing. I'm just keeping him safe until Megan gets back."

"You're such a good friend. Now, recite the species list appropriate for feeding," she said with a smile. "I need to know Adira hasn't ruined you."

"Humans are the most filling and diverse. Their flavors range from savory to sweet, depending on the person. We don't know if it's the personality or the genetic makeup, so sampling is the best way to know what you're getting."

Mom snorted.

"Who told you that last bit of bullshit?"

"Mom, please. There's no need to swear. It's unrefined."

She grinned at me.

"You're smart and beautiful. A perfect combination for a well-fed succubus. Now, who told you that last bit?"

"I don't remember. It was in one of the sessions I've taken."

"More reason to consider homeschooling. I don't know where they get their information from, but it's not entirely correct. We don't need to sample. We can sense it. Smell it. Now, what other species are good."

"Frost giants, obviously. Dwarves. Siren."

I parked the car in front of one of Uttira's few restaurants.

"Can we please be done with this subject? It's rude to talk about other food when we're here to eat human food."

"Fine. Have it your way."

She gracefully emerged from my car, all makeup and glitter, elevated by six-inch heels under her long, sheath skirt. Her gaze took in the small, dark building.

"This is the best Uttira has to offer?"

"You're not in New York, Mom. You're in backwoods Maine where the Council limits the food choices."

She made a non-committal noise.

"Let's give it a try, shall we?"

The moment we opened the door, I knew I was in trouble. Fenris's unique, spice cake scent hit me hard before I even spotted him and his dad dining in the far corner.

Mom inhaled deeply.

"Something smells really good in here."

CHAPTER NINE

I TURNED TO MY MOM WITH WIDE, PANICKED EYES.

"I have to live here when you're gone and see the aftermath of your visit. Don't do anything I'm going to regret."

Her black gaze focused on me then cleared. She gave me a tender smile and smoothed a hand over my hair.

"I've forgotten how intense you can be. I promise not to do anything more to haunt you, Eliana. I've already done enough that you regret."

I hugged her because I had to. My mom hated what she'd done to my dad because it had hurt me. However, she didn't truly see anything wrong with it. Why should she, after all? She'd only been doing what was natural to her. What she needed to do to survive.

"Let's just have a nice dinner, okay?" she said, pulling back. "There's so much catching up we need to do now that I'm here."

She led me to a table, and I did my best not to look in Fenris's direction.

Mom's face was hilarious as she plucked a menu from between the condiment containers in the center of the table.

"Well, this is quaint. And sticky." She set the menu before her and glanced at the offerings.

As done up as she was, she should have looked out of place. But she didn't. She just looked beautiful and commanding. I could tell from our neighbors that they appreciated the effort she had put into her appearance, too. The man was staring at Mom's cleavage while his wife raptly gazed at Mom's face.

"Maybe this wasn't such a good idea," I said.

"Nonsense. Sticky hands are something I grew used to long ago. It's a side effect of having a really good time." She gave me a quick smile. "Did you find something you like?"

I shook my head and stared at the menu while trying to scrub the mental image she'd just painted from my mind.

"I think I'll try their steak," she said. "It looks like it's the popular item around here."

I glanced at the other restaurant-goers and noticed most of them were eating either a burger or a steak. Neither appealed to me. In fact, just the thought of real food made my stomach twist. I could definitely blame that on Fenris's mouthwatering scent permeating the air in the room. Of course, I'd rather have that.

"I'll do the same," I said.

Mom set her menu back in its place and looked around.

"Service here is a little different than I'm used to. Do we wait at the table or order at the bar?"

"Wait at the table," I said.

"How was school today? Learn anything interesting?"

I relaxed into the typical, light Mom conversation we usually shared over the phone. It was weird talking in person, but nice. When the waitress appeared to take our order, Mom spoke for both of us.

"And two glasses of your best red, please," Mom said.

Once the waitress left, Mom leaned in.

"Now that we've ordered, let's get to the good stuff. I'm dying to know what you've experienced so far and what you're curious about. Now that I'm here, I can help."

I frowned, confused.

"Experienced?"

"Yes. Sexually. I'm sure you're well past oral and regular intercourse. Have you progressed to toys yet? I found these cute tails online that are actually anal plugs. They're adorable and feel great to wear, especially with heels. You'll drive the men here crazy if you decided to sport a tail."

My mouth dropped open, and a flush started just over my hammering pulse and spread upward to my face.

"You're probably past that already too, aren't you? Just like me at your age. I bloomed fast and hard." A wistful smile crossed her face. "All the boys in a ten-mile radius had difficulty walking for most of that summer. Oh, the things we did. Have you had group sex already?"

"Mom, please," I managed in a strangled whisper, wishing the earth would open up and hell would swallow me whole. Because it sure felt like I belonged there. My hunger was giddy with all the suggestions she was giving it. And a good part of me was curious, too. However, most of me just felt mortified that she was talking about this in a normal, conversational tone.

"Not here," I said.

She glanced around the restaurant in confusion until her gaze landed on Fenris.

"Is it because there's someone from your school here?" she asked me, finally lowering her voice. "I can assure you Raiden's boy won't care. Wolves have as voracious an appetite for sex as we do. Too bad it's only for their mates."

She gave me a considering look that slowly turned to worry.

"You're embarrassed," she said in sudden shock. "You're not a virgin, are you?"

Her last words had been delivered in a louder than normal tone of abject horror that only a succubus mother could manage when talking about virginity.

The gentle clanking of silverware stopped, and another wave of mortification tickled its way up my spine. Without a doubt, she'd gained the attention of every single person in the restaurant. I didn't turn to look, though, as my face continued to heat.

Mom continued to watch me expectantly, her worry growing. While I knew she loved me unconditionally, her affection didn't make her inability to understand why I hadn't been with anyone yet any easier.

It was crazy to think I'd successfully kept it from her this long. Well, not just me. Adira and the Quills knew, too. But, they hadn't said anything either because the Council hadn't wanted a succubus as powerful as my mom running amok in Uttira. Adira's silence had enabled me to lead Mom to the belief that I was just a picky eater. A stubborn teen rebelling. None of that bothered my mom. However, a virgin succubus my age was unheard of. She'd never leave now, even if her name was cleared with the Council.

I reached into my purse and set my keys on the table.

"I'll see you at home."

Mom didn't try to stop me as I got up and walked out. Although she might not understand why I was upset, she always knew when I needed my space and gave it to me. Just like she had four years ago when I asked to live with the Quills and figure out this succubus thing on my own. I wasn't quite the same girl I'd been back then. I was smarter about the world to which I'd been born. However, I was still just as lost.

The cold winter air licked at my exposed arms, a reminder

that I still hadn't gotten my coat back from Adira. How had everything gone so wrong so quickly? As much as I would like to say my problems began when Megan left, they'd been building long before that. Each time I'd refused Adira's prodding to become more "normal" for a succubus, I'd dug myself a deeper hole. And now, there would be no escaping my fate because Mom knew my big secret.

I hated the pressure that everyone put on me. It wasn't just the adults, either. It was also my peers. Why wasn't I kissing anyone at the Academy? Or dating? Obviously, something had to be wrong with me, according to them. Nothing felt wrong, though, except the way I was constantly judged and found lacking. Why couldn't they all just let me be me?

Lost in my own head, I walked along the road home. At least, I thought I did.

When the scent of something mouthwatering finally teased my attention from my thoughts, I looked up and found myself in the middle of a quiet neighborhood. I knew I should turn around and leave the tempting smell, but I couldn't.

As if pulled by an invisible thread, I moved closer to the stone house with blue shutters. It looked and smelled so inviting. The smoke that curled from the chimney only added to the flavor already in the air.

I inhaled deeply, my hunger already demanding its due, and stepped closer to the home's darkened window. The light from the backyard glinted silver off my black eyes as I approached. In the glass's reflection, I watched myself open my mouth. A thick thread of energy drifted out the partially opened window, filling my mouth and sliding down my throat.

It filled me, warming me and strengthening me in a way that feeding from Mrs. Quill never had. I swallowed and pulled more, too hungry and upset to think of all the reasons I shouldn't. The joy of having a real meal consumed me as thoroughly as I devoured the energy. I never wanted to stop. I never wanted to feel hungry again. I would feed until I burst then—

The energy abruptly ended.

Snapped out of my feeding, I stared at my reflection in horror for a moment before running away from the window. I didn't even know who I'd just fed on. A man? A woman? Someone barely into puberty?

I ran until I had a stitch in my side then slowed to a walk, blocks away from the home.

Angry at myself and everyone who'd pushed me, I kicked at a chunk of snow sitting on the side of the road. It exploded on contact and splattered my jean-clad leg with slush. I snorted in disgust and maintained my anger for another block before my shoulders slumped in defeat.

As much as I wanted to blame Adira, Mom, and Mrs. Quill for what happened, it wasn't their fault. It was mine. If I didn't want to accidentally make love-slaves out of my neighbors, I needed better control. It didn't matter that I had slipped because I was emotionally distracted over things not going my way.

Sure, my mom would make my life hard now that she knew how behind I was, but so what? Ninety percent of girls my age had the same problem. Well, not with being a succubus but with a parent being on their case for something.

I could either become a whiney puddle of life's-not-fair, or I could pull up my big girl pants and figure out how to give myself a life without so much adult interference. Especially from my mom.

Frowning, I thought of Megan and her assurance that she and Oanen were doing what they could to clear Mom's name. I knew Megan was trying, but how long would it take? Whoever was doing these killings was smart because the creatures they were murdering weren't simple to kill. A smart person wouldn't be easy to find, not even for a fury. But, time wasn't something I had. I knew what would start happening now that Mom knew my secret, and I couldn't afford to wait weeks for Mom's name to be cleared. I needed her out of Uttira fast.

I needed to talk to the goblin.

It was a long walk out of town, but I wasn't overly cold, thanks to my recent feeding. When I got close to Megan's house, everything was dark. While I knew of goblins in general, I'd never dealt with one in person. They were reclusive by nature. So, I wasn't sure if a dark house was a good thing or not.

Going around to the back door, I knocked then let myself in with the key.

"Hello," I called. "My name is Eliana. I'm Megan's friend. The one who offered to feed you."

"Elbner knows who you are," a low voice said from the dark.

Red eyes glinted in the hall. A tingle of fear traced down my spine. It didn't matter that the height of those eyes was waist level. In fact, that only made them creepier. I reached out for the switch and flooded the kitchen with light.

The goblin stood where the eyes had been. In one hand, he held a filthy rag. In the other, a small hand broom. Dirt smudged his threadbare clothes and his pointed chin. As I stared, the permanent scowl on the goblin's wizened face deepened.

"It's nice to meet you, Elbner," I said politely, looking around the now immaculate kitchen.

Megan had kept the place neat enough, but the old home had sported signs of age in the yellowing of its walls and cabinets. That yellow was gone. Everything looked fresh and clean. Even the slight stain by the refrigerator handle was gone.

"This is impressive," I said. "Have you slept at all since you got here?"

"Are you here to feed me or talk my ears off?"

"I'm sorry. You're the first goblin I've met, and I don't know the etiquette."

"You feed me, and I work. That's the etiquette."

"Okay. Did you like what I fed you last time? Is there anything that I should change?"

He gave me a contemplative look.

"It was okay. But for the quality of my work, brownie wings would be a suitable gift of appreciation. Dip them in boiled honey and crumble them on top for a bit of crunch. That's how me mum's old owner used to feed her. She ate like royalty and polished his throne nightly in return." His scowl melted into anticipation.

I had to swallow back my bile before answering him.

"Megan is a fury who finds the consumption of brownie wings wicked. For your safety and mine, you must forego the wings."

He grunted, his intelligent eyes never leaving my face.

"You're a clever one, aren't you?" he asked.

"No more clever than you, I imagine." I went to the cupboard and got out a bowl, noting that it was the one I'd used previously and that he'd already washed and put it away.

"Can you tell me anything about your previous owner? Did he feed you wings?"

The goblin snorted.

"Wings are hard to come by."

"Do you remember your previous owner's name?"

I looked up from the oats I was pouring when Elbner made a choked sound. He was trying to speak, but no words were coming out.

"It's okay," I said, doing my best to hide my disappointment. "I know about the spell. It was wishful thinking that you'd be free of it in only a few days. We'll try again tomorrow."

I finished adding the milk and honey and put everything away.

"Is there anything else you need from me?" I asked.

"Your absence. Turn off the light on your way out."

As I left, I heard the chair at the table move across the floor. How could he possibly survive on one bowl of honey and oats a day? Yet, I'd read that's all they required. I wondered if he was in a constant state of starvation like I normally was.

Inhaling the cold air deeply, I realized the hunger that always crawled just below my skin wasn't so noticeable now. Just how much had I really eaten? And what would happen to that person?

Typically, when a succubus fed, it was in the open. The person knew who was feeding on them. But because the person never saw me, I was unsure what would happen if I ran into the person tomorrow. Would they still feel an instant need to be near me? To please me in any way possible? I hoped not because the result of such a deep feeding would be more intense than what had happened with Eugene.

By the time I reached the Quills', my face was cold, I'd lost feeling in my toes, and I wanted nothing more than a long, hot shower where I'd do my best to forget the day I had. However, after ditching Mom at the restaurant, I doubted I'd get any of that.

Instead of going in through the front door, I checked the garage and found my car there then snuck around to the back of the house. This time, I was more careful wedging my way through the bushes and didn't hesitate in the dark. The last thing I wanted to do was face Fenris right now, fed or not. Thankfully, I reached the door without interruption and slid inside the house undetected.

The faint strings of music reached my ears, and I frowned. Music wasn't unusual in the human world. But in Uttira, where creatures tended to have sensitive ears, most didn't play it. In fact, I was the odd one in the Quills' house. That music was playing now meant Mom was still up.

Walking quietly, I made my way upstairs. The sound of music grew louder as I turned down my hall. So did the sound of laughter from at least three different people. I started breathing through my mouth, already dreading what I was likely to find as I approached the entertainment room.

I didn't make it that far.

"Downward dog time," Mom called out behind Oanen's closed door.

I cringed on Oanen's behalf and hurried to my room. He would need to have his room professionally cleaned before he used it again. Even breathing through my mouth, I could taste the lust in the air.

That lust turned to skunk the moment I stepped into my room.

I stared at my bed in wide-eyed horror. Amongst brightly wrapped packages resting on my quilt, Piepen rode an overly large dildo like a mechanical bull. The loud buzzing and the continuous clacking of his tiny teeth did nothing to muffle his wild laughter as he swung one small arm above his head.

"I w-w-wish my mom-m-m w-w-would have giv-v-ven me stuff like this-s-s."

Had I still been starving, he would have been dead. Thankfully, I wasn't hungry enough to consume what was floating in the air. Choking on his awful lust, I crossed the room and yanked his toy out from under him. He squealed his disappointment when I turned it off.

"You could have hurt yourself. This wasn't for you," I said, dropping it back into the box he'd opened.

Guilt stole his indignation as he stood.

"I'm sorry. I've never seen presents before and wanted to know what was in them."

"Never?"

He shook his head sadly.

"My parents were eaten when I was only a week old. Gram and Grand took care of me, but they were wingless and had no jobs."

Just when I was about to feel bad for him, he grabbed himself.

"Why do my nuts feel cold?"

I rolled my eyes.

"Probably because you vibrated all the blood from them."

He began massaging himself, which only made his lust stronger.

"It's for medicinal purposes," he said quickly when I opened my mouth to tell him to stop.

Instead of arguing, I retreated to the bathroom with my pajamas and did my best not to reflect on my crappy day. Tomorrow would be better. It had to be.

Relaxed from a nice hot shower and wearing my comfy button-up pajama top with matching flannel pants, I left the bathroom and found Mom sitting on the edge of my bed.

I looked around the room for Piepen and found him safely peeking over the edge of his drawer.

"Don't worry," Mom said. "He's perfectly safe from me. I don't know how you can even breathe in here."

I shrugged.

"He can't help it."

She smiled.

"You have a good heart, Eliana. It's one of the many things I love about you. And I want you to know that my love for you will never change. Neither will my promise this morning."

I struggled to remember what she'd said. So much had happened since breakfast.

"I'm here to support you in any way I can. Which is why I asked Mrs. Quill to help me with a little quick shopping while she was out picking up some people to feed me. I would have waited for you so I could watch you open them, but I was famished. I see you liked the pink one?"

"What? No. Piepen got into the package before I got here."

She cast a dirty look his direction.

"I told you they were gifts for Eliana. The next time I leave something for her, you will not touch it. Am I understood?"

He squealed and dove under his pillow.

"He understands," I said, answering for him.

"Good."

She stood and opened her arms for a hug, which parted her gossamer robe.

"Mom? What are you wearing?"

She looked down at her white, lacey, see-through contraption in confusion.

"It's a teddy, Eliana." Her gaze flicked to my closet. Before I could stop her, she went to the door and pulled it open.

Her sounds of disapproval made me want to crawl under my covers and never come out.

"This is completely unacceptable. When you said your dresses were gone, I thought it was just the knee-length ones. None of this is you." She turned toward me. "Don't worry about a thing, baby. Now that I've had a little nourishment to take the edge off, I'll be able to speak to Adira with a calm mind. Your wardrobe will be fixed in no time."

She turned to me and kissed my cheek. As she did, her stomach growled.

"Maybe I need to eat a bit more before I face Adira. Would you like to join me?"

"Actually, I'm really tired."

"Okay. Why don't you open the rest of your gifts? Then you can go to bed."

I nodded and robotically went to my bed. My mother loved me. Too much. And she wanted me to be just like her based on the number of "toys" she'd bought me. I didn't know what half of them were, but thanked her for each one and promised to come to her with any questions. Especially about the one that had all the black straps and the weird attachment.

She waited until I put everything away in the unused drawers below Piepen's bed then tucked me in.

"I've missed you so much, Eliana. I want to spend as much time with you as you'll allow. Say the word, and I'm there for you. For anything. Any time. Anywhere."

She smoothed a hand over my cheek and smiled down at me.

"I understand why you've kept things from me...why you're probably still keeping things from me. I'm not angry. I'm not like the Council. We'll find you what you like to eat, and we'll do it your way. Even if I need to hold Anwen down for you."

CHAPTER TEN

A PERSISTENT BUZZING WOKE ME OUT OF ANOTHER SKUNK DREAM. Annoyed, I rolled over to glare at Piepen's drawer in the early morning light.

He made a soft yipping sound as I threw off the covers.

"I told you not to play with the—"

The sight of him naked and blissed out on his pillow robbed me of words. Instead of the big, pink monstrosity, he wore a rubber ring around his waist, the odd nub attached to it centered just over his pelvis.

As I watched, a tiny shower of sparkles erupted from below the nub and landed on the pillow beside him.

"Look! It's changing colors."

I glanced at the multiple smears on the pillow I planned to burn in the near future. If the quantity was any indication, he'd been at this for a while.

"That's probably not a good thing. The humans believe boys will go blind if they play with their bits too much."

"I can't help myself. I want to touch them all the time. I just need..."

Another shower of sparkles erupted, and a dreamy smile ghosted his lips.

"Sparkles make everything better," he said blissfully.

I slammed the drawer shut and hoped his squeal meant he'd fallen off his pillow.

"You better have that thing turned off and in the garbage by the time I'm done showering."

He wisely listened because twenty minutes later, the bedroom was quiet when I emerged from the bathroom. However, the concentrated smell of brownie lust had only grown. I opened every window in my room before opening the drawer.

Piepen sat in an unpillowed corner, his clad knees pulled up to his chest. He gave me a sad look and held up the ring in one hand.

"I would have thrown it away, but I couldn't. I was locked in a dark drawer."

"You broke the rules. Don't expect me to feel sorry for you. And don't expect me to throw that away after what you were doing with it. Fly yourself to the garbage."

He sullenly zoomed across the room and dropped the toy into my trash bin.

"I'll be right back with some food for you. Do not touch anything else in those drawers."

I left the room, fluctuating between guilt and annoyance. When I'd closed Piepen's drawer, I hadn't been thinking. I'd promised never to do that to him and had broken my promise in barely a day. Yet, I'd scolded him for breaking the rules. Rules he couldn't help but break. Unlike me, he wasn't trying to be something other than what the gods made him. A horny little brownie who needed to procreate before his short life was over.

I sighed, wondering if apologizing for what I'd done would

only encourage him to continue his ways or if my silence would somehow curb his instincts.

Like the morning before, I found Mom in the dining room, her back to the door. This time, she was alone. After her parting words last night, I felt a healthy amount of concern for Mrs. Quill. Yet, that concern almost wasn't enough to keep me in the room. After leaving me, Mom had gone back to her "meal" and had eaten very loudly for hours, which had probably contributed to Piepen's driving need to touch himself.

"You're hovering again," Mom said, busting me before I could officially make up my mind whether to leave or not.

"Sorry. I'm just tired." As soon as I said it, I wanted to smack myself.

Mom turned in her chair, setting her coffee aside to worriedly scrutinize me.

"Still? Perhaps I should take you to see—"

"I'm not sick, Mom. I swear."

Her skepticism remained firm in her expression.

"That was over eight hours of sleep."

I gave an aggrieved sigh.

"No, it wasn't. Your company was enthusiastically loud and kept me up. That's all. Will Mrs. Quill be joining us?" I asked, desperate to change the subject.

Mom hesitated a moment.

"No. She and I spoke this morning. I asked her to either feed you or stay away. I'm less than pleased with her choice but know how much her willingness means to you, so I didn't force the issue. Yet."

"Thank you."

She gave me a small smile.

"For you, baby, anything. I made muffins this morning.

Chocolate berry. Give one a try," she said, indicating the sugar topped muffin waiting beside her.

I sank into the chair, already reaching for it. The flavor was amazing. Especially after what had been coating my taste buds since the moment I woke.

"This is amazing," I said around a mouthful.

She chuckled. "I'm so glad you like it. There are five more in the kitchen."

"Only five?"

"I ate the other six."

I laughed. It felt good. I finished my muffin and thought of Piepen waiting for me upstairs.

"Hey, Mom? Can I have your permission to go to the Academy late today?"

"Baby, you don't need anyone's permission to do anything ever. Do what you want, and make no apologies for it. You're too powerful to let other people's rules stifle you."

It was all well and good for her to say that, but she had no idea the lengths Adira would go to keep her students in line and on her right path.

"I just need to know that you'll step in if Adira gives me trouble for being late."

Her eyes flooded with black.

"Does she give you trouble often?" The soft way in which she asked the question made me want to shiver.

"I...uh..."

She blinked, and her eyes cleared.

"Baby, don't protect people who won't protect you." She exhaled slowly and patted my cheek. "Skip school for all I care. It might force Adira to stop avoiding me. I've asked Anwen to let her sister know I'd like a word. However, my phone has remained mysteriously quiet. If you see Adira today, let her know I'm looking forward to speaking with her." Her gaze skimmed my outfit. "She and I have a lot to discuss."

I pitied Adira just then. If she were smart, she would talk to Mom before making her any angrier.

"If I see her, I'll let her know. Thanks, Mom."

After grabbing a bowl full of fruit from the kitchen and running it upstairs to Piepen, I headed out for the day.

The drive to the lake brought back memories of the night Megan came into her powers with flaming glory. My car still had a weird paint job because of it, not that I minded. I wondered briefly how she was enjoying her new-found abilities. Probably a lot more than I'd ever enjoyed mine.

Passing the pull off for the lake, I continued toward the marshes. The flat stretch looked inhospitable with its sea of snow-dusted cattails and long grass, but I knew it was home to hundreds of brownies. Most of them wingless refugees from the real world.

I turned onto a dirt road and followed it to a small parking area that had signs posted forbidding the hunting of brownies, winged or unwinged, in the marshes. Someone had drawn lewd images on the sign, an indication of how much the upstanding citizens of Uttira respected the law.

A brisk winter breeze bit through my thin shirt the moment I opened my car door, and I hoped Adira would talk to my mom soon. I wanted some decent clothes again.

"Hello?" I called, my heels crunching on the gravel. "My name is Eliana. I'm looking for a family to take in a brownie. He's fourteen and recently lost his wingless grandparents."

I hesitated a moment, looking around the marsh. Other than the occasional bird call, there was no sign of life.

"He needs a good home. I don't think he's ever had one

before. If there's a family willing to take him in, call me." I rattled off my phone number.

The bird calls went crazy for a moment, then complete silence reigned.

I got back in my car and drove away, hoping that I made the right choice not to mention he had wings. I couldn't risk sharing that kind of information if there were hunters in the marsh. Or worse, brownie families willing to sell Piepen's wings to earn a little cash. It was common knowledge that brownies would sell their own wings, or someone else's, if money was tight.

By the time I pulled through Girderon's gates, I'd successfully missed the first session. I took my time finding a parking spot, since mine was taken, then went inside. The halls were quiet, a nice change. In no hurry to join the second session, I paused by the pool to watch the mermaids play around with a boat.

While I knew they didn't spend all day in the water, I was still envious that they had at least one class they seemed to enjoy.

"A bit late today, aren't you?" Adira said from behind me.

"Mom wants to talk to you," I said, continuing to watch the mermaids splash. "She wasn't too happy when she said it, either. I'm not surprised, really. She never did like being confined in any way." I finally turned to look at Adira.

"Don't wait too long, Adira. You don't want to push her like you enjoy pushing me. I better get to class."

She didn't say anything as I walked away. As much as I wanted to take that as a victory, I knew better. With Adira, it was hard to tell what was a win and what was a play right into her hands.

Outside the room, I glanced down at my clothes. While skipping school altogether like Mom had suggested would have been much more appealing than facing everyone dressed like this again, I knew Fenris was right about not running from Adira's manipulations. Running never did anyone any good. Taking a steadying breath, I opened the door and stopped short at the sight of Ashlyn's empty desk.

"She gave me a note for you," Yanet said from her spot. "You want me to tuck it into your back pocket so you can read it later?"

The last thing I wanted was the dwarf anywhere near my rear end. I didn't trust the gleam in her eyes.

"No, thank you. I'll just read it now."

I held out my hand, and Yanet set the folded piece of paper in my palm, doing her best to make it as sensually-awkward as possible. Ignoring her suggestive looks, I took the note to my seat and opened it.

I'M sorry for my behavior yesterday and want you to know you did the right thing to bring up my uncle. I doubt anything else would have gotten through to me. Don't take my absence personally. I'm not mad, just being smart. We both know it's best if I avoid you for a day or two.

Still your friend,

Ashlyn

I STARED at the piece of paper, fighting the urge to cry. She was sorry? She had nothing to be sorry for. I should have left the room instead of saying what I had. It hurt her deeply. Some friend I was.

"You okay?" Yanet asked.

"I'm fine," I said automatically. After all, the social nicety that demanded people ask the question also demanded there was only one acceptable answer.

"Because if you need me to distract you, I'm—"

I turned on her.

"I said I'm fine."

She held up her hands, the callouses on her fingers standing out so sharply that I could see the glitter of diamond dust stuck in the ridges of her thumbprint on her right hand.

"Sorry," she said.

I swallowed hard and focused on the note as I refolded it. The intricate pattern of the pressed paper fibers helped distract me from my need to apologize to Yanet. Apologizing would only make her growing fascination worse. I thought of my dad and how he'd pleaded with my mom to stay with him and hardened my heart as I got up to walk out of class. I'd been mean enough to Ashlyn yesterday. I refused to repeat it with someone else today.

Walking back the way I'd come, I hid in the poolside bathroom until the bell rang. As I was leaving, I ran into the same group of druids as they entered.

"You're not taking over our spot, are you?" the one with the thick hair asked with a joking smile.

I shook my head and hurried away before joking turned into flirting. The hall leading from the pool was unusually crowded, slowing my escape. And in a strange turn of events, people didn't seem to notice me as I carefully wove my way through them. The reason for their inattention soon became clear, though.

In the middle of the hall, two boys glared at each other.

Like the rest of the students, I slowed to watch Eras, an incubus a little older than me, push the other boy.

"Dammit, Tarius. I'm not exaggerating or messing around. My meal was primed, and I mean *primed*. Then someone came in and stole it right from under my nose. I want to know who it was. Now."

"It wasn't me," Tarius said. "I wasn't anywhere near the Heights."

I recognized the name of the neighborhood. It was the very

one I'd been in last night. The memory of the energy I consumed set my heart pounding.

Threading my way to the edge of the hall, I tried to make myself as inconspicuous as possible as I passed the pair.

"Spread the word," Eras said. "I'll find the thief even if I have to force-feed every single incubus and succubus in this place."

I fisted my hands and hurried away, his threat echoing in my ears. He'd sensed me feeding, and if I fed near him again, he'd know it was me. Fortunately, I had no plan to ever publicly feed, so my secret and shame would remain my own.

With my mind dwelling on last night's feeding, I wasn't fulling paying attention to the room when I walked into Self-Discovery. I absently sat in my chair as I wondered how long the energy would last me before I found myself starving and wandering the neighborhoods of Uttira, again. Probably not long. Even with the light feedings from Mrs. Quill, I hadn't managed to last more than a few days at a time. A week at most if I fed a little heavier.

Last night's feeding had been more than I'd ever consumed in one sitting before. Yet, I could still feel my hunger lazily coiling in my stomach. I couldn't just wait until I was ravenous again. I had to figure out how I'd feed myself without Mrs. Quill. The unsettling thought left me frowning at my desk.

The bell rang, startling me out of my thoughts. I looked around and saw the room was empty, except for one person.

Fenris.

He was watching me with an inscrutable expression that melted into a rueful smile as our gazes locked. His familiar scent teased my nose, making my mouth water just a little. I did my best to ignore it.

"I wasn't sure you knew I was here," he said, leaning forward against his desk.

It was something I noticed he often did. Whenever he spoke

with someone, he gave his full attention. Sometimes that attention was a bit much.

"Sorry. I was lost in thought."

"Your mom?" he asked.

I cringed, last night's public inquisition about my sexual experience coming back to me.

"No, but thanks for the reminder."

He chuckled.

"There's no need for that blush. We've all been in your shoes."

I snorted.

"I highly doubt your dad has ever publicly asked about your sex life."

"No. It was a public questioning about my sexual preferences. I mean, obviously I'm not straight if I haven't had my mate run yet, right? He offered to bring in more single males for me."

My mouth dropped open, and Fenris's crooked grin grew.

"He didn't care if it was a guy or a girl. He just didn't want me to spend the rest of my life alone. All of which he said at the last pack meeting."

"I'm so sorry, Fenris."

He shrugged.

"Honestly, it didn't bother me. I know I'm an anomaly to him. To all of the pack. It's their problem that they don't understand me. Not mine."

"I wish I had that attitude."

"Why don't you?"

"Because Mom and the Council's lack of understanding means they need to 'fix' me. The 'fixing' is driving me insane. You would not believe what my mom gave me last night."

He flashed a full-toothed smile that made my insides ignite with heat. My hunger stirred, and I quickly looked at my desk.

"I never understood why you always look down," he said.

"Not judging. If you don't want people to see your real eyes, that's your choice. But I've always been curious."

I looked up at him, unsure what to say.

His gaze held mine.

"It's cool when they flicker like that. Does it mean something?"

"Yeah. That they can't make up their minds. Probably because I'm not sure which me I want to be."

He shook his head.

"There's only one you, Eliana, no matter which face you show the world."

His words warmed me further.

"Thank you, Fenris."

"For saying the truth?"

"For taking me as I am."

His scent grew stronger, and this time, it was Fenris who looked at his desk. I noticed a slight tremor in his fingers before he flattened them on the wooden surface.

Something about what I'd said had set off his werewolf lust. I didn't want to press him and ask what, though. I, more than anyone, understood some topics were just uncomfortable to discuss.

"We're not the only ones misunderstood," he said, changing the subject. "I've heard the same conversations happen to a lot of other kids our age."

"Like what?" I asked.

He shrugged.

"More talks in that same restaurant. Parents too focused on their kid's sex life. Are the kids doing it too much? Not enough? The right way? Will the parents be grandparents early? The best so far is don't eat a human if you've slept with them. It's not fair to play on their emotions like that."

I shook my head. Only in Uttira could a person have that conversation in a restaurant.

"Stuff like that makes me miss the human world sometimes," I said.

"Yeah?"

"Conversations were so much politer in public. And the food was way better." I sighed, remembering all the desserts I had consumed before coming here.

"You're thinking about chocolate, aren't you?"

"How did you know?"

"You always get this far away, happy look."

I grinned.

"Humans know how to use their chocolate. You should see the creations they've made." My mouth started watering. "I miss lava cake."

Fenris laughed.

"You have a little drool just there." He reached out and rubbed his thumb over the corner of my mouth.

Hunger kicked me in the stomach, and I knew my eyes went dark.

"You shouldn't touch me," I said. It was part warning, part plea.

His humor faded, and he set his hand on his desk again.

"I get why you have to warn the others away. It's to keep them safe. I'm not like the rest, though, Eliana. You don't have to protect me."

"What are you saying?"

"That it's safe to let me touch you if you want."

I inhaled deeply, my mouth watering at the strength of his scent.

"I'm not sure what you're suggesting," I said. "Based on your scent, it's more than touching. And I'm definitely not interested in that."

He nodded slowly, considering me for a moment.

"When I said holding yourself back from people is lonely, I was speaking from experience. If I show any one female from my pack too much attention, they read into it. They become possessive. I haven't had a decent hug since Megan left."

He said it all with complete sincerity, but the twinkle in his eyes gave him away. He was messing with me. Trying to play on my emotions.

"Is this your way of asking for a hug?"

"Is this you considering giving me one?"

"Nope. But I think I know a dwarf who might be willing."

"And people think Megan was the mean one."

I grinned.

"You can't fool me, Fenris. You're a hopeless flirt, and if you wanted a hug from someone, you'd have hundreds of volunteers."

"Makes you wonder why I want one from you, doesn't it?" he asked playfully.

"Not really. I just think it's in your nature to want what you can't have. It's the whole waiting for a predestined mate thing."

He stared at me for a long, silent moment.

"I didn't mean that in a negative way," I said quickly.

"I know. You just..." He took a long, slow breath. "I like spending time with you. You have more to say than 'do you like my top?' Which I do, by the way."

I looked down at what I was wearing. Another thin number with way too much skin exposed.

"I don't," I said. "It's the start of winter. I wore more during the summer. Adira is insane."

The door opened then LuAnn poked her head in.

"How are you two progressing?"

"We've decided that I'm going to become a male gigolo after

my seventh child, you know, to earn enough money to feed them all; and Eliana is going to attach herself to a hi-roller in Vegas for the buffets there."

LuAnn blinked at him.

"Er. All right. I'm glad you're both embracing your futures. Carry on."

She closed the door, and Fenris threw his head back and laughed.

"What, exactly, were we supposed to be doing?" I asked.

"Not sure, but she seemed to like that answer."

I shook my head at him.

"Male gigolo? I'm pretty sure your future mate wouldn't approve of that. From what I've heard, mates are very jealous of each other."

He shrugged.

"I'm going to break all the molds."

The image of Fenris tangled in the sheets with a pair of blonde women popped into my head. My hunger rose. So did a strange amount of jealousy. Did I want to be one of Fenris's many female groupies? Heck no. I didn't want to worship any man. I wanted men to worship me.

My hunger died at the memory of my dad on his knees. I would never forget his tears or devastation as Mom walked away. I didn't want worship. I wanted—

I sighed, not letting myself think of the impossible.

"Breaking the rules usually doesn't end well," I said.

"What are you talking about? Megan broke rules left and right and made new ones to suit herself. Things turned out for her."

I thought of her in New York, looking for a killer of almost impossible to kill creatures.

"Maybe."

"What future do you want for yourself?" he asked. "A future following other people's rules? Rules where you're stuck in a bullshit excuse for a class because someone else thinks it's the right thing for you? Or do you want to live like you want? Follow your own rules?"

His words, so reminiscent of my mom's, prodded me to dream just a little of a future where I had a real relationship with a guy. Not the feed-or-breed relationships most of my kind had, but a real home. A family.

Fenris leaned farther forward in his chair.

"What are you thinking, right now?"

"Of a future I can never have."

"Tell me."

I hesitated.

"I don't want a life filled with different partners. I want one partner. I want a real relationship."

He tilted his head at me. Monogamous wasn't a word anyone ever used to describe a succubus.

"I can see that," he said. "You, with a special someone. But, you know, in order to get there, you're eventually going to need to let someone in. You know, touching and all that stuff."

He leaned back in his chair and spread his arms wide.

"Go ahead. Give me a touch. Just mind the ribs. I'm ticklish."

"I'm not touching you."

"Chicken."

"I'm not a chicken. There's just no point in touching you."

"Isn't there?"

He stood and took two steps to my desk. He braced his hands on the surface and slowly leaned in. He stopped when his face was only inches from mine. I could count the flecks of gold in his brown eyes.

"The point is to show there's nothing you fear."

The soft rumble of his words almost made me shiver. I itched to answer his dare. To run my fingers along his skin and show him there was everything to fear.

My hand left the desk.

His lips curved into their typical cocky grin.

The ringing of my phone saved us both.

CHAPTER ELEVEN

I silently opened the door to my room, impressed that I'd made it home so quickly and without being seen.

"Are you sure you're okay?" I asked again, holding the phone to my ear.

Megan let out a shaky exhale.

"I'm fine. You would have sounded breathless and shaky, too, if you'd inhaled a whiff of four-day-old dead dragon. It's a smell I'm never going to forget. I don't know how Oanen is still down there. He's going to need a shower after this."

"I like showers!" Piepen squealed, zooming from his drawer.

I sighed and tried to ignore him.

"Please tell me you're getting closer to figuring out who really did this."

"I wish I could. It would have been great if this dragon was freshly dead."

"Uh?"

"The death would have been clear evidence that your mom wasn't responsible."

"Oh, yeah. Well, not that I'm wishing for any fresh deaths, but you're right. It would have been convenient."

"How's it going? Is she being a good mom?"

"Absolutely. She's the perfect succubus mom. She brought me an assortment of toys yesterday. And I'm not talking teddy bears. Also, she assures me she'll get me a teddy immediately. Not the stuffed kind." I lowered my voice. "I'm afraid I..."

There was so much I was afraid of that I didn't even know where to start. Mostly, I was scared that having Mom here and her well-meaning methods of encouragement were eroding my control. If Megan hadn't called when she had, I dreaded the thought of what might have happened with Fenris. Thankfully, I hadn't just fled from the classroom but from the Academy altogether. I hadn't been sure how far Fenris might follow me.

"I'm sure the Council would understand matricide in these circumstances," Megan said after a lengthy silence.

I tried to laugh at her joke, but nothing about my life was very funny at the moment.

"I better go check on Elbner. The less I'm at home being showered by my mother's affection and sage advice, the better."

"Let me know if either he or Piepen has anything useful to say."

"I will."

After I hung up, I refilled Piepen's bowl of fruit then risked peeking in the entertainment room. I regretted it the moment I saw a guy stripped down to his boxers and tied to Oanen's favorite gaming chair. Dressed in her robe, Mom stood in front of him, her back to me. I was about to retreat when the man's gaze met mine.

He made a desperate sound behind his gag, and Mom turned.

"Hi, baby." She tapped the whip in her hand against her leg. "Skipping school or checking in on Megan's friend?"

"Uh, Megan's friend," I said. "And you. Everything okay in here?"

The guy's eyes quickly shifted from Mom to me.

"Yep. Gabe's never been dominated before. It's on his bucket list. I offered to help out." She winked at me.

Gabe's eyes were wide, and he was frantically shaking his head.

"Mom, you know how I feel about being forced to do things. And, you know I feel that way because I see so many people being forced. Please don't do anything he doesn't want."

She gave me an indulgent look.

"Of course I won't. You just happened to catch us before I finished my offer."

She turned back to him and opened her robe wide.

"Would you like Anwen to return you to your home, or would you like to stay and play for a while? I believe Anwen mentioned paying you five hundred dollars as well," she said.

The man's gaze grew a little more vacant the longer he stared at her until he began to slowly nod. She closed her robe before facing me again.

"There you go. Willing." She gave me a bright smile. "Would you like to sit and watch? I'm sure there's plenty for both of us."

Poor Gabe's eyes rounded in panic.

"Thanks, but I need to get back to school. I'll see you at dinner."

"Perfect. Anwen should have a new batch of humans for us by then."

"Actually, I might head for the Roost. You know, my own age and all of that."

She nodded and waved me off. I fled, wondering what the heck I was going to do with myself for the rest of the day. My answer came via a text from Adira just before I made it to the garage.

Your absence is noted. Is there a particular reason you needed to rush from Self-Discovery?

I wanted to kick my tire. Instead, I stopped and asked myself how Mom would respond to the text. I decided she wouldn't. Any reply she thought Adira worthy of she would deliver in person.

Getting into my car, I headed for the Academy. Rather than scurrying to the fourth session like Adira anticipated me doing, I went to her office. However, there was no answer to my knock after several minutes.

Curious, I sent a text to my mom.

Has Adira talked to you yet?

Mom's reply was immediate.

No. Why?

She just sent me a text asking why I left school.

That woman is atrocious. I'll deal with her. You have a good day, sweetie. Do what you want.

I grinned. I had no idea why Mom disliked Adira, but Mom's feelings were clearly strong. If Adira didn't watch herself, she'd end up taking a nap in a ditch soon.

Tucking my phone into my purse, I considered what to do. I really didn't want to go to class. Despite my mom's encouragement to do whatever I wanted, I couldn't help but agree with Fenris's assessment of Adira. The more I ran, the more she would push. Where did that leave me besides stuck and unsure what to do?

The worst part was that the classes were nothing more than a joke with how Adira was making me dress now. When I'd worn my own clothes and people ignored me, I'd actually learned stuff. I missed just quietly sitting there, taking it all in.

An idea took hold, and I smiled before setting off down the

hall. It didn't take me long to reach the pools. Instead of hiding in the bathroom, I sat at the table just beside the water. A few of the mermaids hissed at me, but I ignored them and focused on the siren song filling the air. The melody soothed me, and I relaxed for the first time in days.

A head popped up from the water, rising just enough for her eyes to clear the edge of the pool.

"Why are you here?"

"Because Adira is having control issues."

The vertical slit of the mermaid's pupils narrowed.

"She's not the only one, is she?"

"What do you mean?"

She dived under the water instead of answering.

"It would be better if you left," another girl said, sitting beside me. Even though she had legs, I could tell she was a mermaid by the undertones of green in her hair.

"Where else am I supposed to go?"

"Not my problem," she said.

"I'm starting to think all mermaids are mean."

"What did you expect? Cute and cuddly? We're cousins with piranhas and sharks. Go give one of them a hug and see what happens."

She flashed her sharp teeth at me, stood, then stripped at the edge of the pool and dived into it.

I'd never had a problem with a specific group of creatures before and didn't immediately understand the animosity of the mermaids. Then it clicked. I'd stolen their meal. Something else tickled my mind, but I pushed it away, refusing to acknowledge there was any more to their dislike than me robbing them of their fun with Eugene.

When the bell rang for lunch, I went to my car and ate my sandwich alone.

School sucked.

IGNORING the open solicitations for a good time that guaranteed to feed my hunger, I left the Academy grateful that I would get a few days of freedom now.

"Eliana!"

I paused at the sound of my name and turned to see Fenris jogging toward me. I briefly considered running.

"Don't do it," he mouthed.

I rolled my eyes and waited. His scent hit me hard before he even reached me. Why did he have to smell so good?

"What do you want?" I said with more irritability than I intended.

"I just wanted to extend an invitation to hang out at the Roost. As a friend."

"I don't know, Fenris. I don't think it's a good idea."

"What? Why not?"

It was like he was daring me to bring up what happened during Self-Discovery.

"Because I have other plans."

"Eating chocolate and watching the latest action flick until you pass out at eleven?"

His assessment of my evening was eerily accurate.

"Nine, actually," I said primly. "My mom will probably be using the TV room." Even as I said it, I knew I couldn't go home. Not until really late. Where in the heck was I supposed to go?

"Suit yourself," he said, tucking his hands into his pockets. "If you change your mind, we'll be there past nine."

He smirked and walked away.

I got into my car before anyone else stopped me and followed the line of vehicles from the Academy grounds. Rather than turning to go home, I headed for Megan's.

The goblin was less creepy in the daylight but not any more welcoming.

"Hi, Elbner. If it's okay with you, I'll feed you a little early today."

He silently watched me prepare his meal. When I was done, I walked through the house, looking at his work. I didn't try to compliment him again, but what he'd done was impressive. Everything looked fresh and clean.

"Did you paint?" I asked.

"No."

I touched the couch. The cushions looked fluffier, and the material lighter. I was dying to ask how he did it. Instead, I sat with a sigh. This would be a perfect place to—

A shoe hit the side of my head.

"Ow!"

I turned to glare at Elbner, who was watching me suspiciously from the living room opening.

"This isn't your house," he said. "Out."

"Megan doesn't mind if I stay here."

"I mind. Leave."

He reached down and plucked off his other shoe.

"Okay, okay," I said, standing. "I'm going."

The goblin glared at me as I retraced my steps to the kitchen.

"Can you speak your old master's name yet?" I asked hopefully.

The goblin tried and choked on it.

"Never mind."

Leaving Megan's, I headed back to the Quills'. The house was huge. I'd just find somewhere else to hide out and fall asleep. No big deal.

I could hear the music pouring from the main part of the house as the garage door closed behind me. Reluctantly leaving the car, I continued to hold onto my hope that I'd find a quiet corner somewhere. The moment I opened the kitchen door, I knew that wasn't going to happen. Naked people were in the kitchen.

"Hey, do you know where the wine is?" a woman asked. "Nicolette said there was wine down in the kitchen somewhere."

I pointed to the panel that hid the wine fridge.

"Thanks."

I quickly averted my gaze as she bent over to read the labels on the bottles on the lower racks of the cooler.

"Would you happen to know where the chips are?" a man asked.

"We're out of chips. Help yourself to what's in the fridge."

I left before anyone could ask me anything else. A man and woman were making out near the entry. Another pair was in the shadows behind the stairs Mom was descending.

"Sweetie, how was school?"

"Fine, Mom. Um, should these people be wandering the house?"

She smiled at me.

"It's more fun when they find their own little corners to play." She opened her mouth and pulled in some of the lust just floating around us. The couple by the stairs started moaning, their petting growing more frantic.

"Do you want some?" Mom asked.

"No, thanks."

Her gaze grew concerned.

"When was the last time you ate?"

It was on the tip of my tongue to say I had a sandwich for lunch, but I knew that would only worry her more.

"Last night, after I left the restaurant."

The worry remained in her gaze.

"Nothing since then? And you're not hungry?"

Her words were almost drowned out by the couple's kissing sounds. The collective scent of lust grew, and my hunger stirred.

"Is this normal for you?" I asked, struggling to contain my growing panic. "Feeding off this many people at once? Is this why everyone thinks there's something wrong with me?"

I didn't want to host a group orgy to feed myself, not when I couldn't even manage one person at a time.

"Oh, sweetie, no." Mom hurried down the remainder of the stairs and hugged me tightly. "I'm hungrier than usual because I'm pregnant."

My breath whooshed out of me, and I jerked back to look at her in shock.

"Pregnant?"

She smiled and smoothed a hand over my cheek.

"You will have a new brother or sister in a few months. But that doesn't mean I'll love you any less. I'll always be here for you. And as for what's wrong with you? There's nothing wrong, sweetie. Does a succubus your age eat more often? Yes. But that might just mean you're a late bloomer. You'll see. You'll be feeding three times a day in no time."

Three times a day? My mind went a little numb with that news.

"And I want you to know this baby isn't your dad's. I've respected your wishes and have had no contact with him. I learned my lesson, too. I didn't stay with this baby's father after I learned I was carrying his child."

She hugged me again.

"You look shocked. Let's go upstairs and sit for a bit. We can watch a movie together. There are several new couples up there whose collective lust is delicious. I think they're close to switching partners. That always adds extra notes of sweetness. Anwen did a lovely job selecting them all. This batch will last for hours."

My stomach did a weird happy flip that scared me.

"Thanks for the offer, Mom, but I think I'll hang out with my friends at the Roost."

She released me with a smile.

"I completely understand. Age makes a world of difference. Go have fun with your friends. Be sure to grab a jacket, though. It's getting too cold outside to go without one."

"I, uh. Adira made me give mine to a boy so I wouldn't hide the shirts she's making me wear."

Mom's eyes turned black.

"I'm done being patient with that woman." Mom went to the coat closet and took one of Oanen's spare jackets. "Wear this. I'll deal with Adira tonight."

She kissed my cheek and practically pushed me out the door. The cold hit me hard, punctuating her worry over the weather. I hurried to the garage as I shrugged into Oanen's oversized jacket.

In the car, I set my head on the steering wheel and tried to process what I'd just learned with what I knew. A pregnant succubus was volatile. The Council was a bunch of fools for bringing Mom here. Adira doubly so for continuing her manipulations. What were they thinking?

The question repeated in my mind all the way to the Roost.

Parked on the side of the road, I took a moment to collect myself. My hunger, which had stirred so aggressively in the presence of that much lust, was silent again. I hoped it would stay that way. Yet, a bit of despair rose as I remembered Mom's comment about how often I should be feeding. Three times a day? I'd be hungry all the time. I hoped it never happened.

Maybe because of always feeding less, it meant I now needed to eat less. Holding onto that hopeful thought, I got out of the car.

Despite the early hour, music already thumped loudly from the closed red doors of the Roost. I welcomed the noise and the warmth that wrapped around me as soon as I stepped inside. A few people were already on the floor, dancing. The back table was empty, though.

I debated what to do for only a moment before tossing Oanen's jacket to the nearest couch. The heels quickly followed. Barefoot, I moved to the dance floor, closed my eyes, and lost myself to the music. I didn't know how long I swayed to the changing rhythms, but it was long enough that I began to feel lighter. Freer. I wished I could dance forever.

However, the scent of a certain someone's familiar lust pulled me from my happy place. I opened my eyes and looked around the crowded floor for Fenris. He wasn't in the immediate vicinity, though. I turned a slow circle and found him sitting on the couch, Oanen's jacket beside him.

Fenris's brown eyes locked with mine, and he wasn't smiling. My heart did an odd stutter. The corner of Fenris's mouth lifted. He stood and walked toward me. I slid my foot back, already trying to think where I should run. He slowly shook his head. My pulse picked up speed, and his smile grew.

When he reached me, he offered his hand. The beat of the music called to me. I knew he could dance. I'd watched him with his girls plenty of times. I also knew how dangerous it would be to dance with him.

I shook my head ever so slightly.

"You know you'd like it," he said.

My insides went hot and cold. I turned around, ready to head to the back table.

"Chicken."

The word was spoken right next to my ear. The caress of his exhale against my skin sent a shudder through me. He didn't understand that he was playing with a fire that would damage him for life.

I turned my head. He was so close, I could have licked his lips. The thought brought forth my hunger and changed my eyes. His smile deepened.

"I'm not afraid of you, Eliana," he said.

"You should be. Together, we'd burn so brightly that I'd leave behind nothing but a blackened husk for your future mate. Don't toy with me, Fenris. My kind doesn't play well with others."

He sighed, his gaze shifting between my eyes.

"We'll dance some other time. Let's go say hi to the humans."

He gestured toward the back of the room, my escape. Only, with him tagging along, I wasn't really getting away from anything.

Trying to calm myself, I headed toward Ashlyn's table. Eugene was there with her. Neither looked up from their books when we approached. I realized too late that I shouldn't be talking to either of them and veered for the bathroom. I cringed as I walked into the room, shoeless, and stared at myself in the mirror. What the heck was I doing? Why was I even at the Roost? Nothing good could come of my presence. Yet, did I have anywhere else to go?

My frustration with my life mounted.

The door to the bathroom opened, and Jenna came in carrying my shoes.

"Hey, Eliana. Fenris thought you might want these."

"Thanks." I slipped the first one on as she watched me.

"So are you two a thing?" she asked finally.

"What? No. My kind doesn't do relationships. You know that."

She nodded, looking a little sad.

"I know. It's just, he seems to really pay a lot of attention to you."

I weighed my words carefully.

"I think he just likes paying attention to a girl who's safe so that you guys know he's not playing favorites with any of you."

"Oh." Her expression brightened a little. "I guess that makes sense. No one wants another Aubrey."

I smiled and nodded. Aubrey had been a mean queen bee for sure. I'd seen what she'd done to Jenna.

"Do you want to dance?" Jenna asked. "I saw you say no to Fenris."

"Thanks, but I think I'm going to go. It's a little too crowded for me now."

She nodded and left the bathroom.

I finished strapping on my shoes then checked my phone. It wasn't even six yet. What was I supposed to do now? Hide in the bathroom for the next seven hours?

Lost in thought, trying to come up with a good place to go, I walked out of the bathroom and almost ran into Fenris as he was walking past.

"Ready to dance yet?" he asked, playfully.

"No. I'm going to head out."

"Another dinner date with your mom?"

"Heck no. It's just getting a little too crowded in here for me."

He nodded and looked around the room, his gaze lingering on Jenna and her friends.

"I agree. Let's go somewhere."

"I don't think that's a good idea."

"Why not? Ashlyn says they're fine."

It was on the tip of my tongue to tell him that I was leaving because of him when I heard a raised voice over the music.

"I know one of you assholes stole my meal, and I want to know who."

I looked over at Eras, who stood near the stage, blocking three other incubi from leaving the dance floor.

"He's pretty pissed," Fenris said.

"Why? I mean, I understand it's not polite to steal a meal, but he can just find another one."

"It's not that. I guess whoever fed did it so subtly that Eras didn't even realize it until the energy was gone."

I thought of the lust flowing into me as I stood outside the window. Nothing had felt subtle about it.

"Why do you think it was one of us?" one of the incubi asked. "There's more than one kind of energy feeder."

"Prove it's not you. Pick someone and feed."

Eras was making good on his threat. Fear motivated me.

"Fine," I said, looking at Fenris. "Let's go hang out somewhere."

He grinned widely.

"Come on."

He grabbed Oanen's coat from the couch and handed it to me with a questioning look.

"Adira stole mine," I said over the music.

He nodded and led the way out the door. Outside, the wind stole my breath for a moment, and I tugged the zipper up higher.

"Where to?" he asked.

I shrugged, looking up and down the street. There really wasn't anywhere for us to go. My house was off-limits for obvious reasons. Megan's house was guarded by an angry goblin. Eras was patrolling the Roost.

"I have no idea," I said.

"We can go back to my place and make out if you want."

My head snapped up to glare at him.

"Not helpful. Your scent is strong enough. I don't need words, too."

He tilted his head.

"What do you mean?"

"It's like you're baiting me. Trying to push my control into snapping. And I don't like it. You know what? I changed my mind. I don't think we should hang out. I think you should leave me alone, Fenris."

I turned to leave, or at least tried to. My foot slipped out from under me. I started to tilt.

Fenris grabbed me, turning the fall into a dip. Bent over his arm, I stared up at him.

"Still want me to go away?"

I couldn't answer. My heart was pounding as my hands clutched his biceps. My reaction had nothing to do with fear and everything to do with the tempting position.

"No touching," I whispered.

His expression lost some of his smugness.

"I don't know what I'm doing wrong, Eliana." He gently righted me and released me. "I'm a friendly guy. Usually, people enjoy being around me. If you had the chance, I think you'd push me off a bridge."

His hurt penetrated my hunger.

"I wouldn't push you off a bridge, Fenris. I'd coax you to the edge and encourage you to jump. There's a difference."

He stared at me for a minute then threw his head back and laughed. When he was done, he held out his hand.

"Give me the keys. I know a place where we can go."

CHAPTER TWELVE

ON A SCALE OF ONE TO TEN, GETTING INTO A CAR WITH FENRIS WAS probably at a ten for the dumbest things to do. Mouth breathing wasn't even cutting it. His scent was flooding my senses.

"You need to roll down the windows," I said.

"You're going to freeze."

"Roll down the windows or die, Fenris."

He chuckled then rolled down the windows.

"I didn't know you were that gassy," he said with a smirk.

My mouth dropped open, and I sputtered for a moment.

"It's not me," was all I could manage.

"Well, it wasn't me," he said.

"You're completely ridiculous. I asked you to roll down the windows because your scent is making me hungry, not because—"

I snapped my mouth shut.

"Ah, so it wasn't your smell that would kill me. You're threatening to eat me alive."

He tapped the steering wheel with his thumb for a moment.

162

"I can live with that," he said finally.

"Well, I can't. Are we almost there?"

"Almost."

He took the next left onto another dark wooded road that stopped at a dead end. He turned off the engine, and I gave him a dirty look.

"If this is a setup for a make-out joke, I'm not going to be amused."

He gave me his sexiest crooked smile.

"Do you think about making out with me often?"

"Get out and give me my keys. I'm going home."

He quickly opened the door and got out, pocketing the keys.

"Nope. We just got here. Don't you want to see where we are?"

I looked out the windshield at the dark trees. Given the turns we'd taken, I knew there wasn't much this far out of town.

"Not really. And if you call me a chicken, I'm going to..."

He leaned down into the open door, studying me intently.

"Going to what?" he asked, calling my bluff.

I huffed.

"Fine. Show me where we are."

I got out of the car and gestured for him to lead the way. He looked down at my heels.

"It might be easier if I carried you."

"That would be the furthest thing from easier. Please just start walking, Fenris."

My feet were cold in seconds, but I was grateful for the jacket. It took us ten minutes to reach a cabin in the middle of nowhere. Fenris opened the door and gestured for me to enter.

I hesitated, looking at the dark space.

"Should I be worried?" I asked.

"Do you really want to stand on the porch, shivering, while

we weigh the pros and cons for walking into a secluded cabin in the middle of nowhere?"

"Given that you're a wolf, and I'm a girl in red shoes, yes. Yes, I do."

He laughed and nudged me forward.

"In before you turn into a popsicle."

I only walked a few feet into the cabin before stopping because I couldn't see a thing.

"Just a second," Fenris said, closing the door and moving past me.

A rustle of noise gave away his location. I waited and was rewarded with a burst of light as he lit a candle.

He glanced at me then turned toward the dark fireplace.

"Do me a favor," he said.

"What?"

"Don't run."

"Why?"

"I don't think I'd be able to let you go this time."

My pulse fluttered, and my mind jumped to too many wrong conclusions.

"Why?" I asked again.

"Because your lips really do look blue. Why didn't you say you were that cold?"

I let out a breath of relief and moved closer to him as his kindling lit.

"Because I didn't want to be carried."

"Stubborn," he said without rancor.

I wrinkled my nose.

"How'd you like it if I started carrying you around?"

"That'd be hilarious. You can carry me into school on Monday."

"You're so weird."

He grinned at me.

"Weird. Devilishly charming and handsome. All the same thing."

I snorted this time. Fenris never took anything seriously.

Turning away from the fire, I looked around the small space. It was just a one-room cabin with two chairs before the fire, a bed shoved in one corner, and a kitchen in another.

"Whose place is this?" I asked.

"It was my Dad's. He showed it to me a while ago and told me it was mine. There's a creek that runs along the back of it. Perfect for losing my scent trail when I need to get away and hide for a while."

Fenris added a log to the growing flames then straightened.

"It's not much. But it's quiet and secluded, which is perfect for what we need."

His scent leveled up, and I took a step back from him.

"We? There is no we, Fenris."

He sighed like I'd disappointed him.

"We are both looking for a place to get away, aren't we? But I think you need this place more than I do. Stay as long as you like." He handed me my keys. "I'm going to go for a run. I'll come back later and close the place up when you're gone."

I grabbed his arm, stopping him when he would have gone for the door.

"Fenris, I wasn't trying to be mean. It's just not easy being around you."

He looked down at my hand then met my gaze.

"I know you don't have a mean bone in your body. You just need to trust yourself more. Stay. I'm due for a run, anyway."

He patted my hand then left. If I wasn't mean, why did I feel like such a horrible person at the moment?

Alone, I looked around the cabin. There wasn't much to do

other than sit in a chair and watch the fire. So I did. The crackle of the wood and flicker of the flames was as soothing as it was mesmerizing.

Kicking off my shoes, I made myself comfortable. The log burned down, and I added two more, not yet ready to leave. As Fenris had pointed out, I needed this place. I had nowhere else to hide from my life problems.

The cabin grew warmer, and my eyelids grew heavier.

I knew I was dreaming the moment I was walking through a forest. Only this time, there weren't any skunks. Food, hung by strings, dangled from the trees. Everywhere I looked, there were cakes. Spiced cakes. Chocolate cakes. The further I walked, the more decadent they became. Saliva pooled in my mouth. I needed to eat one. Instead of grabbing it, I opened my mouth and pulled a strand of energy from it. The tree shook, vibrating the ground on which I stood.

It scared me. No, it terrified me. Everything about the dream was wrong, but I didn't understand why.

"Shh..." the tree echoed. "You're safe. Take what you need."

Another cake dangled in front of my face. Lava cake. I wanted it so badly. I opened my mouth and consumed it. And the next one. And the next. They didn't stop appearing, and I didn't stop feeding until I felt bloated with cakes.

I smiled and smacked my lips. In that moment, I knew what was wrong with the dream. My cakes tasted like Fenris.

With a gasp, I sat up in my chair and looked around the cabin. I was alone, the logs nothing more than coals. Yet, the taste of Fenris lingered.

I grabbed my shoes and jacket and hurried toward the door. On the porch, I almost tripped on Fenris's pile of clothes. Pausing, I scanned the trees. Everything was quiet. I bent down and touched the material. Still cold.

"Thank the gods," I whispered.

Calmer, I shrugged into the jacket, slipped on my shoes, then retraced my steps back to the car. It didn't seem to take me long because I wasn't yet freezing when I got in. The seat was cold, though. I started the car and noted it was after midnight and probably safe enough to go home.

I executed a tight Y-turn and headed out the way we'd come. Having lived in Uttira for four years, I knew about where I was. The werewolves occupied a large chunk of land west of town. As long as I headed east, I'd eventually hit a familiar road or the barrier. I shivered and hoped I didn't get that far. Accidentally running into the barrier that kept all the underage creatures locked in wasn't a pleasant experience. I recalled that it had taken days for the smell of burnt hair to fade from my sinuses.

At the end of the road, I turned left. The headlights illuminated the trees on the other side, and I caught a flash of eyes. I really hoped it wasn't one of Fenris's girls. I'd feel horrible if they discovered his hiding place because of me.

I watched the mirror, trying to see what or who it was, but nothing showed up in my tail lights. Unsure what to do, I decided to text Fenris when I got home, just to give him a heads up. It took almost an hour to find my way back, though.

Thankfully, most of the house was dark when I pulled into the garage. I sat there for a minute and debated what to say. Fenris's phone was likely still on the porch, and who knew who was there to see what I sent him.

Thanks for giving me a quiet place to stay. I hope it doesn't cause you any trouble.

I waited, but there was no immediate answer. He was either still out running or finally sleeping.

Tucking my phone into my purse, I went inside and quietly made my way to my room.

"Wakey, wakey. I have something better than eggs and bakey."

I tiredly opened my eyes and looked up at my mom's smiling face.

"Well? What do you think?"

A hand settled on my stomach, and a male rumble of appreciation resonated in my left ear. A full-grown tongue licked my right ear.

I bolted from the bed, clipping the testicles of one of the boys based on his groan. Shaking, I stared down at the pair. They'd been under the covers with me. Naked. The one who wasn't cupping himself grinned at me.

"What's wrong?" Mom asked, looking from me to the boys.

I couldn't believe she was even asking that.

"Why can't you be a normal mom?"

"I think you have the best mom ever," the grinning boy said. "I wish my mom would have invited friends over for me."

"Hush, Michael," Mom said. "Entertain yourself for a moment."

His eyes glazed over, and he reached for his groin.

I quickly studied my ceiling.

"I am normal," Mom said, coming around the bed to grab my shoulders.

"Normal moms don't invite two strangers into their daughter's bed."

"I'm normal for what I am. And I'm worried about you, so I'm just trying to help."

"No, you're not helping. You're being like Adira and trying to force things."

"I'm not forcing anything. If you don't like these two, I'll have

Mrs. Quill return them. Do you prefer girls? It's okay if you do. Knowing your preferences will make it a little easier to pick—"

"I don't want you to pick, Mom. I want you to let me decide who I "see" and when I see them. I'm not like you: hungry all the time."

I realized what we were saying and glanced at the two boys. The groaner was quiet now but still holding his parts.

"Don't worry about them," Mom said. "They know they'll see weird things here and won't remember any of it. One of your druid classmates will do a mind wipe. Part of their studies. See? I'm helping other kids. Don't you want to graduate?"

I couldn't believe she was having a student doing a mind wipe of them. The boys in my bed would be lucky if they weren't drooling when the druid was done.

I looked at the pair.

"And you're okay with this?"

They both shrugged.

"She said we'd wake up in our own beds," the one playing with his bits, instead of protecting them, said. "We'll vaguely remember doing yard work for a rich lady and getting well paid and well laid. Getting a cougar is on my bucket list."

Is that all boys thought about? Money and sex?

"Darling, I'm barely a puma," Mom said with a purr to her tone.

I felt a little gaggy.

"So you brought them here with the promise of sex with me? Like I'm some whore?" I said, more hurt than angry.

"Of course not. They don't have to have sex with you for you to feed. You know that. They can have sex with each other."

"Hey now," the smiler said, losing his humor.

"Hush."

The boys went quiet and looked at each other. I could see my mom's influence and quickly fled before they started touching each other.

"I don't want any part of this," I said just before I closed the bathroom door.

I felt dirty. And cheap. Stripping, I stepped into the shower, which was already running. Mom had probably started it, thinking the two boys and I would end up in there. I shuddered and grabbed the soap.

A sudden buzzing filled the air, and I looked up at Piepen.

"Get out!"

I grabbed the shower wand and tried to spray him. He dodged nimbly, darting from one side of the shower to the other, but not toward the exit.

"I was here first!" he squealed.

A jet of water caught him just as he flew over me. His wet wings collapsed, and he fell with a splat on my chest. He slowly slid downward, his arms catching on the top of my breasts. Then glitter water exploded in a flash of rainbow mist.

"Eliana," he said, his voice filled with awe. "I think we just made a baby."

"Your sparkle dust needs to go somewhere else for that."

I plucked him off me and held him out at arm's length. His eyes roved my chest.

"Look." He pointed at my belly, and I looked down.

A glowing spot the size of a quarter marked the skin just below my boobs. From there, a thin, luminescent line trailed down to my pubic hair.

"Eww!"

I tossed him, grabbed the soap, and started scrubbing.

Piepen's whooping cheers only increased my growing panic. The glow wasn't fading.

"I hate my life!"

I didn't know I was going to scream the words until they were out of my mouth. Setting my forehead against the glass, I started to cry.

The door opened, and Piepen's cheers stopped abruptly. I heard Mom say something to him, and then the door closed again. I didn't care what she did with him. I wanted him and his nasty smell gone. For good.

Picking up the soap, I continued trying to scrub the glowing stain from my skin. It wasn't budging. I cried harder and washed until my skin was raw and I was out of tears. My life had never been a picnic in the park. My early memories of taking care of my dad confirmed that. But even through those times, I'd somehow found acceptance. My life was my life, and I'd dealt with it as best I could, never railing against it. Why did everything feel so horrible now?

Turning off the water, I stood there in complete despair as I realized what had changed. My choices had been taken from me, and I'd never before felt so trapped as I did at that moment. Everything was dark. Everything. Everyone in my life was determined to unmake me. Me, Eliana, the girl who was nice. The girl who didn't want to feed on other people. The girl who just wanted to be left alone.

I grabbed a towel and dried off, still tearing up randomly every time I caught sight of my stomach. If they wanted me to change, fine. I would change. But, the people in my life weren't going to like what they got. I was done being nice.

Wrapping the towel around my torso, I left the bathroom. Mom was sitting on the edge of my bed. The room was otherwise empty.

I barely spared her a glance before going to the closet. My dresses were back. Seeing them almost brought new tears to my eyes. I pushed away the emotion because I couldn't be the girl who wore those cute clothes anymore and started dressing. Jeans. Canvas shoes. A bra that actually covered me. A cami with a button-up top. I felt like I was channeling Megan and managed a smile even though my heart ached.

When I stepped out of the closet, Mom was still there.

"I'm truly sorry for this morning," she said. "I was..." She sighed and shook her head. "I don't know how to help you."

"Try listening. I'm fine. I don't need help. I like myself just the way I am. Why can't everyone else like me, too?"

Mom's expression fell, and her eyes began to tear.

"Don't," I said. "It'll only make you hungrier."

"Then I'll eat."

I shook my head and started for the door.

"Where are you going?" she asked.

"I don't know."

"Your jacket is with a human named Ashlyn. She said she'll bring it over today. Why don't we watch some movies and wait for her together?"

"The last thing I want is another human in this house. I'll go get it."

I moved for my door.

"I'll take care of the brownie for you," Mom said behind me. "He'll be safe. I promise."

Was I a horrible person for no longer caring? Maybe. I walked out without another word.

The house was quiet, as usual. But given it was close to ten in the morning, I wasn't too surprised. I was surprised, though, that I'd slept so late. And, by Mrs. Quill's presence in the dining room.

I stopped short when she saw me and stood.

"Eliana, I know things aren't easy on you right now, but I promise they'll get better."

"Like you promised to care for me always right before telling me you don't want to feed me anymore?"

"We're only trying to help you."

"It's funny how the people who are trying to help me are the ones who are hurting me the most. If you really wanted to help me, you'd stop bringing people here for my mom to eat and tell the Council to set her free. She's pregnant and hungry, she doesn't belong here."

Something like guilt flashed in Mrs. Quill's eyes, and in that moment, the conversation in the library came back to me. The Quills and Adira hadn't been talking about Megan. They'd been talking about my mom and me. Adira had purposefully brought her here to manipulate me into feeding. They'd known my mom hadn't killed anyone and that she would never kill anyone; but they'd used her pregnancy and voracious feeding as an excuse to bring her here. For me.

"Unbelievable," I said softly.

"I know you think you're fine, but you're not seeing what we're seeing. You're slowly dying, starving yourself. And, we love you too much to allow that to happen."

Mom's words about how often a girl my age should feed wormed its way into my mind. I focused on my hunger but could barely feel it. A rare thing. Was I dying? I didn't feel like it. Mostly I felt hurt and angry.

"Please stop loving me. If anything kills me, it'll be that."

She looked like I'd slapped her. I didn't care. I couldn't endure any more attempts to help me.

"Wait," she said when I started for the kitchen. "Take what you need."

She held out a hand, and I knew she was offering to feed me. Instead, I thought of the tree in my dream last night and all the cake I ate.

"I'm really not hungry. Besides, you don't want to break the rules. Adira wouldn't like you ruining her games."

CHAPTER THIRTEEN

THE TEN-MINUTE DRIVE TO ASHLYN'S WAS JUST LONG ENOUGH FOR me to cool off a little so I could knock on her door with my usual smile. She answered almost right away.

"Hey, Eliana. I told your mom I was fine bringing the jacket to you. Come in." She waved me inside as she stepped back.

"I don't mind. I needed to get out of the house."

Ashlyn offered me a sheepish smile and closed the door behind me.

"Same," she admitted. "I thought going to school would help the boredom, but I feel just as confined."

I wanted to smack myself.

"I'm so sorry, Ashlyn. I wasn't thinking."

"It's okay. I'm guessing there's a pretty good reason for me to not want to visit the Quills if you needed to get out of the house."

She gestured to the living room.

"Want to sit and talk for a bit?"

I took a step then hesitated, looking at her again.

"I swear I'm fine now," she said, reading my hesitation. "Skipping class yesterday was just precautionary. That, and I needed a little time, you know?" She glanced at the pictures on her wall. The smiling faces of her family made me hurt for her.

"I'd love to sit and talk for a while," I said, really meaning it.

"So what drove you out of your house?" she asked, leading the way.

"My mom. I woke up with two boys in my bed. Naked. What kind of mom does that?"

Ashlyn grinned and sat across from me on the couch.

"A succubus mom, I would guess. What was your reaction?"

"About a two-second sprint from my bed. I think I accidentally stepped on one of them. His privates, based on his pained breathing."

She laughed, and I couldn't help but smile a little. Then, my humor faded.

"I hate living here," I said softly.

She grew quiet and looked around the room.

"Me too," she admitted. "I'd do anything to get out of here. Anything but give up who I am."

The only way out of Uttira for a human was a mind wipe. Since Ashlyn had been born here, she wouldn't be left with anything. Not even her name.

"We have more in common than I thought," I said. "I hate being here, but in order to leave, I would need to stop being who I am, too."

"So what are you going to do?"

I leaned back into my chair and considered my options.

"Up until now, I've followed their rules, to an extent. I don't like makeup, but I wore it to get them to ease off of other things. I don't like revealing clothes, but I wore those, also to keep the peace. I'm done compromising, but I don't know what that means for me. Fenris said not to let Adira see she's made me sweat, and I agree with that. But, I think I need to show her that she's made me angry. I'm no Megan. While I know I won't make Adira quake in her frost giant shoes, I've seen the way Adira avoids my mom. If I'm angry, I think my mom will be angry. And Adira and the rest of the Council don't want my mom angry."

"What about your mom? She's the one who tucked you in with two boys."

I shook my head.

"I don't know. The Council is keeping her here. I'm hoping that Megan will clear Mom's name so she can leave."

Even as I said it, I had my doubts. Would Mom leave? She kept saying how much she liked being here. The Council might have let a beast in that they won't be able to get out.

"What about you?" I asked. "What are you going to do?"

"The only thing I can do. Wait until I turn eighteen so I can be bound. It's not ideal, but at least I'll have a chance at leaving this place then. Even if it's only for Council errands."

I could feel her energy. The despondence.

"I don't think this is the conversation you had in mind," I said.

She gave me a rueful smile.

"Any conversation is better than sitting in a quiet house with nothing to do."

I stood.

"Let's go do something."

"Like what?"

"I'm out of chocolate, thanks to my mom. Let's go to the Threadbare Trader and see if Mags has anything we can use to make some dessert. I had an amazing dream about cakes last night, and now I kind of want the real thing."

We both grabbed our jackets, and I drove us to the shop. Mittens lined the walls, and Mags sat in her usual place behind the counter. She looked up from what she was knitting and greeted me with a smile.

"Haven't seen you in a while, Eliana. And who's with you?"

"This is Ashlyn."

"What kinds of mittens are you two looking for?"

Mags sold banned foods to the teens of Uttira. For the adults and any humans stupid enough to wander into this place on their own, she sold mittens. Overpriced and very soft mittens.

"No mittens. I want enough chocolate to make a cake, please," I said, not caring that I wasn't playing along with her usual banter.

Her gaze flicked to Ashlyn then back to me.

"You're getting bolder. You might bring the wrong person with you one of these days. What will you do then?"

"Find another way to get chocolate."

She gave me a hard look.

"I'm sold out. Not sure if I'll get any more in. The mitten business is pretty lucrative on its own."

I leaned over the counter toward her.

"I've been coming here for three years, and in those three years, every time you said you're out, you magically manage to find just enough for the right price. I'm very tired of being manipulated by adults. If you have any chocolate, get it and sell it to me for a fair price."

She stood and left the room.

"Uh, are you okay?" Ashlyn asked.

I turned toward her, and she gave me an odd look.

"I'm fine. Why?"

"Your eyes. They're black. I'm trying to figure out if you're angry or hungry. You know, should I run, or should I hide?"

I smiled a little and blinked. My vision lost some of its focus.

"You don't need to do either. I'm not that kind of hungry, and all my anger is reserved for the people waiting at home."

Mags emerged from the back, looking more irritable than usual.

"Here's the chocolate. Ten dollars."

Ten dollars was far less than I'd ever paid before, but I quickly handed her the money and motioned Ashlyn to the exit.

"Don't come back soon," Mags said just before the door closed behind us.

"Is she always so friendly?" Ashlyn asked on the way back to the car.

"Pretty much. She usually says she looks forward to seeing me again, though. By the way, I have a lot of mittens if you ever need to borrow a pair."

"A lot of mittens but only one coat?"

"If I asked for another one, Adira would pick it out for me."

"And that's bad?"

"For me, yes. You saw what I've been wearing to school this week. My next jacket would have probably been a see-through raincoat."

"You should ask Mrs. Quill to take you shopping again."

I recalled the shopping trip we'd taken with Ashlyn to cheer her up after her uncle died. It had been Ashlyn's first trip out of Uttira—Council sanctioned, of course—and she'd loved it for the most part. So had I.

"I don't think she would," I said, opening my door.

"Why not?"

I buckled and started the car as she did the same.

"They're playing games again like they did with Megan. Only now, I'm their pet project."

"Uh-oh."

"Yeah. So, while I could ask for another fun shopping trip, I doubt I'd like what it would cost me. Did Eugene tell you that

Adira invited him to the Quills for dinner so I could feed on him?"

"What? No."

My grip on the steering wheel tightened.

"I refused, of course."

"Of course," she echoed.

"And Adira said I would regret my decision. Now, the Council supposedly suspects my mom of killing trolls because she's pregnant and hungry. In reality, I think they brought her here to punish me. The jokes on them, though. I know my mom, and she won't put up with Adira's manipulation games much longer."

"So Adira brought your mom here just because you wouldn't feed on Eugene? That seems a little extreme."

"She brought my mom here because they think I'm starving myself. That I'm not eating enough."

"Do you think there's anything to their concern?" she asked.

"No. Why?"

She shrugged.

"Just say it," I said. "You know I won't get mad."

"Honestly, I'm not sure how to put it into words without making it sound like I'm criticizing you."

"I know you're not. Try. Maybe it will help me understand what they see."

"Well, you're not like the other succubus at school. You're small. Not just in size but your presence, too. The other girls can walk in and own a room. Even knowing the tricks of your kind, it's hard not to look. With you, it's easier."

"Not that easy. You fell for it on Thursday."

"True. But it was because I had my guard down. I wasn't looking for it with you. You don't tempt me now, and I'm not sure you could if you tried. It's like you lack a spark."

I considered what she was saying.

"Are you mad?" she asked.

"No. I'm trying to look at myself objectively. I think you're right that I'm missing the spark that they have. But I think it's by choice, not starvation. I don't want to be like them and command a room with a look. If I'm noticed, I want it to be like this," I said, waving a hand between us. "Something real."

"I don't know, Eliana. I've overheard the other girls talk about how often they feed, and it's a lot. They also get insanely hangry when they skip a meal. Even the guys are like that. You heard about Eras, right? He's going crazy because he went hungry for a night. How are you not hungry all the time like them?"

"I am hungry all the time. I just learned to control it."

"In the human world that's called anorexia, and it's dangerous. I'm not saying that I'm siding with Adira or Mrs. Quill, just that you need to take a long look at yourself. You're hungry all the time and refusing to eat. What's that really doing to you? You're one of the few friends I have here, and I don't want to lose you. I've lost enough."

I knew I shouldn't, that it was dangerous, but I reached over and placed my hand on Ashlyn's and pulled some of the sorrow from her. The non-sexual energy didn't nourish me, but it did make me weirdly hungry for lava cake.

"I'm sorry for all that you've gone through and the pain you still feel. I hope it fades in time and you find some true happiness." Even as I said the words, I knew how impossible finding happiness would be here. Either she would spend her life alone, or she would bring another human into this hell with her. And I didn't see her as the type of person to do that.

She pulled her hand out from under mine.

"Thank you. I'm sure I'll be fine."

Was there any word used more falsely than the word fine?

"Still want to bake a dessert?" I asked as I parked in front of her house.

"Absolutely. The brownies we made with Megan were amazing."

The comment made me think of Piepen and how very not amazing he was.

"How much do you know about brownies?" I asked. "The ones with wings."

She let us into the house and waited until I closed the door before answering.

"Not much. They're one of the few creatures I haven't had to interact with. Mostly, they keep to themselves and stay hidden. Why?"

I thought of the glowing line on my belly and shrugged.

"Megan sent a brownie to me, and he's more than I can deal with right now. I went to the marshes and asked if any family would take him in."

"You saw brownies at the marshes?"

"No. I just stood there, talking to the marsh. But I know some of them heard me. There weren't any birds around but a lot of bird song. I gave them my phone number. I mean, I know some of the wingless ones have jobs in town, right? They should be able to call me."

"The ones that work in town don't go back to the marsh. Too dangerous. They could give away where the young ones with wings are hiding."

Defeat kicked me hard in the ribs. Why couldn't anything go right for me?

Ashlyn must have seen something in my expression because her gaze turned sympathetic.

"Maybe we could try asking the new liaison for help."

"Don't worry about it. I'll figure something out after we get our chocolate fix."

My phone started to ring before we even had the mixing bowls out. I glanced at the number and wrinkled my nose.

"Your mom?" Ashlyn asked.

"Worse. Adira."

Ashlyn gave me a sympathetic look as I answered.

"Why aren't you spending time with your mother?" Adira asked without greeting.

"Because she's a hardened serial troll killer, of course."

There was a beat of silence on the other end.

"Your new attitude is unappreciated. Did you retrieve your jacket?"

"The one you made me give away? Yes, I have it again."

"Good. Then go home."

"No."

"I see."

"No, you don't. But I do. As soon as we hang up, you're going to do something to try to get me to leave this house prematurely. However, it won't work. Do you know why? Because I've already put up with as much as I can deal with today. Do what you need to do, but remember that Ashlyn's under Megan's protection before you start handing out ultimatums in an attempt to get your way in whatever game you're playing."

I hung up the phone before she could answer.

"What do you think Adira's going to do?" Ashlyn asked, measuring out some flour. I started in on my recipe, too.

"It's hard to tell with her. She never does anything that would be obvious, you know? I don't think you have anything to worry about, though."

"I know. I'm more worried about what she'll do to you."

"My mom's already mad at Adira. I don't think Adira will rush to do anything to make her angrier. She's not stupid."

My phone started ringing before I managed to crack my eggs. Thinking it was Adira, I didn't rush to answer it. When I saw it was Mom's number, I frowned and said a wary hello.

"Hey, baby. I wanted to apologize again for this morning. I know I messed up, and I promise I won't surprise you with any meal options in the future."

"Thank you."

"Did you get your jacket?"

"Yes. Thank you for talking to Adira and getting my clothes back, too. I should have thanked you right away."

"Nonsense. You were upset. I understand. Do you think you'll be home soon?"

I looked at all the ingredients we had spread over the table.

"Probably not. Why?"

"I want to talk to you about something, and I'd prefer to do it soon."

I opened my mouth to ask if something was wrong with Dad when another thought occurred to me.

"Adira," I said. "She called you, didn't she?"

"She did."

"She's trying to manipulate me into leaving Ashlyn's to spend more time with you."

"Is spending time with me a bad thing?" Mom asked.

Guilt hit me hard.

"Mom, it's not about you; it's about Adira. She needs to stop trying to force me to do things."

"She told me you're feeding on non-sexual energy, Eliana. Is that true?"

"Yes, but not for food. I was just doing it to help people out."

"You need to come home now."

I pulled the phone from my ear and stared at it in shock. My mom had just used a mom-voice on me. She never did that. Ever.

"Respectfully, I think it's best if I don't come home for a while. I don't think either of us is in the right frame of mind for whatever talk you want to have."

There was a beat of silence before she answered.

"You might be right. Be careful, Eliana. You have no idea what you're doing to yourself with these false feedings. I'll see you at dinner."

I hung up the phone with a shaky exhale. Adira's words from the last dinner she attended at the Quills' were starting to haunt me. She'd said I would regret my choice, and she was doing everything in her power to make that happen. A gut feeling told me that she was far from done.

"I really hate Adira," I said to Ashlyn.

"Yeah, it was a real dick move for her to call your mom. You okay?"

My phone buzzed with a text. Instead of answering it, I started cracking eggs into my lava cake batter and answered Ashlyn.

"Not really. Adira just made a huge mess for me, and I'm not sure what'll happen next."

"Nothing good, most likely."

"You're probably right."

I finished mixing my lava cake and got it into a pan. When I was wiping my hands, my phone buzzed again. Giving in, I checked the messages. Instead of being from Mom or Adira, they were from Megan.

Freedom is one phone call away. Get ready to say goodbye to mommy-dearest!

She'd sent a second one three minutes after that.

Everything okay?

Everything was most definitely not okay. Adira was using

Mom to try to control me. And just then, I realized what that meant for me. Freedom was far from one phone call away. Even if the Council officially pardoned Mom, they wouldn't make her leave.

I needed to come up with a plan of my own before I lost myself in the aftermath.

Everything is fine, I sent back. *See you soon, hopefully.*

Putting aside my concerns for the future, I focused on the now.

Ashlyn and I made a mess of her kitchen and decimated her baking supplies, but managed to make three different dessert options.

"Oh, these are so good," Ashlyn said around a mouthful of warm brownie.

I shuddered.

"I don't think I'll ever be able to eat a brownie again. Piepen's scarred me for life." Probably literally the way my luck was going.

"I'll take one for the team and eat all these myself. How's the lava cake?"

"Good." And it was good. It just wasn't as good as my dream lava cake, which was a huge letdown.

"You're still thinking about your mom and Adira, aren't you?"

I set my fork down and sighed.

"Yeah. Dealing with Adira is bad enough. Now she's trying to turn my mom against me."

"You know you're welcome to stay here as long as you'd like. The threat of Megan's retribution will be enough to keep Adira from doing anything too awful."

As tempting as that would be, I knew I couldn't stay forever. Eventually my hunger would raise its head and put Ashlyn in danger.

"Thank you," I said. "But avoiding everything won't make my problems go away."

WITH MY CONTAINER of lava cake in my hands, I entered the kitchen from the garage. Scents of grilled meat and vegetables filled the air. Mrs. Quill looked up from her place at the stove.

"Did you have a nice visit with Ashlyn?" she asked.

I stared at her for a second, wishing our lives were still at the point when I actually thought she cared.

"The visit was fine until Adira called, trying to play her games again. I can't wait to be free of this place." I put my cake in the fridge and started for the door.

"I'm sorry you're hurting, Eliana," Mrs. Quill said.

I waved and kept walking. Her sorrow didn't help anything. Her support would have, but heaven forbid she do anything against Adira's wishes.

From above, I could hear the thumping beat of muffled music. Resigned, I made my way to my bedroom and ignored the growing scent of lust. How many people did Mom have in Oanen's room? I was no longer sure a professional cleaning would be enough. He'd need to gut the space by the time he and Megan returned.

Another thought hit me hard. When he and Megan returned to Uttira, he likely wouldn't be coming back here. He'd probably go live with Megan.

I wanted to groan. Was I going to be stuck with my mom forever?

Continuing past his room, I noticed the door to the entertainment space was open and looked in. Piepen flitted in the air, watching the TV raptly. His jerky movements, and the tiny glowing firework that exploded just in front of him, had me rolling my eyes. I would need to burn that couch when Piepen was gone.

I glanced at the TV then quickly hurried to my room. I should have known how Mom would keep an adolescent brownie entertained while she was busy. Thankfully, Piepen's skunk scent was almost completely masked by what was seeping from Oanen's room.

In the peace of my own space, I sighed and went to my closet to change for a dinner I didn't want to attend. Adira would expect it, though, even if she wasn't there. Based on her call, Mrs. Quill was giving her sister full reports of how much time I was spending in my mom's presence.

As if summoned by my thoughts, my mom knocked on my door and entered without waiting for a response.

"Hey, baby. I thought I heard you come home."

"Not sure how you can hear anything with your music so loud."

Mom smiled.

"The music sets the mood for the humans. You know that." She tilted her head, watching me consider the dresses. "Are you going somewhere?"

"Mrs. Quill is almost done with dinner. They expect me to change into something fittingly succubus."

"I see. There's no need for that anymore, though. I think it would be better if we stopped with the pretext of eating human food unless we're using the experience as it's meant to be used."

I frowned at her, confused.

"It's a form of foreplay, baby. Putting the fork in your mouth, licking it, swallowing what it provides. It's a phallic representation to your male companion."

"And you've just ruined eating for the rest of my life."

"Don't be so dramatic. Human food is a tool, not nourishment. If you're hungry, I have a buffet in my room. Why don't you come and sample a little? You might find something you like."

"Thanks, but I'm not really in the mood for an orgy."

She sighed and stood.

"Fine, but I'll leave my door open just in case you change your mind."

"I won't."

She'd no sooner left than Piepen came buzzing in, his iridescent wings fluttering behind him.

"You're home!" he cried, zooming at me.

"Stop."

He halted midair, just shy of my hand.

"Baby, don't be like that," he said. "I got what you need. Come here and let big P treat you right."

"I think I just threw up in my mouth. Stop talking like that."

"Like what? You don't want your baby daddy sweet-talking you?"

"Baby daddy? You are not—"

He zoomed over to my bed and landed face up on my pillow.

"You know what you need? A ride. Hop on, mama," he said, patting his tiny hips.

"I should sit on you and end my suffering, you annoying little P."

"Hey now," he said, sitting up. "Don't be like that. Is the baby giving you trouble?"

I threw my hands in the air just as my phone started to ring. I grabbed it, thankful for any reason not to continue the conversation with Piepen.

"Yeah, what's up?" I answered.

"Everything okay?" Megan asked.

Piepen chose that moment to start humping my pillow. I covered the phone to yell at him before answering her.

"Not really. I need to find Piepen a better home."

Piepen squealed and started pleading with me to let him stay until the baby was born. I rolled my eyes.

"You do what you need to do," Megan said.

"Thanks."

Piepen came flying at me in all his naked glory.

"I gotta go," I said quickly then hung up.

"No, Piepen. Enough is enough. Get back to your drawer pillow and stay there, or I'm going to put you in a cage. And for the last time, I am not pregnant with your baby or anyone else's. I'm still a virgin, and so are you."

I slammed my door on the way out of my room.

CHAPTER FOURTEEN

Winter's wind cooled my face but not my temper. A faint howl echoed in the distance followed by another further off. How great would it be to just change what I was and run free? No. Instead, I was stuck at the Quills' in my own personal hell. What would Dad say about all of this? He'd lecture on promiscuity then ask if I'd spoken to my mother lately.

Sighing, I brushed the snow off of a bench and sat. I was who I was. Not a product of my upbringing but of my experience and the personal decisions made because of those experiences. People, whether human or not, weren't just food. Each life mattered regardless of birth or background. Why couldn't the Council see the same thing I did? We were all connected. People who knew people who knew people. Every time I heard a human say, "it's a small world, isn't it?" I was reminded of those connections. Yet, people with influence and power tended to forget that.

Was it fear that kept them rigidly holding to their beliefs that only their way could be the right way? Heaven forbid I be allowed my differences or be shown any acceptance because of them. My thoughts ricocheted back at me. Was I being the stubborn one? Was I unhealthy? I wished that everyone would stop telling me what to do and let me figure it out on my own.

I kicked at the snow at my feet and looked up at the stars.

"What are we looking at?"

The voice, so close to my ear, made me jump.

Swiveling, I glared back at Fenris.

"What are you doing?"

"Creeping around in the dark. That's what we werewolves are known for. That, and chasing girls dressed in red."

I glanced down at myself.

"I'm wearing green."

"I thought you might want to go change for me."

His humor in the face of my troubles irritated me.

"Do you ever take anything seriously?"

His expression sobered.

"Yes. What's wrong?"

"I have an insane, sex-obsessed mother, and she's staying here. I hate my life and wish I had my mark so I could just leave this place."

He stepped over the bench and sat beside me.

"I'm sorry," he said quietly.

"Don't be. None of it's your fault."

"Fault doesn't matter when someone I care about is hurting. Want to talk about whatever's going on?" He bumped me lightly then stilled and sniffed.

I glanced at him.

"Is that you?" he asked, leaning in and sniffing again.

A flash flood of heat consumed my face when his nose almost touched my chest. He inhaled deeply. He didn't pull back when he tilted his head to look up at me.

"What is that smell?" he asked.

I could barely think with his face so close to mine. Dirty thoughts filled my head, and my pulse skipped several beats.

"Eliana?" he said softly. "What happened?"

I planted my palm over his face and pushed him away. He chuckled and sat again.

"One of my many problems happened. You know about the goblin at Megan's. Well, he arrived with a brownie. A fourteen-month-old brownie who can't stop touching himself and makes me dream of skunks making babies."

Fenris snorted a laugh, which he quickly smothered with a swipe of his hand.

"Please, continue."

"It's far from funny. He saw me naked in the shower more times than I care to recall."

"Naked?"

"Very."

"Lucky little flitter."

"More than you know. This last time, I hit him with water and he fell right between my...well, he was so excited by it he exploded."

Fenris arched a brow at me.

"Exploded?"

"Yes. It's as dirty as it sounds. That's what you smell. He just keeps going. He thinks we made a baby and is saying the most ridiculous things now. I just can't anymore. He needs to go. So does my mom. Either the goblin needs to talk, or Megan needs to find the killer because I'm two seconds from losing my sanity."

"It can't be that bad."

"My mom made me breakfast in bed."

"See? That's motherly."

"Breakfast was two naked boys tucked in with me when I woke up."

He exhaled heavily and looked out at the trees. We listened to the distant howls, and I wondered if he could understand what they were saying.

"I'll make you a deal," Fenris said finally. "If I can find a happy home for your pocket pool playing pixie—"

"Brownie."

"—you repay me by showering me with your undying gratitude."

I stared at him for a moment. His brown gaze, while still filled with humor, held mine with complete sincerity.

"What exactly are you asking for?"

"I want a hug a day until Megan gets back," he said.

"Hugs?" Hugs were dangerous. They were full-body contact, usually front to front. I could feel my hunger stir just at the thought of all that touching.

He shrugged slightly.

"What can I say? It's in my nature to like affection."

"Are you making a canine joke?"

"Are you thinking of petting me?"

My vision sharpened, and he grinned.

"No. No petting," I said, blinking in an effort to return my vision to normal. "While I appreciate the offer to help, hugging is too dangerous. For you, not me."

"I disagree. I think you hugging me could help us both. I'd get my daily dose of affection, and you'd be doing something that would appease your mom enough to get her back on your side instead of Adira's."

"Hugs aren't going to appease any of them. It's gone way beyond that. Give me a real reason why you want a hug, and I might think about it."

He studied me for a minute.

"Because you hate your life and think no one cares. You need to remember your mom, Adira, and the Quills aren't the only people in your life. You have friends. And I'm willing to remind you of that for as long as it takes until Megan's here to remind you herself."

He nudged me then stood.

"Come on. Let's get you back inside before you freeze."

We walked the path back toward the house. Before we reached the door, I groaned.

"I forgot to feed the goblin."

"Don't worry about it. I'll take care of him before I start looking for the brownie's new home."

"You're going to start tonight?"

"Sure. Just be ready to pay up tomorrow."

THE SOUND of my phone pulled me out of a deep sleep.

"Hello?" I answered groggily.

"Get out of bed, beautiful. Your meat-beating brownie issues are solved."

My sluggish brain struggled to process what Fenris was saying.

"My what?"

"I found your brownie a new home as promised. Meet me at the marshes in thirty minutes, or we'll miss our chance."

I looked at the time on my phone, saw that it wasn't even six in the morning and that Fenris had already hung up.

He couldn't be serious, could he? How had he found a family overnight? Had he slept? Had I? Mom's party had kept me up until close to three. My eyes felt gritty like I needed at least another two hours. But thirty minutes barely gave enough time for me to drive to the marshes.

My eyes, which had closed again, flew open, and I scrambled from bed.

"Piepen, get dressed. We need to hurry."

He sat up in his drawer, his shaggy hair wild around his head.

"Is it the baby? Is it time?"

"What? No. Get dressed."

He flopped back onto his pillow.

I rushed to the closet, threw on some clothes, and was out the door with a naked Piepen and a handful of brownie clothes two minutes later.

"I'm going to freeze my bells off," he said when we reached the garage.

"I think you mean balls, and they wouldn't be cold if you'd gotten dressed like I'd said."

"No, I mean bells. They make beautiful music when I—"

"Don't want to know, Piepen. Just get in and get dressed." I tossed his clothes into the back seat with him and hurried to pull out of the garage.

He bombarded me with questions as we drove. Wisely, I didn't say much.

"You're making me nervous," he said, landing on my shoulder. "Why won't you tell me where we're going? Are you going to lock me in a cage and eat my wings?"

"No. I'm going to do the opposite so you can truly be happy."

"I am happy. I'm with my woman who's carrying my baby. What more could a man want?" He stepped closer to my cheek and stroked a hand over it. "Well, I could think of something," he said, lowering his high-pitched voice pseudo-seductively. "How about you pull over and I make you really happy?"

"Stop touching me, brownie, or you'll find out what's it's like to be a mosquito."

"Someone's cranky. Probably because you missed your dose of vitamin P."

I flicked him from my shoulder. He squealed indignantly but recovered in the air just before hitting the passenger seat.

"Keep this up and I'm going to leave," he said.

"Come back here so I can flick you again."

"You're being mean."

And I felt a fair share of guilt for it under my annoyance. However, I wouldn't apologize for my behavior. Any hint of affection from me, and the brownie would never leave.

A sullen silence filled the car, and I watched for the marshes. Piepen didn't say anything when they came into view. More than likely, he didn't know what they were. I glanced at him in the mirror, and my guilt grew. His clothes weren't that warm. Would he be okay out here? Brownies didn't have heated homes like we did. Or pillow beds. I started to worry that my need to get rid of him would be what killed the poor little thing.

His gaze met mine as I put on the blinker.

"Pulling over so we can make up?" he asked.

My worry went out the window.

"Nope."

He frowned at me and watched the road. When I reached the parking area, I saw Fenris. He stood by the reeds, wearing nothing but a pair of jeans. Steam rose from his torso. I tried not to stare at the ridged expanse. I tried to tell myself that he had to be freezing like that. But mostly, I just imagined what it would be like to—

"Stop staring," Piepen said, flitting in front of my face so I had to slam on the breaks.

He yanked up his shirt and pointed at his belly.

"If you want abs, you can look at mine."

The passenger door opened before I could swat Piepen.

"Everything okay?" Fenris asked.

"No, but it will be. Where are they?"

I opened my door and got out, shivering despite my jacket. Piepen followed, staying close to my head.

"Where are who?" he asked.

"Your new family," I said.

His eyes rounded.

"New family? You're my family."

"Hello, Piepen," a female voice said, drawing our attention to the reeds in front of the car.

An older couple, both with their wings, hovered just within the brown stalks. Their grey hair and creased faces worried me a bit. Hopefully, they weren't too old to handle Piepen's energy.

"I'm Madeline, and this is my husband, Marshal. We'd like to give you a home and a family."

Piepen looked at me, shock and dejection showing on his little face.

"What about our family?"

"We don't have a family, Piepen."

"The baby," he said stubbornly.

I had to take a slow breath before answering.

"For the last time, there is no baby."

"How do you know?" He looked at the older couple. "I gave her my very first magic dust."

They both made sounds of awe as if he'd done something special instead of disgusting.

"It's a special gift to receive," Marshal said. "You're marked for life for certain."

I thought of the stain still on my stomach and really hoped it wasn't permanent. Hopefully, the lifespan he was talking about was theirs.

"How long ago did it happen?" he asked.

"Yesterday," I said.

"Oh, you'd be entering your second trimester then," Madeline said. "Enough for someone with good ears to hear a heartbeat." She looked at Fenris.

I did, too. He was standing there with his hand loosely over his mouth as if he was seriously following the conversation. I knew better. The tramp was laughing his butt off.

However, with all attention on him, he managed to remove his hand without showing a hint of his amusement and walked over to me.

"I'll take a listen," he said in all seriousness before dropping to his knees in front of me.

He reached up and slowly unzipped my jacket.

"So I can hear better," he said.

It didn't matter the reason. All I saw was a man on his knees before me, undressing me. My eyes went black, and hunger clawed its way to the surface, fierce and demanding.

"Worship me, wolf," I said.

Fenris looked up at me, a hint of a smile showing on his lips.

"What exactly does that entail?" he asked, playfully.

I liked playful.

"Stop hitting on my woman," Piepen yelled.

I bared my teeth and started to look up at the little gnat who needed to die.

Fenris grabbed my hips, commanding my attention.

"Before we work out the details of this worship you want, I think we should check to see if you're carrying another man's child."

He set his ear against my lower belly. My hunger craved more. It demanded his lust, and his complete...

Obedience.

I closed my eyes, realizing I'd slipped again, and pulled my thoughts back to the moment. Fenris was helping me. Piepen needed to go. And stress was making me act weird. Nothing more. I wasn't hungry; I was tired.

My hunger stirred to contradict me.

"No heartbeat," Fenris said, standing. "Sorry, Piepen."

I hurriedly rezipped my jacket.

"We can try again," Piepen said, flying close to me. "Don't give up on us."

I rolled my eyes and struggled to find the remnants of my shredded patience.

"There is no us, Piepen. I took you in because Megan asked me to. Now I'm asking you to leave, willingly, so you can live a happy life with your own kind. There's a brownie girl out there who is as desperate to make little brownie babies as you are. Go find her and be happy."

His little eyes watered.

"This isn't you. You're upset that I—"

"You're right. This isn't me. I'm not the type of person who gets so angry that I close someone in a drawer or threaten to rip their wings off. I brought you here to keep you safe. From me. Please. Just go with them."

Hurt flitted across his features.

"You didn't mean it, though," he said.

"Yes, I did. I was that angry."

His wings wilted a little with defeat.

"Can I come see you some time?"

"How about I come see you? It'll be safer that way."

He nodded sadly and turned toward the old couple. I didn't feel a twinge of sorrow as they led him away. Only relief.

"Still want to be worshipped?" Fenris asked when we were alone.

"Shut up, and get in the car," I said.

"Yes, ma'am."

He got into the passenger seat and grinned at me as I buckled. I knew he found the whole thing amusing. I didn't. It was my life, and Piepen had nearly destroyed it.

I knew the thought wasn't entirely fair as soon as I had it. Piepen, alone, wasn't responsible for my out of control spiral. The adults in my life had a fair share of blame with all their meddling, too. Although, without their meddling, I probably wouldn't have started talking to Fenris and would still be stuck with Piepen.

Glancing at Fenris's bare chest, I tried to decide which of the two creatures would have been the safer option.

"Where are the rest of your clothes? I'll drop you off there."

"My clothes are in the Quills' garden. But I'd rather you drop me off at the cabin. You can bring the clothes to school tomorrow, or I can swing by afterward to pick them up."

My fingers tightened on the steering wheel at the idea of him stripping down to almost nothing so close to the Quills' house.

"Thank you for your help," I said, trying to control the direction of my thoughts. "I don't think I could have survived another day with Piepen."

Fenris chuckled.

"For such a small guy, he had a lot of feeling. My nose was close to bleeding."

"Brownies live intense little lives. How did you find Marshal and Madeline?"

He grinned.

"I sat in the parking lot and howled until someone came to talk to me."

"The power of annoyance."

"I prefer to call it persistence. Did your night go better after I left you?"

"Not really. My mom stayed up until 3 a.m., having an orgy two doors down from mine. I didn't get much sleep. And no doubt, she'll probably be awake by the time I get home and will have some new way to torture me ready. Got any ideas for how to get rid of her?"

"Not really. But you're welcome to hang out at the cabin with me for a while."

I sighed.

"I'm looking for more of a permanent solution."

He considered me for a moment.

"I can smell your exhaustion. Just under three hours of sleep isn't enough. Take a nap at the cabin. Things might look better afterward."

"You didn't get any sleep at all. I'm not going to take over your cabin again."

"We could share."

I shook my head before he even finished talking.

"Too dangerous. My guard is down when I sleep." Obviously, my guard was lacking when I was tired, too.

"And what do you think will happen?" he asked.

"With the way you smell, probably the worst thing possible."

"I can't read your mind. What's the worst thing possible?"

"That I'll feed from you."

"I was thinking murdered in my sleep by a sex-crazed brownie because I took his goddess away from him, so I'm not sure how a feeding would be the worst thing possible."

"I'm not Piepen's goddess, and feeding from you would be horrible."

He tapped his knee with his thumb.

"If I smell good, I assume I'd taste good. I'm struggling to connect the horrible."

"Horrible for you. Why are we even talking about this?"

"Because you're tired and need a place to crash, and you're being stubborn."

"You don't understand what a feeding could do to you. You saw how obsessed Eugene was after an almost feeding. You'd be a mindless slave if I fed from you."

He snorted.

"It's not funny."

"It kinda is. You already almost fed from me twice. Have I acted any differently around you? To you?"

"Well, no."

"Then why are you worrying? We both know that different creatures have different levels of susceptibility to each other. My kind does the whole fated mates thing, right? So maybe you can't persuade me because my genetics just aren't interested in anyone who's not my mate."

Hadn't Mom said something similar in the restaurant? Not that I was considering feeding from him, I quickly told myself. It would just be nice to know I wouldn't hurt him if I did slip.

"But what if you're wrong?"

"I don't think I am. You can't hurt me, Eliana. Trust me."

I sighed and thought of a nap in his cabin with him still there. My hunger slithered under my skin, more responsive than it was the day before. Maybe it was because I was tired. That just made sleeping at his cabin more dangerous.

My brain was saying no, but my eyes were saying yes with each tired blink. When I reached his road, I knew I'd need to sleep before driving home even if it was just in the car.

I parked and cut the engine.

"I can see you're going to say no. What kind of friend would I be to let you drive home like this?"

"The kind that let me drive here."

"Come on, chicken. I promise not to bite."

My insides went hot at the thought of Fenris biting, nibbling his way up my leg.

"You're right. I'm too tired to drive. Or fight you. Can I borrow a blanket and just sleep in the car for a bit?"

He laughed and got out, walking around the car to open my door.

"Not a chance. Come on. Everything will be fine."

I got out and waited for him to close the door.

"If you ever want, I can take your car somewhere to get this fixed," he said, pointing to the bubbled paint. "Just let me know when you're ready to be without it for a few days."

I nodded and tiredly followed him.

My gaze was glued to his back. The play of muscles as he walked mesmerized me as I listened to the crunch of his feet on the snow.

"How are you not cold?" I asked.

He looked over his shoulder at me.

"What can I say, Eliana? I'm hot, and all the girls are in awe."

I rolled my eyes at him.

"Hot or big-headed?"

He grinned.

"They usually go hand in hand, don't they?"

He opened the cabin door. This time, in the daylight, I could see the room and closed the door as he went to light the fire. He had flames within a few minutes then crossed the room and pulled back the blankets.

"In you go," he said.

I looked at him then the bed.

"I don't think that's a good idea. You take the bed. I'll take the chair by the fire. I'll be warmer."

He shrugged. "Suit yourself."

I watched him crawl into bed and turn his back to me. Within seconds, his breathing evened out.

Exhaling slowly, I went to the chair and closed my eyes.

Once again, I was in the woods surrounded by cakes. They smelled so good. Better than the ones I made with Ashlyn. My mouth watered, but I didn't eat. I was too afraid of what the sleeping me would do to Fenris.

My hunger grew as I walked, clenching at my stomach so painfully that I whimpered.

"Take what you need," the forest rumbled.

I shook my head and kept walking. The hunger didn't ease.

"Stop denying yourself," the forest said. "I exist only for you. Take what you need. There will always be more."

A cake dropped in front of my face, brushing my nose, flooding my senses with its sweet scent.

I knew I shouldn't, but I took a bite. Then another. Warmth surrounded me, blanketing me in comfort as I ate deeply of every sweet possible. I gorged myself until I thought I'd burst. Then the forest disappeared. The warmth didn't. It stayed with me while I slept deeply.

When I woke, I was in the bed, tucked under the blankets. I looked around the room warily. Fenris was gone, though.

Confused, I got out of bed and checked my phone, which was in my purse still by the chair. Five hours had passed. I rubbed my face and stretched, wondering how long Fenris had slept before he'd left. I frowned and glanced at the chair then the bed. Had he moved me when he'd woken up?

"Hey, sleepyhead," Fenris said, opening the cabin door.

A cold wind stole into the room with him.

"How did I get in the bed?" I asked.

"You walked to it and crawled in," he said. "Are you hungry

for human food? I ran to my house and grabbed some stuff." He lifted a brown paper bag that had a wet spot in the middle.

I glanced at the teeth marks in the paper.

"Sorry. I shifted and ran with it. I didn't want to leave the fire for too long. You were cold."

"Were you in the bed when I crawled into it?" I asked, not letting him distract me.

He grinned.

"Only for a little while. You hog the covers."

I studied his eyes, looking for any trace that I'd done something I shouldn't have. They looked the same, though. No haunting earnestness. Just the ever-present glint of humor.

"I could maybe eat something," I said. "As long as it isn't anything sweet."

The idea of eating anything sweet just then turned my stomach.

"Not sweet. I made sandwiches."

We sat in the chairs by the fire. I was one bite away from finishing the best ham and cheese sandwich I'd ever had in my life when my phone rang.

Seeing it was Megan, I answered.

"Eliana, you need to get to Elbner," Megan said as soon as I answered. "Tell him I know his master was Zayn Sias. I know Zayn was the one responsible for all the creatures who died with a smile. Tell Elbner I'm making it common knowledge. Once you do that, you should be able to take him to the Council as a witness. Got it?"

"Yes. Zayn Sias. Got it. Thank you."

I hung up and looked at Fenris with growing hope.

"Megan's figured out who's doing the killing. I need to get to the goblin and deliver him to the Quills. Once he confirms Mom didn't do it, I'll be free again."

"I'll go with you."

"No. It's okay. I got this."

I grabbed my purse.

"Thanks for letting me sleep here. You're right. It did make things better."

I ran from the cabin, excited to get back into my car. I was almost free.

CHAPTER FIFTEEN

ELBNER SHIFTED HIS WEIGHT FROM ONE FOOT TO ANOTHER AS HE stood before Mr. Quill. I could see the goblin's mistrust as his gaze flicked to each of the room's occupants. He didn't want to be here. However, now that Megan knew the name of his previous master and that the druid named Zayn was the one responsible for the mysterious deaths, Elbner was no longer held silent by any spell.

"Tell us what you know," Mr. Quill said.

"Zayn Sias is a druid of vast power. He is the one who took the life energy of the smiling trolls, not that woman," Elbner said with a glance at my mom.

She perched elegantly on the couch in Mr. Quill's office, listening without comment. Adira, Mrs. Quill, and Raiden were there, too.

"What is he doing with the energy?" Adira asked.

Elbner shrugged.

"He didn't confide in me. I cleaned the homes of those who surrendered their souls before they died and was fed for it. I did what I was told and didn't ask questions."

"We understand. Thank you for coming forward. If anything else comes to mind, please let us know."

Mr. Quill looked at me.

"You may return him to Megan's house."

I glanced at my mom.

"Does this mean Mom's free to go?"

"That is something we will discuss with your mother. Thank you, Eliana."

Hating that I was being dismissed like some child, I left the room with Elbner. After the door closed, I looked at the goblin and lifted my fingers to my lips. He remained quiet as I set my ear to the door.

"I believe some groveling is necessary," Mom said.

"If you feel it necessary, you may," Adira said.

There was a tense minute of silence where I hoped Mom was strangling Adira.

"Why do you think I am the one who needs to grovel?" Mom asked, disappointing me.

"Because you've been given a chance to spend time with your daughter. A daughter who requested you remain far from here. We made that possible," Adira said.

Mom laughed.

"You're trying to spin this like it was all for my benefit?"

"Haven't you benefited? Not only have you had time with your daughter, but we've made sure to provide you with everything else you needed. You've wanted for nothing."

"And what is it you want in return for this magnanimousness?"

"We're worried about Eliana. Despite all of our efforts, she's not hunting for her own meals. And when she does feed, she isn't taking enough to survive."

I wrinkled my nose. They were acting like I was on death's door when, in reality, I was walking around as well as could be.

"Yes. You've mentioned this already," Mom said.

"Since you've come, we're seeing more resistance from her. More life. More energy. We think your presence is good for her."

I almost snorted.

"Are you asking me to stay?" Mom asked.

"We are willing to invite you to extend your stay based on a few conditions."

"Oh? And what might those conditions be?"

"No feeding on anyone beyond the people we provide."

"And if you stop providing me enough?"

"You're welcome to leave, but you should know your re-entry to Uttira will be barred once you leave. And I'm well aware you're overeating. While I understand why you're doing it, my concern right now is the child you already have and what starving her during your pregnancy did to her."

A sick feeling settled in my stomach as I understood what Adira was saying. Mom had only fed on Dad during her pregnancy with me. She'd mentioned it during one of our many conversations. Given how mom was feeding now, I wondered how unhealthy that had been for her.

"I did not starve her or myself. Don't judge what you don't understand."

I could hear the threat in my mother's voice.

"I'll stay. Whether under your terms or my own will depend on your interference, Adira. I suggest you leave my daughter to me."

Backing away from the door, I hurried down the hall.

"Some secrets are best left unheard," Elbner said softly beside me.

I couldn't have agreed more.

After dropping him off at Megan's, I drove aimlessly for a bit and ended up parking in front of Ashlyn's house. She must have seen my car because she opened the door as I walked up the sidewalk.

"That looks like an I-need-chocolate-and-a-friend face."

"It is. Do you have a few minutes?"

"I have loads of them. Come in."

She took my jacket and led me to the kitchen. While she dished up some dessert, I talked.

"Piepen's gone. I handed him over to a good family this morning, thanks to Fenris."

"That's great news, right?"

"It is. So is my mom's name being cleared for the troll murders in New York."

"I sense a 'but' coming."

"Adira asked Mom to stay because they still think something's wrong with me." I lifted my arms. "Do I look more sickly since the last time you saw me?"

She considered me for a moment.

"No. You actually look a little better. More mad, but less pale. It might be related," she said with a small smile.

I returned it, appreciating her effort to cheer me up. If only a smile would fix everything.

"Do you think your mom's going to stay?" Ashlyn asked. "I mean, she left you here once because you wanted her to."

"I don't know. She is pretty excited to be here."

I thought of all the times she'd stood up to Adira for me. How protective she was. How supportive. Would she walk away from that? She didn't love me any more or less than she had when she'd left me the first time. She might leave if I asked her to, but I wasn't naïve enough to think things would go back to the way they were. Despite Mrs. Quill's offer to feed me, I knew Adira wouldn't allow that long term. I needed a way to deal with both Adira and Mom.

Sitting back in the chair, I sighed.

"It all comes down to their belief that something is wrong with me because I'm not behaving like all the other succubi my age. To reassure them that I'm fine, they want me to start feeding. Which I won't do. Not the way they want me to do it."

What if there was another way to reassure them? What if I proved I'm healthy? But how? If I were a human, it would be as easy as bringing me to a doctor.

I grinned and stood.

"Thanks for giving me a quick place to think. I'll text you with how everything turns out."

I was out the door before she moved.

Back at the Quills', I raced upstairs and knocked on Mom's door. The moaning and music inside continued uninterrupted as the door opened. Mom stood there in her typical robe. When she saw it was me, she smiled.

"Baby, I was hoping I'd see you soon."

"Can I come in and talk to you?"

"Of course," she said, sounding surprised.

She stepped aside, and I strode in, ignoring the four people in Oanen's bed and the couple on his couch. Although the sight made me uncomfortable, the lust clogging the air didn't bother me much.

I turned to face Mom.

"I was at the office door when they tried to bargain with you," I said without preamble.

"Oh? And what do you think of me staying?"

"I love you. Having you here makes me feel protected in some ways. Threatened in others." I gestured at the people behind me. "I don't want this in my life."

"What exactly don't you want? The food?"

"No, Mom. I know I need to eat. I don't want to coerce anyone or to have anyone suffer the mindless adulation that comes after I feed. I lived with the aftermath for twelve years. I will not do to anyone what was done to my dad. I love him too much to allow that to happen.

"My fear is that, if you lived here, I'd eventually make love slaves out of people and hate myself for it. I want you to be in my life, Mom, but it needs to be with a mutual understanding."

"What understanding is that?"

"That I'm fine and healthy just the way I am."

"I don't think you are, though."

"I know. Which is why I'm proposing you have me checked out. If a human doctor isn't good enough, then have Raiden sniff me. Whatever it takes. If I get a clean bill of health, you help get Adira off my back; and you can live in Uttira as long as you want."

Mom studied me, the pity in her gaze growing by the second.

"Baby, I knew the moment you walked into the dining room that something wasn't right. I didn't need Adira or Anwen's stories to tell me what it was, either. You're fading away. No human doctor will be able to verify that. Raiden would, but I wouldn't put you through that humiliation." She took my hand and gave it a squeeze. "I'm staying. On my own terms, not theirs. And I'll help you figure this out. Now that I know why you're not feeding like you should, we'll work through it."

"Work through it?"

"Yes. I know you don't like what I did to your father. I've avoided him because you asked me to. If you could see how he is when he's with me, you'd change your mind. He's happy when he's with me. Feeding me. It gives him purpose."

I pulled my hands from hers, disbelieving what I was hearing.

She thought he was better when he was under her thrall? Had she listened to nothing I'd said?

"Dad had a purpose before you came into his life."

"Teaching others about his god isn't a purpose, baby. It's an occupation."

"Ugh! Can you even hear yourself?" I shook my head. "You stole Dad's life. I'm not letting you steal mine. I get to choose how to live it."

"And as your mother, I get to choose to save it."

"I want you to leave," I said angrily.

"You want me to leave? Hop in that bed and show me you can feed. Better yet, lose the virginity you're clinging to. Your innocence isn't helping you. It's corrupting your thinking. Do that, and I'll leave."

I stared at her for a minute then walked out of the room before I did or said something I might regret later. My anger blinded me. How could she be so unreasonable? So unrealistic?

"There you are," Adira said, coming up the stairs. "I have some good news."

"Not now, she-devil," I snapped. "You can ruin my life some more tomorrow. I've hit my quota for the day."

I was down the stairs and in the kitchen before what I'd said even registered. There would be repercussions for my disrespect, but I found I really didn't care. There were repercussions even when I tried to follow the rules.

In my car, I texted Ashlyn.

I need a place to cool off. Can I come over?

Adira sent me to the Roost. Sorry.

I tossed my phone to the seat and tore out of the garage, sliding on the slush. If Adira thought sending Ashlyn to the Roost would keep me home with my mom, she had another thing coming.

Reaching the Roost in record time, I got out of the car and slammed the door. The music thumping in the air did nothing to soothe me. I pushed my way through the doors and scanned the thin crowd.

"Someone's looking hot and tempting," a boy said.

I turned my dark gaze on him.

"I suggest you run away, boy, or fall now to tremble at my feet. I am the destroyer of men."

The boy paled and ran out the door. The rest of the dancers moved to the far side of the room. I turned away from them and looked for Ashlyn. She sat in her usual spot in the back row of booths, looking down at a book.

I stalked across the room and slid into the bench across from her. For the first minute, I focused on calming my breathing then on my vision. Through it all, Ashlyn remained quietly focused on her book. A book she was actually reading and not just holding as a decoy. I realized it was one I'd never seen her with before.

"Is that new?" I asked.

"Yep. Adira used it to bribe me here. You okay?"

I sighed.

"Not really. I just argued with my mom and called Adira a she-devil."

Ashlyn snorted.

"I don't imagine that went over well."

"I didn't stick around to find out. My mom's staying, Ashlyn. She won't leave until I have sex with someone and feed."

"Uh..."

"Don't worry, I'm not here looking for volunteers. I'm here looking for ideas."

"Ideas?"

"Yeah. Ways to get rid of my mom that don't involve having sex with someone."

My bench seat shifted under me, and someone peered over the booth's divider.

"We can maybe help with that," a girl said.

I recognized her from the bathroom at Girderon and from the other night in the Roost. She was one of the three druid girls. The one with all the jewelry.

"How?" I asked.

"A transference spell. It's like a portal, but only one way."

She had my attention.

"Is it dangerous?" I asked.

"No. The spell and the portal can't kill anyone. Worst case, the person ends up a little off course."

"Could you send my mom outside the barrier?"

"If she has her mark, sure. But her mark also means she can get back in."

I slowly smiled, remembering Adira's warning to my mom. My mom had her mark, but the Council would be keeping her out of Uttira with a different spell now.

"Don't worry about that," I said. "All we need to do is get her outside the barrier."

The druid nodded, sending her dangling crystal earring swinging.

"We'll need to gather some things to do the spell."

"How long will it take?"

"We can have everything ready tonight. We'll need a place we can do the spell in private, though."

Two more heads popped over the divider.

"Not my house," the druid with the thick hair said.

"Mine, neither," the one with the glitter makeup said. "My brother's home, and he'll tell."

I glanced at Ashlyn.

"We can't use her house," earring girl said. "It's warded

against spells. But, we can meet early at the Academy and use the pool bathroom. The spell won't take long."

"And what do you want in return?" I asked, knowing nothing was ever done for free.

"If we get caught, you take the full fall," glitter eyes said.

"And you owe us a future favor, collectively," thick hair said.

"Eliana," Ashlyn said. "This isn't a good idea."

I exhaled slowly. I knew it wasn't a good idea. I knew we'd probably get caught. But everyone was saying I was too small, fading, as if I was too weak. Maybe doing something this drastic would show I wasn't. At the very least, it would help Mom understand how serious I was about not feeding or having sex.

"No one gets hurt, and Mom is safely removed from Uttira," I reiterated. "If you can do that, I'll be your fall girl, if needed, and owe you a favor, collectively."

The bejeweled girl grinned.

"See you in the morning, succubus."

The trio left their booth and joined the dancers. As I watched, several of the dancers shook their heads and wandered off.

"They're making anyone who overheard forget the conversation," Ashlyn said. "You shouldn't trust them."

"If druids were powerful enough to hurt my species, I doubt my mom would still be alive. Their magic is limited. Just like we have limits. I'm sure it'll be fine."

Ashlyn looked doubtful.

"How long do you have to stay here?" I asked.

"Four hours."

I settled in for a long wait and listened to the music. The dance floor gradually filled up, and a familiar group walked in the doors.

This time, it was Jenna who had her arm around Fenris's waist while he was laughing and talking to the others. Then he stopped, and his gaze immediately found mine from across the room.

Why did that make my pulse leap? I checked my hunger, but it felt lazy and sated.

Fenris untangled himself from Jenna and started toward me. When he reached the table, he didn't say anything. He just opened his arms and grinned.

I stared at him for a second then realized what he wanted.

A dumb hug.

Sighing, I got out of the booth. No matter how much my brain said it was no big deal, my insides went crazy as I stepped into his embrace. He wrapped his arms around me and pulled me close.

"One-sided doesn't count," he murmured against the top of my head.

I slid my arms around his waist and tried not to feel how his hips pressed against me. Then I breathed in and tried not to bury my nose in his shirt. He smelled so good it was a struggle not to drool.

"You're important, and you have friends, Eliana. Say it."

I tipped my head up and wrinkled my nose at him. He chuckled.

"Say it."

"I'm important and have friends."

"And you don't hate your life," he said.

"And I don't hate my life as much as I did yesterday," I said, ad-libbing.

He grinned, gave me an extra squeeze, and released me.

I glanced at his girls, who were just behind him. Jenna didn't look mad. Maybe a little sad, but not angry.

"Sorry you're having a hard time," she said.

"Thanks."

"Want to dance with us?" Fenris asked.

"No. But thanks for the offer."

They left me with Ashlyn, who glanced up from her book as I resumed my seat.

"Did you just grab his ass?"

"What? No." I paused, doubting myself. "Did I?" He *had* smelled distractingly amazing.

She laughed.

"Don't ever change," she said. "You do reluctant succubus too well."

I rolled my eyes at her and turned to watch the dancers. Or, more accurately, Fenris's butt. Ashlyn had planted a seed, and try as I might to look away, I couldn't.

The double doors opened, and Eras and his gang walked in. His eyes immediately went black, and he inhaled deeply. He turned his head to his friends and said something that had them scattering throughout the room. One of them was slowly making his way to our table when Fenris stepped away from the dancers and spoke to him. Whatever he said had them both looking at me. The guy nodded and walked away.

No one else tried to approach us, so I stayed and listened to the music until the Roost closed. As did Ashlyn and Fenris's group.

"Want to keep the party going?" Fenris asked. "We're going to the hot spring caves. A good soak would fix whatever troubles you."

"It's the most relaxing thing ever," Jenna said.

"Especially without Aubrey," one of the other girls added.

"Could I go? Without dying some horrible death?" Ashlyn asked before I could decline.

Fenris grinned at her.

"I'll make sure you don't die any type of death if you come with."

The rest of the group looked at me. I trusted them not to do anything to Ashlyn. But I could see from the look in her eyes that she wouldn't go if I didn't. Yet, I knew what tagging along would entail. A lot of tempting nudity. Though my hunger was quiet now, would it stay quiet?

"I don't know," I hedged.

"Do you really want to go home?" Fenris asked.

We both knew what waited for me there.

"Not really. Fine, I'll tag along."

"Great. Try to keep up," Fenris said, walking his girls to their cherry red convertible that had the white top up against the cold.

"Let's drive together," I said to Ashlyn. "I'll drop you off here so you can get your car then follow you home."

"Thank you," she said, walking with me to my car. "I'm so excited for this. I've heard of the caves, but I've never seen them."

We got in, and I quickly pulled out to follow the wolf-mobile.

"You do know that they don't have swimsuits, right?" I asked.

"Oh. I wasn't thinking of that."

"I'm sure Fenris was. Just keep your bra and panties on, and you'll be fine."

"What about you?"

"I don't plan on swimming," I said.

"You sure? You could use a little relaxing."

"If I relax, so does my control."

"Oh."

"Don't worry about it. You'll be fine."

"I was more thinking of you."

During the rest of the drive, we avoided talking about the spell I wanted the druids to do the next day. Instead, we talked about clothes, the other humans and their schedules, and the next batch of desserts Ashlyn wanted to make. I appreciated that they were all chocolate-based.

Before long, the convertible turned off onto a wooded road that ended in trees just like the cabin road. The lights from town didn't reach this far, and once the convertible's lights went out, it was a lot darker and more secluded than Ashlyn was used to. I could tell from the hint of fear that drifted from her.

"We can turn around," I said, pulling up behind the convertible.

"Nope. I want to do this."

"You can change your mind at any time."

"I know."

Fenris's group was out of the car before I parked. He opened Ashlyn's door and leaned down.

"It'd be better if I carried you to the caves," he said. "We're in werewolf territory, but that doesn't mean there isn't anything wandering around."

She glanced at me.

"I trust Fenris to behave with you," I said. "Just don't fall for any lines about needing affection."

He laughed, and Ashlyn blushed when he picked her up.

Leaving the vehicles, we started through the trees. Fenris and his girls moved with quiet grace, leaving the night undisturbed, whereas I sounded like a parade. I didn't mind the walk, though. The cold nipped at my exposed skin, but it wasn't terrible. And my toes were fairly warm, thanks to wearing my sensible flats again. However, Ashlyn's teeth started chattering before we reached the caves.

"Almost there," Fenris said softly.

Snow started to fall. It was more of a crystalline glitter rather than large flakes.

"Pretty," Ashlyn said.

"It's from the springs," Jenna said.

The girls stopped walking at the edge of a clearing and

started stripping in the snow. Ahead, I saw a mound of rocks around a small cave opening. Steam rolled out of the entrance and drifted upward only to turn into sparkly snow.

I looked at the small gap with a frown. That was the hot springs? It didn't seem like much.

Fenris set Ashlyn down.

"I'd recommend removing what you can here. Everything you bring inside the cave will get damp because of the humidity."

Ashlyn glanced at me, and I grinned at her uncertainty. I'd warned her. She made a face then took off her shirt. I averted my gaze as she set it on the ground and stood on it after she removed her shoes.

"You, too, Eliana," Fenris said.

"I wasn't planning on swimming," I said quickly.

"Unless you planned on sitting out here and freezing the entire time, you're going to want to strip. It's not fun walking back to the car in wet jeans."

He reached for his fly, and I quickly turned around, ignoring his knowing smirk.

A shirt landed at my feet.

"You can stand on that."

I removed my shoes and socks, using his shirt to keep my toes from freezing. Then, I shimmied out of my jeans.

"I'm taking Ashlyn in," Jenna said. "Her lips are turning blue."

"We'll be right behind you," Fenris said.

When I glanced over my shoulder, he and I were the only ones in the clearing. And he was wearing boxers.

"You wear underwear?" I asked before I could stop myself.

He grinned widely.

"Only on special occasions. When the girls brought this up, I planned on asking you to come with us. I knew you'd rather I have something to leave on."

"Thank you," I said, really meaning it.

My hunger still liked the sight of him in his underwear, though, and I struggled to tear my gaze from his muscled torso.

Facing away from him once more, I removed my button-up shirt then started pulling the t-shirt over my head. The bright glow of Piepen's thin line of brownie batter stopped me. I tugged it back into place and turned toward Fenris.

"I'll go in this."

"Okay." He was beside me in two steps. "Come on." He picked me up without warning.

My eyes went black at all the skin to skin contact.

"Fenris, put me down."

"Two seconds. You can do it."

I opened my mouth to argue, and he was already setting me on my feet at the rocky opening.

"The ground is warmer here," he said. "Your cute little piggies would have squealed if you'd tried walking." He gestured toward the opening. "Go ahead. I'll bring up the rear."

I stared at him for a moment, trying to decide if I should still scold him. He knew what the contact did to me, but his intent had been sweet.

Shaking my head at his knowing grin, I bent down and entered the cave. The cooling mist immediately coated my skin, and I was glad I'd removed my jeans.

The floor sloped steeply for the first few yards then eased to a gentle decline. We gained headspace quickly, but it wasn't easy to see anything beyond the light of the opening. My steps slowed as soon as that faded.

Fenris's hand gripped my hip and nudged me forward.

"Keep going. You'll see light ahead soon."

He steered me with light touches until my heart was racing painfully in my chest. Just when I thought I wouldn't be able to take any more, the air grew even warmer and a light appeared ahead.

I brushed his hand away and hurried forward to an opening in the tunnel. Torchlight glinted off steamy pools of water. The air was heavy with warmth and moisture.

Ashlyn waved from one of the pools, surrounded by Fenris's girls. Jenna lifted an arm from the water and waved, the move proving that not everyone had shared Fenris's consideration about underclothes.

My cheeks, already warm, heated further as I waved in return then started studying the nearest wall.

"Since Eliana doesn't want to swim with the group, I'm going to show her the rest of the pools," Fenris said. "We'll be back in a minute."

CHAPTER SIXTEEN

WAS IT SMART TO GO OFF ALONE WITH FENRIS? PROBABLY NOT. BUT I knew it wouldn't be smart to stay with the others, either.

I followed him deeper into the cave system through another tight opening. Again, the light faded, and I had to reach out to keep my hand lightly on Fenris's back.

Touching him was a little easier than him touching me. But only because I was keeping the contact to a bare minimum. We walked a long while. In the dark, my hearing was more acute. The scrape of our feet along the path was the loudest noise for a while. And my breathing. Then, I heard the burble of water. That sound grew, along with the heat, then both faded again.

Twice more, we passed pools before Fenris stopped.

"Stay right there," Fenris said.

I waited until another torch flamed to life.

"How do they light when everything is so wet in here?" I asked.

"We got special torches from some druids. They always light and never burn down."

I looked around this smaller opening in the cave. Right

alongside the path, there was a pool big enough for about four people.

"Get in," he said.

"What? No way. I really don't want to swim."

He grinned and walked to the edge of the pool, lowering himself into the water. I watched him extend his arms along the edges so he was taking up a third of the space.

"There's not enough room to swim. This is soaking with a purpose. The waters are hot and full of minerals. Good for the body and the mind. If you were any more stressed out, you'd supernova."

The water tempted me. A lot. I glanced back at the way we'd come. The tunnel was dark.

"You're far enough away from Ashlyn that you won't sense her."

I looked at him.

"And we've already established that I'm mostly immune to you."

"Mostly?"

"I didn't want it to sound like a challenge if I said I was fully immune to you."

I grinned, considering him. He'd proven I could trust him. Sure, he did some things that worried me occasionally, but he respected my wishes whenever I voiced them. And, he was right. He did seem to be mostly immune to me.

"What if you're not?" I asked, tempted but still too worried to risk him.

"What if getting into this water is just the thing you need to melt away everything troubling you? What if this is the soak that changes your life for the better?"

I snorted a laugh at his hopeful thinking. He was right, though, about the "what ifs." There were so many possibilities it was impossible to know what might be. Fearing the unknown was holding me back from what I really wanted in this moment. And that was relaxing in the pool.

Taking a calming breath, I stepped to the edge of the pool and stuck my foot in the water. It was hot. Almost uncomfortably so. But once the sting faded, it felt wonderful.

Fenris watched me lower myself into the water, a crooked grin tugging his lips.

Settling with a sigh, I let my legs float in the vacant space beneath me and leaned my head against the ledge to anchor myself.

"This is amazing," I said, feeling all of my tension melt away.

With the humidity and heavy minerals, it was hard to smell Fenris's typical lust-laced scent. Which meant no temptation. I closed my eyes and just relaxed.

Everything from the last few days faded. My mind didn't wander, it just went blank.

"I love this place," I said.

"Me, too."

Fenris's tone stroked the hunger in my stomach.

"No talking," I said.

He chuckled. My hunger still stirred, and I wrinkled my nose. Instead of saying anything, I lifted a foot to poke him in the ribs with a toe.

He caught my foot and started rubbing it. I groaned, feeling real bliss. I never wanted to leave. I wanted to live in the hot springs forever. If I stayed long enough, maybe everyone would think I was a cave troll and not a succubus. Then, they would leave me alone.

I smiled at the thought.

"I like it when you smile," Fenris said. "Give me the other foot."

I willingly surrendered it.

"I like it when you're relaxed, too," he added.

His fingers kneaded the arch of my foot then worked their way to the ankle. When he started in on my calf, I sighed contentedly.

"I think we might need to take a break," he said, rubbing behind my knee.

I made a sad face without opening my eyes.

"You need to stop thinking so much," I said.

He chuckled, and his fingers touched my cheek.

"Now I know you've had enough. Come on, linguine, let's get you out of the water before you go past al dente."

I snickered at his joke and wrapped my arms around his neck when he picked me up.

"Open your eyes, Eliana."

Listening, I looked up at him as he stepped out of the pool with me. There was a tender look in his brown eyes. I liked seeing it there. For me. It told me that he really cared. Not the pretend kind of caring that Adira and Mrs. Quill had. Or the forceful caring that Mom had. Fenris didn't want to see me hurt or suffering.

I reached up and placed my hand on his cheek.

"Thank you for caring," I said.

"Always, beautiful. Let's cool you off a little."

He set me on the smooth stone path and sat beside me. The rock began to leech away the water's warmth and breathing got a little easier. My face started sweating, though. Grabbing the end of my shirt, I lifted it up to wipe away the sweat.

"What is that?" Fenris said.

His fingers touched my stomach and traced their way to the edge of my underwear.

I glanced down, seeing his tanned fingers on my pale skin

rather than the glowing line. My insides went molten, and hunger surged forward. I turned to Fenris.

Lightning fast, I had him on the floor and was straddling his torso. With one hand braced on his chest to pin him in place, I took his hand and flattened it over my stomach.

"That is yours," I said. "If you dare to take it."

I found myself pinned underneath him. He had my hands restrained against the floor over my head with his legs weighing down mine. I tried to pull myself free, but I couldn't.

"Don't fight, Eliana," he said. "Breathe. Feel the stone under you. The coolness of it."

It was his earnest expression along with the temperature of the smooth rock underneath me that brought back a semblance of clarity.

I blinked my eyes, pushing back the hunger.

The crooked, teasing smile returned to its usual place on his lips, melting away his worry. But I'd seen it. His fear. I closed my eyes and turned my head.

"Please get off me," I said, struggling not to cry.

"Hey, no being mad at yourself," he said.

"Mad?" I snorted. "I'm disgusted with myself. You were being nice, and I—"

I swallowed hard, and a tear escaped from the corner of my eye.

"Don't cry," he said.

His weight lifted, and he grabbed me, settling me in his lap before I could get away. Tucked against his chest, I focused on the beat of his heart and tried not to give in to all the tears fighting to get free.

"You didn't do anything wrong," he said, resting his chin on top of my head. "I only stopped you because I thought you'd be upset if you went through with it."

I jerked my head up and stared at him.

"You think?"

His crooked grin looked a little tormented.

"There was no right move for me back there. I went with the option I thought you'd want once you cooled off."

He'd been thinking of me. Again.

"You did make the best choice. I'm just sorry you had to make any choice." I climbed off his lap and tugged my shirt back into place. "I shouldn't have come here."

"I disagree."

He patted the spot beside him.

"Let's give you more time to cool off before we join the others."

He was right. I could still feel the hunger crawling under my skin. The last thing I wanted to do was unintentionally tempt Ashlyn. I sat beside him, shifting around to find a comfortable spot on the rocks.

"So, about that glowing stripe down your middle. Want to tell me about it?" he asked.

"Not really."

"It smells like the brownie."

"Because it's from the brownie."

He tilted his head at me, his grin widening.

"His explosion? His very first magic dust that marked you for life?"

I groaned.

"I'm just repeating what Marshal said. I didn't fully understand the conversation in the marshes, but now I do. It's cute."

"Cute's the last thing it is," I said.

"Show me again."

"No. My mark of shame will remain forever hidden."

Fenris snorted a laugh.

"Mark of shame? It's not your shame but his. He obviously missed by a long shot because the line starts under your bra."

"I really hope it's not there for life."

"I really hope the smell fades."

I groaned again and made a pained face.

"It's not that bad, I promise."

Fenris's name faintly echoed down the tunnel.

"Come on. I think the girls are done."

He extinguished the torch, and his fingers laced through mine.

I followed him through the dark, appreciating the irony of the moment. Without Fenris, I would have been lost.

I USED every kind of body wash I owned the next morning to try to scrub Piepen's mark from my skin. It didn't fade. Not even a little. I hoped all the washing would at least help with whatever Fenris could smell.

While wrapped in nothing but a towel, I walked from my bathroom, enjoying the freedom of dressing not only in private but also in whatever I wanted. After last night's chilly walk through the trees, I wasn't in the mood for any type of skirt.

Dressed in jeans and a brightly colored top, I slipped on a neutral pair of flats then returned to the bathroom. I took the time to style my hair in soft curls but skipped the makeup. It'd be nice to have a normal day at school. Well, semi-normal.

A cool breeze tickled my skin, and I saw the bathroom window was cracked open just a bit. With Piepen around, most of my windows had been opened at one point or another. I closed it, remembering all that had happened yesterday.

Taking a last look at myself, I weighed the wisdom of my decision to use the druids to remove my mom. It was rash and dangerous. But, mostly, just for me. And that's exactly why I needed to do it. Adira and Mom thought I was incapable of embracing the non-human side of my nature. Having the druids cast a spell to get my mom out of Uttira was me embracing my succubus side in the way I was willing to embrace it. None of that made the decision any easier. I loved my mom. If only she didn't have to be so...her.

I left my room and knocked on Mom's door. I couldn't cast her out without saying goodbye. However, there was no answer. Easing it open, I glanced at the bodies that lay in sprawled tangles on the bed and floor.

"Mom?" I called softly.

One of the men lifted his head.

"Tell her I need her," he said tiredly. "I ache for her. I need to please her and hear her sweet cries of pleasure."

I looked at him with pity.

"I'll tell her," I said. "Go back to sleep so you're ready for her when she returns."

He nodded and rested his head back on the woman's thigh.

Leaving them, I went downstairs and found Mom sipping coffee in the dining room. She gave me a small smile as I joined her at the table.

"I thought I might need to corner you this morning to get you to talk to me after yesterday."

"No. I think I've been cornered enough, don't you?"

"You came home pretty late last night. Did you do anything interesting?"

"I hung out with some friends. You know, healthy socializing."

"That's great, darling. You look a bit more energized this morning. Did you feed while you were out?"

The memory of last night's dream rose to mind. I'd gorged on cakes in the woods again. I highly doubted that Mom would count that as feeding, though.

"Speaking of feeding," I said without answering her, "one of your humans is aching for you. He could barely keep his eyes open as he begged me to find you and ask you to return to him."

"Don't worry. I told Anwen they were almost used up. She'll find me some replacements today. This batch will be mind-wiped and returned to their lives."

My stomach turned at the thought. They'd go back to their lives but always feel like something was missing. They'd crave what they couldn't even remember. I didn't see how that was any better than what she'd done to my dad.

"I love you, Mom. I just wanted you to know that," I said, standing.

"I love you too, baby. Everything I'm doing is because of just how much I love you. Do you want something to eat before you go?"

She slid a plate I hadn't noticed toward me. I glanced at the large slice of triple chocolate cake and shook my head.

"Thanks, but I'm not really hungry. I better get going. I want to get to school early."

I went to the kitchen and made myself a quick sandwich for later then headed out the door.

The pool was quiet when I entered the room and started across the tile. The humidity reminded me of the hot springs. Leaving the caves hadn't been as fun as going to them. With wet hair and damp skin, it had been a trial to redress in the cold. My teeth had been chattering by the time I'd gotten my jeans up. Fenris had to help me with the button, but he hadn't lingered or commented about my glowing line. I'd seen his amusement, though.

He and Jenna had both offered to carry me back. But not trusting myself, I'd walked on my own. Overall, it'd been fun. And relaxing. It was definitely something I wouldn't mind trying again. Alone.

Drawing close to the bathroom door, all my tension returned. Doubt and fear pulled at me. Was I doing the right thing? I thought of the man in my mom's room. If I didn't stand up for what I wanted, how long would it be until I had an exhausted group of people in my bed?

The druids looked up from their places on the floor when I entered. Ashlyn, who stood near the side, slightly hidden by the paper towel dispenser, waved at me.

"Perfect timing," the leader said. "We just finished setting everything up."

They'd drawn a circle of runes on the floor. I recognized a few of the gods' symbols but nothing else. Just outside the runes, there were several bowls that held different objects. One looked like a bowl full of ash. I hoped it wasn't human remains.

"What do you need me to do?" I asked.

"You and the human should stand off to the side."

"Ashlyn," I said. "Her name is Ashlyn."

"Great. This is Meg—," she pointed to thick hair, "—Anne—," she indicated glitter makeup, "and I'm Lauv. We'll do the spell, and when I point to you, you'll need to speak your mother's name. That's it. Nothing to it."

"How many times have you successfully performed this spell?" Ashlyn asked.

"More than a dozen times inside the barrier. Finding volunteers with a mark to travel outside the barrier is a little harder."

"So never?" Ashlyn pressed.

"The spell is the same," Lauv said. "It's just the location that changes. Are you changing your mind?"

Ashlyn and Lauv both looked at me.

"No. I'm not changing my mind."

"Good. Ashlyn, you're heavier than Eliana. Go stand against the door so no one interrupts."

Ashlyn moved past me, but not before giving me a warning look. That she was against what we were about to do was clear. That she was still here for me despite that fact said a lot.

I took her spot by the paper towel dispenser and waited.

The trio of druids positioned themselves so they were cross-legged, knee to knee within the circle. Lauv took a larger, empty metal bowl and set it in the center. Anne grabbed a handful of small twigs from outside the circle and placed it inside the empty bowl, starting a fire with a single word.

They began chanting and speaking syllables that didn't make sense to me. As they spoke, they added objects to the flames so that the color changed from orange to red to purple then blue.

Then the chanting stopped, and Lauv nodded at me.

"Wait, put the ash in," Meg said.

"The hell? Shut up," Anne hissed.

Meg grabbed the ash and tossed it into the flames. There was a burst of light, and Lauv gestured at me again.

"Nicolette Lynn Barchim," I said quickly.

All three stared at the flames for several seconds.

"It should have flared again, shouldn't it?" Meg asked.

"Who knows," Anne said. "You opened your noisemaker when you weren't supposed to. You know how exact these things are."

"So it didn't work?" I asked.

Lauv shrugged.

"We won't know until we know, you know?"

I wanted to roll my eyes at her. Instead, I looked at Ashlyn to see what she thought. However, the space by the door was empty.

"Where did Ashlyn go?" I asked, looking around the bathroom.

"She probably bailed when the flames started turning colors," Lauv said. "Most humans don't like magic. Weirds them out."

"She was born and raised here. I doubt she was weirded out," I said, already sending her a text asking where she was. "How do we know if the spell worked?"

"Call your mom," Anne said.

"Don't be stupid," Meg said. "If she calls her mom just after her mom is transported, her mom is going to know it was her."

"You'll find out when you go home tonight," Lauv said. "Until then, play it cool and don't acknowledge us if you see us in the hallways. Got it?"

"Yeah, sure."

I left the bathroom while they were still cleaning up the remnants of the spell. There were more mermaids in the pool now, but none of them paid me any attention as I hurried away.

The halls were only slightly crowded as I made my way to the first-hour session. A few people gave me disappointed looks, but no one commented on my clothes or lack of makeup. I'd never been more grateful to resume my unremarkable existence.

Sliding into my chair, I waited for Lucas to begin the Human Studies lecture. Yet, it was hard to remain focused on his words once he started. My mind kept going to Mom, wondering if she was standing outside the barrier in her robe. I hadn't thought about that and hoped she wasn't cold. Surely, the liaison would notice her on her rounds and give her a ride somewhere. What if the liaison reported what happened to the Council and the Council invited Mom back in?

I wanted to groan and hoped that wouldn't happen. It would

unlock a new level of hell in my life. There'd be an investigation. I'd have to come forward just to protect the druids. I should have listened to Ashlyn.

No. I'd done the right thing.

My mind went back and forth the remainder of the hour. When the bell rang, I was the first one to escape the room. I needed to talk to Ashlyn.

However, when I entered the self-paced study's room, Ashlyn wasn't there.

Yanet was, though. She watched me enter with a slight look of disappointment.

"I made you something," she said, reaching into her pocket. She withdrew a diamond ring.

"I can't take that, Yanet."

"I know. Just thought I'd show it to you in case you wanted to go home and put something nicer on."

"Um, no. I think I'll stay like this. Thanks."

Her gaze swept me head to toe, and she stuffed the ring back into her pocket. It was almost laughable if it wasn't so sad. Her attitude wasn't solely the fault of the clothes and makeup I'd been forced to wear. A good portion of what she'd felt had been from me. My natural lure had kicked in with the right clothes. The same lure that should have kicked in last night when I'd been with Fenris. Was he actually immune?

The bell rang, and I turned to the front of the room.

Ashlyn still wasn't there.

A thread of worry wormed its way into my middle and only grew as the minutes slowly ticked by without any word from Ashlyn. I needed to talk to those druids and figure out what they'd done. Ashlyn didn't just not show up. Okay, she'd done it once, but she'd left a note that time.

I could feel my panic spiraling, and I was once again the first one out of the room when the bell rang. I jogged through the halls, threading my way through my peers while looking for any of the three druids. The halls started to clear without any sign of them.

Ignoring the bell, I went back to the pool bathroom. It was empty. I hurried out, ignoring the heckling calls of the mermaids, and went to my third-hour session, unsure what to do.

I opened the door to a nearly empty room. Fenris straightened in his chair at the sight of me.

"Didn't think you were going to show," he said.

"What? Why?" I asked. Could he smell the smoke on me? Did he know what I had done?

He grinned.

"Relax. Your heart is going to jackrabbit right out of your ribcage. Last night was no big deal, and I'm glad you're not avoiding me because of it."

"Right. Last night."

I realized he was talking about how I'd almost fed from him and quickly took my seat.

"So, what are we supposed to be doing today?" I asked, changing the subject.

He shrugged.

"Discovering ourselves, I guess. How are you feeling? You look a little flushed."

"I'm fine. How are you?"

He leaned back in his chair and considered me.

"What's going on? You weren't this tense even before the hot springs." He started to look troubled. "Did something happen that you didn't want to happen? Something we should talk about?"

I swallowed hard against the fear squeezing my throat.

He knew.

CHAPTER SEVENTEEN

"Look, I'm sorry about last night, but you looked miserable." He leaned forward in his seat, almost angrily. "And I couldn't just leave you alone like that. I had to stay and help you. I needed to."

Of course. Last night. I wanted to smack my forehead. Instead, I took a calming breath and offered him a grateful smile.

"No, you were right. I did need the hot springs. And I'm sorry for what happened, but you were great. Not many people would have had the sense to turn me away like that."

"Hot springs. Right."

Confused by his annoyed tone, I watched him wearily lean back in his seat.

"Is something wrong? Girl trouble?" I asked, realizing he might have problems of his own that he was dealing with.

"You could say that. I don't think this is the right time to talk about it, though."

"Okay." I looked around the room, trying to think of a suitable subject change. One came to mind, and I wrinkled my nose.

"Do I smell any different today?" I asked.

His expression lost a little of its dejected cast.

"Different how?"

"You know, is the brownie batter smell gone?"

A slow grin spread across his lips, and he crooked a finger at me.

"Come on. Let me have a smell."

I got up and crossed to his desk. He turned in his seat and tugged me closer so I stood between his knees.

"I could smell the soap when you walked in," he said. "But is it covering up your little friend's present, or did it remove it?"

"Just get on with it already," I said impatiently.

His hands settled on my hips, and my pulse hitched. When he leaned in, my insides went hot. It was a dumb idea to have him smell me. As dumb as asking the druids to get rid of my mom. When was I going to learn?

Yet, seeing his dark head so close to my chest made me hungry for so much more. I lifted my hand, itching to run my fingers through his hair.

The door opened, and LuAnn poked her head in. Her glance caught it all. Fenris's nose planted between my boobs. My hand hovering inches from his hair. My black eyes.

"I wasn't going to touch him," I said quickly, pulling my hand back.

"It's okay if you do, dear. I'll leave you two to it."

The door quickly closed.

Face flaming, I glanced at Fenris. His grin was so wide I was pretty sure I could see his molars.

"You weren't going to touch me, huh?"

"Shut up, Fenris." If possible, my face grew warmer.

"Oh, now I gotta know where."

"Nowhere."

I tried to step away, but his hands stayed firmly planted on my hips.

"Hmm, let's see. It's snowing outside, and 'tis the season...were you thinking of my jingle balls?"

I wanted to disappear, but his hold wouldn't allow that. Staring down into his thoroughly amused gaze, I wrinkled my nose at him.

"I'd like to unfriend you now."

He laughed then leaned in to sniff my chest again.

"It's still there," he said after a moment. "Try wiping it with lemon juice tomorrow. The acid might help cut some of the smell. And the glow."

He released me and leaned back.

"This whole thing just made your day, didn't it?" I said, noting his unrepentant grin.

"You have no idea just how much."

"Well, I'm glad you're amused." I returned to my chair with a scowl. "No doubt LuAnn will report this to Adira, and that giant pain will find some new way to twist our lives around because of this."

"Would it be so horrible if she found ways for us to spend more time together?" he asked. Though he was wearing his usual smile, I could sense the hurt I'd inadvertently caused.

"No. Of course not. I do like spending time with you, Fenris. I just don't like being forced to do anything. No one does."

Once the bell rang and the distraction that was named Fenris wasn't in the immediate area, I focused on finding Ashlyn. The druids were nowhere to be found during lunch, and Ashlyn's car was still in the parking lot when I checked.

Debating my options for only a moment, I sent Adira a text.

Ashlyn wasn't in second session, but her car is in the parking lot. Should I be worried?

I'll look into it. Focus on your studies.

I rolled my eyes and went to the next session, watching the clock until the final bell rang. When I went out to the parking lot, Ashlyn's car was gone.

Breathing a sigh of relief, I went home. It wasn't until I pulled into the driveway that I remembered Mom.

I parked in the garage and turned off the car but didn't go in. I stared at the kitchen door and tried to sort through what I felt. Yes, I was sad. I wished my mom hadn't sided with Adira's crazy idea that I was dying and needed to hop in bed with someone to save myself. But mostly, I was relieved. It was hard enough fighting Adira's manipulations, but facing Mom's disappointment and worry day in and day out would have been too much. I would have given in eventually and hated myself for it.

It was better this way.

I repeated those words in my head as I left the car and made my way into the kitchen. Mrs. Quill was by the fridge and turned at the sound of the door.

"Eliana," she said with a smile. "Dinner will be ready at six. I'm making something special to celebrate."

"That sounds good. Thank you, Mrs. Quill."

I managed a return smile, and as I hurried away before she could say more, I told myself her excitement was a good sign. It meant everything had a chance of going back to normal. But why did her good mood make me feel like I was on the verge of tears, then?

The house seemed so empty as I made my way upstairs. Too quiet.

I'd barely had the thought when I heard a laugh ahead. My steps slowed. Further down the hall, the steady, familiar beat of music started.

"Mom?" I called in disbelief.

She stepped out of her room and came to me with arms wide. "Baby, you're home."

Stunned, I didn't fight her welcoming hug.

"I'm so proud of you. I knew the moment I smelled him in that restaurant, he would be just what we needed to tempt you from your hunger strike."

I pulled back in confusion.

"What are you talking about?"

Mom smoothed her hand over my hair, still smiling at me.

"The lusty werewolf boy that Adira paired you with in your Self-Discovery class. Was he able to walk after your feeding?"

I jerked out of her arms.

"Fenris? You think I fed off of Fenris?"

"Didn't you?"

"Of course not. I wouldn't do that to him."

She sighed.

"That's disappointing, but don't worry. I'm sure things will go better tomorrow. And if not him, maybe I'll find someone else whose scent is a little more potent. The way you avoided eye contact, I thought for sure he'd be the one."

I stared at her for a stunned moment.

"You? You're the reason Fenris was suddenly in my class?" I covered my face with my hands, so frustrated I could scream. "You shouldn't even be here anymore."

"Baby, I told you, I'm staying until I know you can take care of yourself. We'll work through this together. After I eat, I'll go out and—"

"No. I don't need you to go out looking for my next meal."

"Apparently you do, or the Council would have found a reason to force me out. But they haven't. Instead, they offered me, the ravenous pregnant lady, a deal. What does that tell you, baby? You have a lot of people worried about you. I'm staying until I know, without a shadow of doubt, that you've finally embraced who you are."

Angry, I walked around her and shut myself in my room. The spell had obviously gone all wrong if Mom was still here and Ashlyn was missing.

A thought stopped me. If mom was here, then maybe Ashlyn was outside the barrier. Maybe she was finally free. I hoped that was the case. I needed to be sure, though. I checked my phone again and saw I still had no message from Ashlyn. I sent her another text.

Starting to really worry. Let me know when you get this.

I paced from my door to the bed and back again. Stupid druids and their stupid spells.

As much as I wanted to believe Ashlyn was outside Uttira and happy, I knew better. The druids had made it clear that getting mom out would depend on her having the mark of Mantirum that allowed her to leave. Ashlyn didn't have the mark. That meant she was somewhere inside the barrier. I could check the perimeter, but there wasn't a road circling the thing. And because the area's size was magically altered to give us more space, it would take me weeks to walk the entire perimeter. There was also another reason not to bother with searching on foot. She would have texted me back if she was wandering around inside the barrier.

Mom called out to me when I hurried past her partially open door, but I didn't stop. Jogging down the stairs, I yelled that I'd be back later then cut through the kitchen with a wave to Mrs. Quill.

The drive to Ashlyn's house wasn't long enough. When I pulled up to the curb, I still hadn't decided what I'd do if she wasn't there. However, the sight of her car in the open garage gave me hope.

Not lingering in the car, I rushed to the door and knocked.

It was opened several moments later by Anne Regan, the new liaison officer.

My hope shriveled.

"Is Ashlyn here?"

"No. I'm looking for her, actually. When was the last time you saw her?"

"This morning just before the first session bell. Was her car here when you got here?" I asked.

Anne shook her head. "The Council asked me to move it. I heard you're the one who brought Ashlyn's absence to Adira's attention."

I nodded, feeling sick.

"Yeah. She wasn't in second session. She's almost always there. The one time she wasn't, she left a note to explain why. She didn't this time. It's not like her to just disappear."

"Do you know anyone who'd want to harm her?"

I blinked at the woman.

"Uh...everyone? This is Uttira," I said.

"Right. I meant, is there anyone who has a personal reason to harm her?"

"Not that I know of," I said. "Where should we look next?"

"We aren't going to look anywhere. You're going to go home while I continue my search."

"Miss Regan, it's dangerous for her to be anywhere but her home, her car, the Academy, or the Roost. She doesn't have a lot of time."

"You seem really worried about her."

"I can count the number of friends I have on one hand. She's one of them. She's suffered so much but has always been there for me. I need to be there for her."

Anne nodded.

"If I don't find her at the Roost, I'll contact the Council and recommend we organize an official search. Now go home. Let me take care of this."

I reluctantly returned to my car. The chances of Anne finding Ashlyn were as slim as me finding her. Ashlyn was the proverbial needle in a haystack at the moment. I needed to focus on finding the druids. But where to start.

A knock on my window startled me from my thoughts.

Looking out, I saw Anne, so I quickly rolled down the window.

"I'll follow you home to make sure you get there," she said.

"What about Ashlyn?"

"I just called the Roost. They haven't seen her all day. It's time to talk to the Council."

I rolled up my window and started the engine as my thoughts raced. I felt certain Ashlyn's disappearance was a result of the spell this morning. Had the druids guessed the same? If so, that would explain why they'd suddenly vanished from school as well. It frustrated me, though, that they would run instead of staying to determine what went wrong with the spell and where it might have sent Ashlyn. They were our best bet at finding her right now.

If I told the Council what happened, would it be easier to locate the druids or harder? I recalled how they'd easily memory wiped people at the Roost and decided it would be harder. At least, the liaison was looking for Ashlyn in the meantime. While she did that, I'd keep looking for the druids.

Despite my decision, the sick feeling in my stomach grew the closer we got to the Quills' home.

I parked in front of the house and let Anne in through the front door. Using the intercom, I asked Mr. and Mrs. Quill to meet us in Mr. Quill's office.

Anne didn't say much as we walked upstairs, but I could sense her fear. I wondered if it was fear for Ashlyn or fear for herself. Neither would help her find my friend. Both could attract predators while she was out searching, though.

I brushed my hand against the petite blonde's hand and pulled a healthy amount of her negative emotions from her.

"Don't let yourself feel fear," I said when she glanced at me. "Be wary. Be smart. Don't be bait."

She slowly nodded.

"Thank you."

"Just find Ashlyn."

The office door was open when we reached it. Adira and the Quills were all inside. Anne walked in first, and I boldly tried to follow.

Adira portaled, appearing just beside the door before I fully entered.

"We'll talk later, Eliana," she said, closing the door in my face.

I stared at the wood. Then, deciding I didn't care if I was caught or not, I pressed my ear to the panel.

"Miss Regan," Adira said. "It's good to see you. Any update?"

"I wish I had good news. I've checked the girl's home and don't see any signs that she was there since she left it this morning. I think it's time we organize an official search. We need to recruit as many friendly creatures as we can to help find the girl."

"We appreciate your determination to find her," Adira said. "However, I caution against using that method. If you spread the word that a human is missing, it won't only be friendly creatures out looking for her, and our chances of recovering the girl whole will rapidly fade."

"What do you propose then? Do nothing? Her chances of being found whole are already rapidly fading."

"I'd like to suggest we make Raiden aware of the

disappearance. He is discreet and trustworthy. And he'll be able to use her scent to track her."

There was a long moment of silence.

"Fine. But we contact him now. If he can't start immediately, then we find another trustworthy nose to sniff her out."

I thought of Fenris and moved away from the door. Should I involve him? If both he and his father were looking for Ashlyn, they might find her faster. Faster still would be getting more information from the druids. I chewed on my lip then started back down the stairs, believing that finding the trio was still Ashlyn's best bet.

Before I reached the door, the air shimmered, and Adira appeared. She looked surprised to see me.

"Eliana. Are you going out for the evening?"

"Probably. Any news about Ashlyn?"

"Don't worry about Ashlyn. Just focus on your classwork and your friends."

"Ashlyn is my friend."

"Ashlyn is food, Eliana. Protected and treated well, but still food."

I stared at her, wishing I was strong enough and fast enough to strangle her.

"I'll be sure to share your opinion with Megan," I said.

Adira nodded, not looking the least bit threatened.

"I'm so proud of the progress you've made in the past few days. I can see having your mother here is a very positive influence on you."

"Positive?" I sputtered.

Someone knocked on the door, and she answered it, cutting our conversation short.

"Raiden," Adira said in greeting to the tall, dark-haired man. "Thank you for coming so quickly."

"Of course." He looked at me. "Eliana. It's nice to see you."

"You too."

His gaze swept the room.

"Nicolette is upstairs," Adira said. "She's not the reason I called you."

I could sense his relief as his guilty gaze locked with mine for a moment.

"Don't worry. I don't want her around either," I said.

"Eliana," Adira scolded. "Your mother loves you and is here to help you."

"No. She's here to help you. Not me. Good luck, Raiden," I said before walking out the door.

I got in my car and headed to Megan's, debating my next move. One thing was certain: I couldn't do nothing.

At Megan's, I sent Fenris a text.

Can you meet me at Megan's? Alone?

I probably didn't need to say alone because he was always looking for a reason to leave his girls behind, but this time I needed to be sure.

Be there in ten, he sent back.

While I waited, I went inside to feed Elbner. The house was dark and quiet, though.

"Elbner?" I called.

No answer.

After I mixed up his meal, I went in search of him, turning on lights as I moved from room to room. The house was amazingly clean. It smelled good, too. Even the guest room, which had been a little creepy to sleep in, had web free, shadowy corners. However, there was no sign of Elbner anywhere. Had he left now that he'd shared the information about his previous master?

I was just about to text Megan to see if she'd heard from him when shouting erupted outside.

The kitchen door slammed behind me in my rush to see what was going on.

Two heads swiveled my direction.

Elbner looked furious, and Fenris looked amused. And barely dressed. He stood in the snow, barefoot and only wearing a pair of low riding jeans that made my stomach clench.

"Did you bring a shirt?" I asked.

"I can only fit rolled up jeans in my mouth," he said.

"Why don't you come inside?" I offered.

"The mongrel is not allowed in this house," Elbner said. "Or this yard. Go, tramp!"

Fenris's grin widened.

"Elbner, Fenris is Megan's friend. Mine, too."

"The mutt is no friend of Elbner's. Leave now, or I will neuter you."

"Try it, bite-sized," Fenris said.

I hurried between the pair, hands out to keep them apart.

"What is going on?" I demanded, looking at Fenris.

"I was wronged!" Elbner shouted, shaking an angry fist. "You and the fury are both lucky I'm still here."

"How were you wronged?"

"I wasn't fed yesterday."

Fenris snorted.

"You little liar. I fed you your oats and milk."

"Oats on a plate and milk in a cup," Elbner said with a scowl at me and a gesture at Fenris as if to say, "see what I have to deal with?"

"Elbner, I'm sincerely sorry," I said. "I'm pretty sure Fenris slept through the caring for helpful creatures lecture and missed the part where the oats and milk were supposed to be mixed in a bowl and topped with honey."

"Ignorance is no excuse."

"I completely agree. I swear to properly educate him if he ever needs to fill in for me again. I have your oats ready for you inside if you want."

Elbner considered me then Fenris.

"Fine. I will continue to serve Megan, but this is a black mark against her care for me. Don't let it happen again." He started for the house. "And the dog still can't come in."

The door slammed closed behind him, and I looked at Fenris. He was grinning from ear to ear.

"So, you're going to educate me?"

"Try to educate you. How do you not know how to feed a goblin?"

"Oh, I know how. I just chose not to when he accused me of trespassing after hitting me in the head with his shoe."

I groaned.

"I'm sorry."

"It's not your fault he's small and unstable."

"It's my fault for not warning you he likes throwing shoes at uninvited guests."

Fenris's smile vanished.

"Did he hit you with his shoe?"

"Calm down. It didn't hurt me any more than it hurt you. We have bigger issues to deal with."

"We do?"

"Ashlyn is missing."

"How? When?"

I wasn't yet ready to talk about how so I focused on when.

"I saw Ashlyn this morning before first session. But she wasn't in second session and hasn't answered any of my messages all day. She doesn't do that."

"Have you told Adira?" he asked, tucking his hands into his jeans.

"She's with your dad now. They want him to try to track Ashlyn. But we both know how big this place is. It might take him longer than she has."

"You have a different idea, don't you?"

"Maybe. There were these three druids Ashlyn and I talked to the other night in the Roost. Meg, Anne, and Lauv. I think they can help find Ashlyn faster, but I don't know where they live. Do you?"

"No. I can ask around, though."

"Discreetly," I said.

"Don't want the Council catching wind of the fact you're thinking of using magic?"

"No."

"A location spell is a good idea, though. And probably something better left to more experienced druids. You might want to mention it to Mr. Quill."

"I will. But just in case they don't think one human worth the expense of hiring a professional, can you still ask around?"

"Of course."

He removed his hands from his pockets and raised his brows expectantly at me.

"What?" I asked.

"Am I going to have to chase you down every time?"

"Chase me? Why?" As soon as the words left my mouth, I understood. "Oh, right. Forget the missing human and the fact that my mom's still in Uttira and that Adira purposefully put us together in Self-Discovery because said mom thought your lust-smell would do me good. Fenris needs his hug."

"That's right, I do."

He wiggled his fingers and squatted down a little.

"I'm not running into your arms."

"Come on. Bring it in hard and fast, lightweight. Don't you want to see if you can knock me over?"

At the moment, knocking his grinning face to the ground did sound a little fun. But I took the dignified route and walked into his embrace.

"One of these days, you'll come running for a hug," he said into my hair.

"Don't hold your breath."

"Oh, I'm not." He inhaled deeply. "New shampoo?"

"Are we done hugging yet?"

"The timer doesn't start until your hands are on my back. Or lower. Whatever's more comfortable for you to grab."

I rolled my eyes and wrapped my arms around his waist. It felt good to be hugged by Fenris.

"So we have your mom to thank for getting us out of real work at the Academy?" he asked against my hair.

"Not that I'd call any of the work there real, but yeah. It was her. And don't thank her. You should be as upset as I am at being manipulated."

"I dunno. She got me what I wanted."

"And what's that?" I asked, warily easing out of his hold.

"An hour of freedom. Celebrate the small stuff, Eliana. Don't let the big picture worries drown you."

CHAPTER EIGHTEEN

Cakes were great until they tasted like skunk butt. I spat out the cake and started wiping at my tongue. The taste wouldn't go away. The dangling cakes did, though. They vanished like popping bubbles as skunks came marching in, two by two, to start humping.

I woke with a gasp and sat straight up in my bed.

"Good morning, beautiful. Your prince has returned."

The prince in question was lying like a starfish on my pillow, pointy side up.

"Piepen, where are your clothes? And what are you doing here? You have a new home. Go back to it."

His little face scrunched up in a scowl, and he gestured at his naked self.

"I flew all night so you could wake up to this, and you start in on me as soon as you open your eyes. Woman, learn to be grateful."

I raised my hand to flick him away. He squealed and rolled off the pillow.

"Okay, Okay," he said, lifting his hands. "I can see your

hormones are swinging hard. Maybe you'll change your mind when you see what I brought you."

He flew to the window, which was partially open, and lifted a bag from the floor. It weighed him down so much he could barely fly up to the bed. He made it and collapsed panting.

"Did you come in through my window?" I asked.

"Of course, my Juliette."

I needed to check my windows better before bed. I didn't remember leaving it open.

"You are not my Romeo, Piepen. And I can't accept any gifts from you."

"Well, it's not really for you. Go ahead and open it. See for yourself."

I loosened the cord on the cloth sack and stared down at a matching set of manual breast pumps.

"For the baby, when your milk comes in." He smacked his lips and stroked himself. "The baby and I are going to eat like kings."

Dropping the string, I glared at Piepen.

"I have exercised an incredible amount of patience with you, Piepen. But that ends now. Get your prepubescent butt out the window and back into your own bed immediately, or I will drive you to Megan's house and feed you to Elbner. Am I clear?"

"You seem tense. Maybe I should rub your—"

"Continue speaking and die, brownie," I said.

Piepen paled and escaped into the predawn light. I growled, got out of bed, and slammed the window closed, this time making sure to turn the lock.

Too angry to sleep, I went to the bathroom and turned on the shower. While the water warmed, I stripped out of my warm pj's, grateful I'd been wearing my old ones again. Turning to place them on the counter, I blinked at my reflection. My emaciated self was back. Sort of. I didn't look as wasted as I had a few days ago. Still boney, though. Only now, I had a dumb glowing strip down my middle.

I leaned toward the mirror, wondering what the heck was going on. Why was I seeing myself like this? Was it because everyone kept telling me there was something wrong with me?

They were getting into my head. Squaring my shoulders, I looked at myself in the mirror.

"You are not sick or dying, Eliana Barchim. You are stronger than them all."

I showered quickly and got dressed for the day, noting that my clothes fit me just fine. Everyone was crazy.

The faint sounds of groaning reached my ears a moment before the low beat of music drowned it out. I grabbed my phone to check the time and saw it wasn't even six yet. I was about to toss it to my bed to go pound on Mom's door when the phone started to ring. I saw Megan's name, recalled the text I sent her last night about Mom being free but not leaving, and quickly answered.

"What do you mean she's not leaving?" she asked. "Does she have a choice?"

"Apparently she does now," I said.

"What does that mean?"

"Adira thinks she is seeing a positive change in me with my mom being present. She also thinks I look healthier. I don't look healthier; I look angrier. The Council obviously can't tell the difference. I think they're confusing me with you."

Megan laughed.

"Give them hell, then," she said.

"Oh, I plan to."

"So, other than your mom staying, how are things back home?"

My stomach dipped as I thought of Ashlyn's disappearance.

"Not too bad," I said quickly. "I found some brownies who were willing to take Piepen in. He was a little upset, but I think he's adjusting. I'm planning on visiting him later today. And, Elbner is making great progress on your house. For being such a grumpy, unkempt thing, he sure has that place looking nice. He's even started scraping the loose paint off the outside."

"Wow. I'm impressed," she said. "He knows that it's winter, though, right?"

"It doesn't seem to bother him."

"Other than that, anything new?"

"Nothing worth talking about," I said quickly, thinking of Ashlyn again. "How about you? Is it true that a druid was involved in the deaths?"

"Yes. That would be Zayn. He's not wicked, though. That much I could sense."

"Be careful around him, Megan. It's not safe to trust druids."

"It's not safe to trust most of us."

"Isn't that the truth."

We talked a bit about New York before I had to leave so I could make it to the Academy on time. I didn't care about classes as much as I cared about looking for the druids and getting answers about Ashlyn.

However, there was no sign of them in the pool bathroom before school or in any of the halls. I struggled to behave normally as I waited for time to move so I could get to Self-Discovery.

Fenris sat in his usual seat, the room once again empty except for us.

"Any luck finding the druids?" I asked, sliding into my seat.

"Nothing yet, but I've been putting the word out that I'm looking for them. Quietly, as promised."

I sat back in my seat and stared at the clock. Where was

Ashlyn? Was she safe? Was she running out of time? Was it already too late?

"You okay?" Fenris asked softly.

"Not really." I scrubbed a hand over my face and turned my thoughts to an annoyance Fenris could help me with. "Piepen crawled through my window at dawn, turning a really good dream into a nightmare."

"What was the dream?"

I blushed a little.

"I was eating cake like a pig. It was so good, though. I love that dream, and he wrecked it with his nasty lust smell."

Fenris's grin widened.

"It's not funny. I woke up to him propositioning me. And that's not the worst of it. He brought me breast pumps, Fenris. He still thinks I'm pregnant. What do I need to do to get through to him that I'm not now or ever will be his baby mama?"

Fenris smoothed a hand over his mouth in an effort to stop his erupting laughter.

Sitting there with him, having a "normal" conversation, I realized something had changed. His scent. I breathed it in, trying to figure out what was different. It still smelled sweet and spicy, reminding me of my cake dreams, but it wasn't as overpowering. Had he found a way to control it to make things easier on me?

"We'll pay Piepen another visit after school and talk to him," Fenris said, having reined in his humor. "If he's not reasonable, maybe his new guardians will be. It's not safe for him to be wandering anywhere outside of the marshes. His new family will help convince him of that."

I had my doubts they'd be able to contain Piepen's infatuation.

"He needs a girlfriend. Big time."

"Thinking about playing brownie matchmaker?"

"If it keeps him where he should be and not creeping into my windows at night, yes. I don't even know how he got in. I could have sworn I checked all the windows."

"You know better than that," Fenris said. "We're all taught how to sneak into human homes from a young age. A simple window lock wouldn't keep the majority of the residents in our fine town out of your home."

"Perfect. Now I have another reason to talk to the druids. I need warding spells on my windows."

"I'm surprised you don't have them already."

"Not many people would have the jingle bells to break into the Quills' home."

He laughed.

"I think you mean balls."

"You say it your way; I'll say it mine."

With a grin, he leaned back in his chair.

"So what do we do today to get LuAnn all excited that we're making progress?"

"Nothing, preferably. I have enough drama in my life right now. No need to add to it."

"I don't know about that. If we do nothing, they'll think we're relapsing and push harder. If we give them a little more, they'll leave us alone."

"Ha. They might leave you alone, but not me."

He raised a brow as if to say, what exactly did they do?

"Okay fine. They were treating me like I'd won the human lottery."

"See. Perfect." He turned in his chair and patted his lap. "Let's do a brownie check again."

I wrinkled my nose but dutifully got up and went to Fenris. Instead of nudging me to stand between his legs, he pulled me into his lap and buried his nose between my boobs just as the door opened.

This time, LuAnn didn't speak. At least, I think it was LuAnn. The door closed before I could turn my head and look.

Fenris inhaled deeply, sending a shiver through me.

"Do you have to be right up in there to smell it?" I asked, not moving.

"Yep," came his muffled reply.

I rolled my eyes and held onto his shoulders as he continued to breathe in whatever he was smelling. Finally, he lifted his head.

"Your scent is getting stronger," he said. "It's helping to overpower Piepen's, but I don't think his is getting any weaker. Did you try the lemon? I couldn't smell any lingering hint of citrus."

"No. I forgot."

He said nothing, and I realized how close we were. And that I was still on his very warm lap. It was comfortable. Cozy.

My pulse picked up speed, and I inhaled slowly, noting the increased scent of his lust. My hunger lazily stretched.

"It would be better if I didn't sit on your lap anymore," I said, removing my hands from his shoulders.

"Better for who?" he asked, not yet releasing his hold on my waist.

"You, Fenris. I don't think I could forgive myself if I hurt you after everything you've done to help me."

A smile tugged at the corner of his mouth.

"You haven't hurt me yet."

"I have lost control, though."

"Are you saying I make you want to lose control?" He playfully wiggled his eyebrows.

"Why do you have to turn everything into an innuendo?"

"Because you're pretty when you blush."

He finally released me, and I quickly returned to my seat.

"So tell me about your cake dreams," he said.

I rolled my eyes and started talking.

WITHOUT FENRIS TO distract me with conversation, I dwelled on Ashlyn, Megan, Mom, and Adira for the rest of the day. Ashlyn was gone because of a spell I asked the druids to cast. If something bad happened to her, not only would it tear me apart, but it would make me wicked. Which would mean one stupid mistake could cost me two of my friends. Oh, I knew Megan wouldn't hold it against me, but her fury would.

Then I'd be on my own to deal with Mom and Adira. Well, not alone, exactly.

From the driver's seat of my car, I watched Fenris jog from the exit and wave at me. A moment later, he got in. I still wasn't sure how he'd talked me into letting him come with me to feed Elbner then look for the druids around town.

"Ready to dodge a few shoes?" he asked.

"If you stay in the car, Elbner probably won't throw any."

I could tell by Fenris's grin that he wasn't going to stay in the car.

"So I might have some good news," he said as I backed out of my spot. "I got a text from an unknown number. It's an address. Most likely a druid's address. Not sure if it'll be one of the three you're looking for, though."

"It's okay. Something is better than nothing."

"True. Now about those cakes. Which one is your favorite to eat?"

I rolled my eyes at his obsession with my cake dreams and

started discussing the pros and cons of each of the flavors I'd tasted in my dreams.

"It sounds like you're torn between the spice cake and the lava cake," he said.

"The Death by Chocolate is pretty tempting, too."

"You'll have to let me know if you start dreaming of other flavors."

I glanced at him, wondering why he cared.

He shrugged slightly.

"Maybe there's a relationship between what's going on in your life and what you're dreaming about."

I reached Megan's house before I could figure out how something that tasted as amazing as lava cake could possibly be related to the poo-show that was my current life.

Elbner was outside in all of his ornery glory when I pulled into the driveway. The vines that had been clinging to the front of the house were gone as was the loose paint. The goblin looked up from where he was filling cracks in the foundation with foam and watched me park by the back door. Megan had been smart to send him to her home. Not only was her house looking great, but I bet it would be warmer now too. However, as Elbner continued to scowl at my car, I wondered what she'd do with the little man when she returned. The goblin's personality was far from pleasant.

I warned Fenris to stay in the car then went inside to make Elbner his daily meal. When I reemerged, I saw Elbner standing next to the car, glaring through the window at Fenris, who was grinning like a madman.

"Is there anything else you need, Elbner?" I asked. "Paint? Cleaning supplies? A warmer coat?"

"No. Elbner needs nothing but the mongrel gone."

"All right. I'll get him out of here. See you tomorrow."

I got in and backed out of the driveway without making eye contact with the angry goblin.

"Did you have to grin at him like that?" I asked once we were on the road.

"Yep. He threw a shoe at me, and it bounced off the glass. It was hilarious."

I shook my head at Fenris and followed the road back into town. He directed me to the address, and we parked in front of a very standard looking ranch home.

"You can stay here," I said, reaching for the door. "This will only take a minute."

He followed me out of the car.

"Like I'm going to let you walk up to a strange house alone. You're not the only thrill-seeker in this relationship. They might have candy."

I snorted.

"I highly doubt whoever lives here is stupid enough to try luring anyone in with candy. We're the predators."

He flashed a toothy grin.

"It's cool hearing you say that."

I rolled my eyes and knocked on the door.

"I'm very aware of *what* I am," I said softly. "I'm just choosing to be *who* I am if that makes sense."

"It does to me."

The door opened, and a man a few years older than us stared at us.

"Can I help you?" he asked.

"I'm looking for Meg, Anne, and Lauv. Are any of them here?"

"Nope. Anne and her friends went out camping. Winter solstice and all that. I hated that shit when I was their age. It's fucking cold in a tent."

"I hear you," Fenris said.

"Do you know where they are?" I asked.

"Nope. But Anne has her phone. You can call her."

I gave him a sheepish look.

"I would, but I don't have her number." Suspicion crept into his gaze. "I swear she knows me. And I really need to talk to her."

"About what?"

I struggled to think of something quickly.

"Spell work," Fenris said. "The Academy kind. Maybe you could pass on a message to her?"

The man nodded and pulled out his phone.

"Sure."

"Tell her that Eliana needs help finding some missing spell ingredients. And I'm running out of time."

I didn't know what else to say without tipping my hand that something was wrong. So I gave him my number and just had him ask her to call me.

"Got it," he said. "I'm sure you'll hear from her soon."

"Thanks."

Walking away from the door, I noticed Fenris's unsmiling expression.

"You okay?" I asked.

"I wished you would have let me give him my phone number."

"Why? I'm the one who needs to talk to her."

"Yeah, but now some random guy has your number."

I laughed.

"I'm pretty sure he already forgot it.

Fenris shook his head. "I'm just as sure he's going to be messaging tomorrow to see if Anne got back to you. It'll be a conversation opener. Just wait and see."

"You're so wrong."

We both got into the car.

"Want to bet on it?"

"Sure. If he doesn't message me, I'm off the hook for hugs."

Fenris actually winced, then grinned.

"Okay. And if I'm right, the daily hugs double."

"Fine. It's a deal."

"Ready to get rid of your last lover boy before I have to help you with this new one?"

I gave Fenris a dirty look then headed for the marshes. While I knew Piepen's infatuation was due to his age and nature, I couldn't help but feel a little guilt over my part in it. Would Piepen be so obsessed if I hadn't accidentally fed from him?

Probably.

The marshes were quiet when we parked, but I wasn't fooled. Piepen was out there somewhere.

"You sure you want to say goodbye to all of this?" Fenris asked, gesturing to the reeds. "There could be a nice little home out there somewhere for you and the baby."

"Get out and help me like you promised."

He grinned and left the car with me. Neither of us said anything as we stood in the parking lot. Thankfully Piepen didn't leave us waiting long.

With a squeal that sounded like my name, the small brownie who'd marked me came flying out of the reeds. I barely had time to register that he was aimed to land right on my face before Fenris stepped between us.

I heard Piepen's outraged shout when he realized he was hugging the wrong person.

"No one stands between me and my woman," Piepen yelled.

"About that," Fenris said. "I think we need to have a man to man talk."

Piepen shot up over Fenris's shoulder and looked at me.

"Why did you bring him?" he demanded.

"Because I needed help," I said.

Fenris turned and held up a hand.

"Would you mind waiting in the car?" he asked.

I retreated into the lingering warmth of the vehicle and watched Fenris lead Piepen to the edge of the marsh. He spoke quietly for a while. Piepen stopped flying and perched on a cattail stalk, his wings dropping behind him as he looked down at his hands. Then his dejected gaze flew to Fenris's and his wings started to perk up again.

As I watched, more brownies appeared in the stalks. All males from the looks of them. All of them raptly listening to whatever Fenris was saying.

My curiosity got the better of me, and I rolled down the passenger window a crack.

"Desperation has its own scent. Females can detect it even if their sense of smell isn't evolved like mine. It turns them off in a big way. If you want to win a woman over, you have to get rid of the desperation."

"How?" Piepen asked.

"You're not going to like the answer," Fenris said.

"Tell me. I'll do whatever it takes."

"You need to win over another woman."

Piepen looked over at me. I could see the longing in his gaze and wanted to hide. When he turned back to Fenris, he looked determined.

"For Eliana, I'll do it. She's a goddess."

"Remember, you have to let a woman come to you, not the other way around. It won't be easy. It'll take a lot of time and a lot of patience."

"I understand." Piepen held out his tiny hand to Fenris. "Thank you for your advice."

Fenris shook his tiny hand then headed for the car, a slight smile tugging at his lips. When he got in, he rolled up his window and winked at me.

As I started the car, I glanced at Piepen, who was watching me. The little guy nodded in my direction then flew away.

"Did you just encourage him to keep harassing me?" I asked.

"He thinks that's what I did," Fenris said. "But what I really just convinced him to do is find another girl. He'll be married with a baby on the way before he figures out what happened."

I should have felt bad for Piepen, but my relief was too consuming.

"Thank you," I said. "For your help with Piepen and the druids. Do you want me to drop you off at your cabin?"

"Nah, the Roost is fine. I've been avoiding the girls too much, and they're complaining to my dad."

"You mean hugging me today won't be enough to keep him happy?"

"Hugging doesn't cut it in my world," he said.

"Right. The mate run."

"Yep."

He started tapping his leg, an indication we'd touched on an uncomfortable subject. I didn't know what else to talk about, though, so the rest of the ride passed in an awkward silence. When I pulled in front of the Roost, he immediately got out but then leaned down to look at me.

"Thanks for the ride and the distraction. See you tomorrow."

"Yep. Tomorrow."

He closed the door and walked into the Roost without a single comment or backward glance.

Worried, I sat there for a moment before starting home. Fenris didn't do silence, and he never forgot to flash his flirting smile and try to talk me into joining his herd at the Roost. Was his delayed mate run really bothering him that much? I felt bad for him and wished there was something I could do. Sighing, I added it to my list of things to try to fix.

Mom was waiting for me in the kitchen when I walked through the door.

"I was just about to call you," she said, standing.

"Did they find Ashlyn?"

"Not that I've heard. I'm sure she'll be fine."

My steps slowed as I noted her glittery, floor-length dress and short white fur coat.

"Are you going out?" I asked.

"Since we've rid ourselves of the useless pretext of partaking in human meals, I thought we'd go to the Roost. Back in my day, it was called the Fledgling. Dumb name. No one wanted to go there. Mrs. Quill said it's changed drastically since then and that everyone your age spends their spare time there. I'm eager to see that for myself."

"It's a teens-only place," I said. "Except for the staff."

"Don't you worry about that," she said with a wave. "I already cleared it with Adira and swore I wouldn't feed while out of the house. This is just for a look so I can see where Adira has you spending your time."

That she and Adira both were okay with this meant they were up to something. What, though? Probably to get me to feed. Everything revolved around that with them.

Mom watched me expectantly, and I smiled, already knowing this plan of theirs would backfire spectacularly.

"You know what? Sure. Let's go to the Roost so you can see the wild nightlife of the young and imprisoned. You'll love it."

I turned around and went to my car, opening the door for Mom.

She smiled and patted my cheek before getting in. I hurried to join her and got her talking about New York and all her amazing parties during the short drive. Her amazingly high-end parties.

"Here we are," I said, parking on the sidewalk almost a block away.

Mom leaned forward to look up at the neon sign in the distance.

"The sign's a little tacky, I know, but it gets better inside," I said.

She didn't say a word as she got out and followed me down the sidewalk.

"It's usually not this packed," I said. "Most of the time I can park by the door. There must be a decent crowd tonight."

When I parked by the door, it was because I normally arrived early enough to avoid the late crowd. I'd probably go to hell for the way I was bending the truth, but at the moment, I didn't care.

Music floated on the air and became blaringly loud once I opened the doors. Two sirens were on the stage already, singing for a crowd of maybe twenty, which included Fenris and his girls. None of the humans were here yet, so I headed for the back booth and slid in.

"Don't lean back against the seat," I said. "It might be a little grimy. They don't clean very well in here."

Despite her best efforts to hide it, Mom's horror was showing as her gaze swept the space.

"And if you have to go to the bathroom, check the bowl before you hover. I've had as much as I can stand with brownies," I said as if the two topics were related.

The horror in her eyes grew.

"Do you want something to drink?" I asked. "I can run upstairs to get it."

"Upstairs?"

"Yeah, you didn't see it when we came in? There's a staircase over there that leads up to the loft and the bar. There's not a lot of sitting room, but it's a great place to watch the dancers."

Her gaze drifted to the dance floor again.

"This is a crowd?"

I frowned, doing my best impersonation of confusion.

"Don't you like it?" I asked.

She made a sound of disgust. "It's no wonder you're starving. There's nothing here. This is no feeding ground for a creature of your distinction."

She got out of the booth and motioned for me to join her.

"That woman is a menace," she said. "This place is a complete waste of your time."

She started for the door, and I got up to follow her, more than a little satisfied I'd won this round.

A tingle of awareness raced over my neck before I reached the door, and I turned to see Fenris watching me.

With a smile, I waved and pushed the door open only to walk into the last person I wanted to face.

Eras.

CHAPTER NINETEEN

I jerked away from him even as his hands closed around my arms.

"No need to be testy," he said, maintaining his grip. "Is that your mom?"

I followed his gaze and saw Mom pacing toward the car. She had her phone to her ear and looked like she was arguing with someone. Probably Adira.

Eras gave me a little shake.

"When did she get into town? It wouldn't have been last week, would it? Say Thursday?" His grip hardened, bruising my skin, as he pulled me closer. "Did your bitch mom steal my food, Eliana?"

I laughed, a low sound that didn't seem to belong to me.

"Forget your lost meal, Eras. It's only the first of many in your pathetic lifetime."

His gaze went vacant, and his grip loosened. Jerking my arms free, I turned my back on him and headed for my mom.

"We've seen the results of your way. Now we try mine."

Mom's words made my stomach drop because I had no doubt

she was talking about me. She dropped the phone in her purse and watched my approach with a wide smile. My dread climbed higher.

"Good news," she said. "I'm already working on finding you a proper place to learn to feed."

"A what?"

"Don't worry. Not here. I know how you feel about feeding where you live, so I spoke to Adira about an outing."

"No."

"No?"

"It's not about where I feed. It's about who I feed on. I'm not feeding on some stranger."

"That's the whole point of going to the city for a while. You'll cultivate a circle and be able to make your own choices."

I opened my mouth to reiterate my refusal.

"Enough, Eliana. You're going. You need to see how it's really done."

THE FOLD in my sheet blocked the morning light from my eyes. I stared at the material, watching it move as I breathed without really seeing it. The remnants of dreams filled with cakes and forest couldn't dispel the feeling of complete destruction from last night's announcement and the determination in Mom's gaze.

It was going to happen. Exactly what I'd told her I didn't want to happen. She was going to take me somewhere that would shred my control. And, unable to resist, I would feed and turn into exactly what I hated. I could already visualize the number of people who would be lying limp on the floor at my feet.

Something inside of me had cracked last night when I'd realized that. Cracked in a bad way.

With everything that had happened in my life of hardships, I'd always had an ability to rise above and make the best of whatever I was handed. But that thing inside me wasn't right anymore. It was too broken this time. I was too broken. My mind still knew what I needed to do. Get out of bed. Shower. Go to school. I just had no will to carry through with any of it.

The door to my room opened. The whisper of footsteps and the soft rustle of material gave away who it was. Mom.

Her movement stopped, and I listened to the rasp of a window sliding closed before the mattress dipped and her hand smoothed back my hair.

"Morning, baby. Did you decide not to go to school today? It's past seven."

"There's no point to school," I said, impassively.

"I agree completely." She patted my shoulder. "You go ahead and rest. Tonight's going to be a big night for you."

She kissed my cheek then left the room.

How could I hate and love someone so much at the same time?

I lifted myself out of bed and threw some clothes on. Warm pants. A sweater. Then, I grabbed my overnight bag and packed an extra set of clothes. After using the bathroom, I left.

Mom didn't come out of her room. Based on the music, she was already having breakfast.

Mrs. Quill looked up from her coffee in the dining room as I proceeded to the kitchen.

"Are you going somewhere, Eliana?" she called, noting the bag.

I didn't answer.

The car was cold, and I shivered for the first few minutes as I drove out of town, trying to remember the turns. It took me a few tries to find the road that led to the hot springs cave. However, the drive out there didn't take nearly as long as wandering through the trees, looking for the crystalized snow. My feet were completely numb by the time I found the clearing. I stripped my outer layers of clothing and stuffed them in the bag.

Barefoot, I made my way inside the caves, sliding my hand against the cold, damp walls. The warm air enveloped me, but it didn't dispel the bone-deep chill from the walk. My teeth chattered, and my feet ached as I made my way deeper into the darkness.

Letting my memory guide me, I ignored the first pool and kept going until I found the pool Fenris and I had used previously. It took time to find the torch and even more to figure out how to light it. When the flames finally did light the space, I looked around at the oasis with a numb sort of detachment.

How could this nothingness inside of me still hurt so much?

Leaving my bag, I stripped from my shirt, ignoring the soft glow from the line on my stomach, and slid into the waiting pool.

The hot water soothed me, stripping away my emotional numbness to let the tears flow. It wasn't a pity party. It was a farewell to the remaining innocence I'd clung to far longer than most. That shred of virtue wasn't in the form of my virginity, though that added to it. It was my inexperience. The things I'd managed not to do so far. The things Mom would ensure I did tonight. Things that would save me in her mind but damn me in mine.

I didn't know how to come to terms with that, which is why I came to the hot springs. To see if there was some way to find peace with all of it. So I let the waters drain me of tears and whatever other emotions bubbled up. When I grew too warm, I left the pool and lay on the rocks.

That's how he found me.

I couldn't be sure how I knew he was there, standing in the shadows of the tunnels, but I turned my head and found him watching me. His sad brown gaze held mine.

"You worried me," he said, stepping forward and squatting down beside me.

I reached out and touched the jeans covering his knee. He didn't wear anything else, and I knew what that meant. He'd run here in his fur and put on the only clothes he had because he knew what I wanted. What I feared. And he respected it. And me. Why couldn't all the people in my life be as considerate as Fenris?

"Sorry I worried you," I said, letting my hand fall. "I just needed to get away."

"Your mom and Mrs. Quill called my dad to find you. They think you're trying to run off."

I snorted.

"Without my mark, I'm trapped in Uttira. Where do they think I could go?"

He shrugged.

"They lost Ashlyn, so I think they're afraid you found a way."

I thought of Ashlyn with a pang of regret and a pinch of hopelessness. The druids hadn't contacted me. Fenris's father obviously hadn't found anything, or Mom and Mrs. Quill wouldn't be so worried. Ashlyn's disappearance was another piece of my life where I had no control, and I hated that.

"I wish I could vanish like Ashlyn."

Fenris brushed some wet hair back from my face then scooped me into his arms, settling me comfortably on his lap. My hunger stirred, but I ignored it and leaned against his chest, accepting the embrace.

"They're making it really hard to not give up," I admitted. "I keep trying to come up with a silver lining, but I think I'm out.

Instead of focusing on finding Ashlyn, Mom and Adira are plotting my début trip to New York."

"Haven't you been there already?"

"Not to feed."

"Oh."

"Yeah. Oh." I sighed and lifted my hand, setting it on Fenris's chest, right over his heart. I could feel the steady pulse under my palm. What would it take to make his heart beat for me? With Fenris's resistance, it would probably be impossible. But with humans...

"I'll steal them all. The heart of every man and woman I come near. I'll feed. I'll be powerful. And I'll hate myself."

"Why?" he asked. "You are what you are. You're not bad. You can't choose how you eat."

"Can't I? I was doing fine before Mom got here. I know Adira didn't think so, but I was feeding and okay with it. Well, not okay with it, but I was managing. I just want Mom to go back to New York and things to go back to the way they were. But Mom and Adira both have it in their heads that I was dying. Starving." I lifted my head to look at him. "Do I look starving to you?"

Fenris's gaze held mine for a long, silent moment.

"You've never looked starving, but I don't see you with just my eyes, Eliana."

I stared at him for a moment as his words sunk in.

"What are you saying? That I am sick?"

He pulled me against his chest again and held me close, rubbing his hand up and down my arm like he was trying to give me all the comfort in the world. However, instead of feeling comforted, I was feeling terrified. I knew his answer before he spoke it.

"Yeah," he said. "You are sick. But I think you're getting better. And, without their help."

I thought of the reflections I'd glimpsed of myself in the mirror. Although the last version of me had still looked unwell, she'd appeared a little better. Barely. Was that the real me? The succubus me?

"You're stronger than they give you credit for," he added.

I pulled out of his arms and sat beside him, needing space to think. Or, rather, to try to comprehend this new view of my life. Was I really starving? And if so, why did my reflection seem better when I was eating less? I hadn't fed since stealing Eras's meal, and that was almost a week ago.

"If you thought I was sick, why didn't you tell me?"

"You weren't ready to hear it."

"I doubt anyone is ready to hear there's something wrong with them." I struggled not to be angry with him as my thoughts collided. How many times had I fought against Adira's insistence that I feed? Would I have taken her insistence more seriously if I'd known? Would I have done something differently? I doubted it. I didn't feel sick. Not then and not now.

"Why do I look fine if I'm starving?" I asked.

He shrugged slightly.

"That might be something to ask your mom when you go back."

I leaned my head against the stone wall and watched the steam move in the torchlight. He didn't say *if* I go back, but *when*, because we both knew there was nowhere else for me. Like I'd pointed out, I was trapped.

"What am I supposed to do?" I asked, more to myself than Fenris.

"If you don't want to go to New York, don't."

I snorted.

"Right. That'll fly."

"Have you told your mom what you told me? That you'll hate yourself once you feed like she does?"

I thought back to all of the conversations I'd had with my mom. While I'd strongly hinted at it, I didn't think I'd ever come out and said it as bluntly as I had with Fenris.

"I'm not sure," I admitted.

"Then don't wait for my dad to find you and drag you home. Face her on your own terms, and tell her what you really feel."

I turned my head to look at him.

"The fallout is going to be catastrophic," I said. "She'll take what I'm saying to mean that I would rather die than be like her."

"Isn't that what you're doing?" he asked softly. "Slowly dying because you're trying not to be like her? Maybe if she knows the problem, she can help find a solution. Talk to her. See if there's another way to feed."

"Fine."

We left the caves, but rather than going straight home, Fenris drove us to his cabin. My teeth chattered the whole way, part of the reason he'd insisted on driving and the cabin.

"Are you going to let me carry you?" he asked when we reached the end of the road.

"N-nope. You already h-had your daily affection. T-too much will go to your h-head."

"Doesn't count. I didn't hug you back," he said with a grin.

I rolled my eyes and got out of the car. We both knew that was a lie. He'd definitely hugged me. Maybe not at the same time I hugged him, but it didn't matter. I knew if I gave in now, it would become a game with him. For whatever reason, Fenris was a very touchy-feely kind of person.

He led the way to the cabin, glancing back at me constantly. I tried not to begrudge the steam rolling off his exposed torso. Or stare at all the muscled flesh on display. Thankfully, I had enough to distract me.

With my wet hair, I couldn't keep myself warm enough; and my teeth were clicking together with increasing force. I didn't lie and try to tell him I was fine. I was freezing and wanted to get inside quickly. However, I didn't give in and ask for help, either.

When the small building came into sight, Fenris jogged ahead. I entered a minute later to the crackle of a fire just getting started. Using my hip, I closed the door and shuffled to the chair.

"You never said. After the last time I was here, did anyone find this place?" I asked.

"Nope. It's still my secret hideout from the ladies," he said with a grin. "Well, the rest of the ladies. Do you want something to drink or eat?"

My hunger lifted its head, and I glanced away from him as he straightened.

"No, I'm fine. Thank you."

He sighed.

"We've already established the opposite. There's no need to be polite about it." He claimed the chair near mine. "Have you ever considered feeding from me?"

My eyes nearly popped from my head as I turned to look at him. He chuckled.

"The idea shouldn't be that shocking. It's not like I'm suggesting sex," he said. "You said I smell good, and we've proven that I don't turn into a Eugene junior when you hug me. What if I'm like Mrs. Quill, and you could feed from me without any issues?"

I was shaking my head before he finished.

"Oh, there would be issues, Fenris. Lots of issues. Your resistance to me is hypothetical, and I don't ever want to test it. It wouldn't be safe."

He studied me for a moment then looked at the flames.

"Fine. But if Mrs. Quill is immune, others could be as well. You should ask your mom that, too. I don't like the idea of you going hungry."

I reached over and patted his hand that was resting on the arm of his chair.

"Don't worry. It'll be fine. Once my hair dries, I'll talk to Mom like you suggested. If she reacts like I think she will, I'll be feeding on humans in New York tonight."

Saying it made me feel dead inside. I really hoped Fenris was right and Mom would listen.

"And if she accepts what you say, will you go back to feeding from Mrs. Quill?"

The immediate surge of resentment I felt at the idea worried me. Would I be able to go back to feeding that way? I wasn't so sure I'd be able to forgive her abandonment of me.

I walked into the house, struggling between my desire to turn around and leave again and my need to reclaim my life. Fenris's parting words helped bolster my courage and kept me moving forward.

"Go show them how strong you really are," he'd said. "And when you're done making them cry, I'm here for as many hugs as you need."

I pressed the intercom and listened to the click of it echo through the house.

"Mom, I'd like to speak to you in the kitchen, please."

Releasing the button, I claimed a seat at the island and waited. The location was strategic. She would need to come to me, not the other way around. And it was close to my car if I needed to take off again.

The thought had barely left me when the door to the garage opened.

"Hello, Eliana," Adira said.

I frowned at her.

"What were you doing in the garage?"

"Oh, last week, I noticed your paint had some heat damage. I haven't had a chance to address it. When I saw you come, I took the opportunity."

"You fixed it?"

"No, I transported the car to someone who can."

"You took my car?"

It didn't matter that I hadn't paid for it or that she'd been the one to give it to me. It was my car. My only means of escaping this house not on foot.

"Only for a few days. You won't even miss it."

I strove to find the words to adequately convey my hate of her manipulative nature. Before what I felt could spill forward, Mom walked in.

"Baby, you had us all worried," she said, coming to me and giving me a tight hug. She pulled back to look at me.

"You're shaking."

"Yeah. I'm angry." I pulled out of Mom's arms. "Adira took my car."

Mom glanced at Adira then back at me.

"She said it was damaged and that she wanted to fix it. I didn't think you'd mind since we plan to be out of town for a few days."

"A few days?"

I closed my eyes and took a calming breath. Losing my cool now wouldn't help me.

When I opened my eyes again, Mom was watching me with concern.

"Do I have any choice?" I asked. "At all? I'm given what to wear. Told how to behave. Now, I'm being forced to feed. Forced when you promised you would never force me."

"Sweetie, I'm not going to force you. I'm taking you to New York to show you how I feed in the real world. Feeding in Uttira is like fishing in a barrel. I can understand why you find it repulsive."

"No, you don't understand. I'm repulsed by what we do to the humans we feed from. Not during, but after. We ruin their lives, Mom. Erasing their memories doesn't make it better. Go watch any of your playthings from this past week and see what they're doing now.

"They'll be moving around like normal, but something will be off. And if you're brave enough to ask them, they'll tell you they don't know what's wrong. That they feel like they're missing something. Something important. Something big. Something life-changing. They'll be missing you, Mom. You. And you aren't even thinking of them. It doesn't go away. For the rest of their lives, they'll be craving you, unhappy in any relationship because it's not you. And they won't even understand why.

"I don't want to be a part of that. I don't want to make slaves of humans."

Mom gently squeezed my arms.

"Baby, it's not like that. We bring humans more pleasure than they can possibly achieve on their own. It's a magical experience. One they would give anything to repeat. Of course, they're going to miss that and want it back."

"Human addicts miss cocaine, too. That doesn't mean it's good for them."

She cupped my face.

"Baby, listen to me. We are not a drug. We are gifts waiting to be given to those who are worthy. I promise you'll see that in New York."

I stared at her as my anger and resentment shriveled into a ball of numb acceptance.

"Fine. Take me, then. Show me how to feed and watch my self-loathing deepen. I hate what I am, and I hate what you want me to do. And if it's a choice between hurting others or hurting myself, I'd rather starve."

I pulled from her hands and started to leave the kitchen.

"Where are you going?" Adira asked.

I turned back to look at her. She hadn't moved during my conversation with my mother.

"My room. Or am I not allowed that small freedom anymore?"

"Of course you are," Mom said. She looked at Adira. "Bring her car back or find her another one while hers is being repaired. She's not a prisoner."

I left them both, no longer caring about the car. Adira had proven her point. She controlled me. Mom might not see it yet, but she would eventually. And, it would probably be right after Adira had manipulated her into forcing me to feed.

Closing my door behind me, I paced my room and paused to look at myself in the mirror. If only Adira hadn't been the first one in the kitchen. Her presence and the removal of my car had doomed any chance of a rational exchange with my mom. One where I would have had the chance to ask about the odd reflections I'd glimpsed or ask if there were other races I could safely feed from.

The murmur of voices in the hall drew me to my door.

"Every time I listen to you, I get more push back from her. I'm done. Return the car or I will find it myself. I have nothing better to do with my evening than wander Uttira looking for it. Do we understand each other?"

"I understand you very well, Nicolette," Adira said. "Try not to forget that I'm the reason you're here."

The intercom clicked, and Mrs. Quill's voice rang out, asking Adira to come to the study immediately.

"Awful bitch," Mom muttered before her door closed.

I opened my door and debated which was more pressing. Speaking to my Mom alone or finding out what had Mrs. Quill calling for her sister in such a worried tone?

Mrs. Quill and my fear for Ashlyn won. I ran quietly down the hall and stopped by Mr. Quill's office door. At first, I couldn't make out what was being said. Then a voice, angry and female, came through clearly.

"Enough," Megan said sharply.

"We acknowledge that you were unable to sense his wickedness, but that doesn't absolve us of our obligation to determine what he is planning to do with all that life energy," Adira said.

"From now until the end of time, Oanen belongs to me," Megan said, her voice ringing with the full power of a fury. "Any task he chooses to perform on behalf of the Council, he does with me at his side. And since I have spent time with Zayn Sias and have found him to be completely without any trace of wickedness, I will not waste my time tracking him down. Casting spells with life energy is not against the laws of Mantirum or mankind. Your persistence in finding the druid seems unusually driven. I think, perhaps, I would like to question you about that as well as your insistence in naming Nicolette Barchim guilty of a crime she was proven not to have committed."

I grinned and pressed my cheek closer to the wood.

"We understand your warning," Adira said. "Congratulations on your ascension, Fury."

"Thanks, Adira. We'll see you soon."

"Soon?" Adira said, letting her panic show. "What do you mean?"

There was a pause then someone swore.

"We cannot afford to have her return," Mr. Quill said. "Not yet."

"No, you're right," Adira agreed. "Everything would be chaos if she returned now."

I smirked at the fear in Adira's voice. It was about time she realized she couldn't push everyone around.

"Is there any word from Raiden on the missing human, Ashlyn?" Mrs. Quill asked.

"Nothing," Adira said. "We have a choice to make. Employ a druid to attempt a locator spell or let the Fury start questioning people when she returns."

"You know what will happen if she goes out seeking the wicked here," Mr. Quill said. "Many of our young will die because of mistakes made in ignorance or plain stupidity."

"What do we do, then?" Mrs. Quill asked.

"If we can't find a way to stall her, we encourage Megan and Oanen to come here to visit you," Adira said.

"Here?"

"Nicolette won't be able to resist a newly mated pair. Hopefully, her hunger will keep them distracted long enough for us to find the missing girl and spare some innocent lives because I highly doubt whatever happened to Ashlyn was wicked enough for a trip to hell."

I hurried away from the door, retracing my steps while my mind raced. I'd wanted Megan back for so long that I'd never stopped to think what that might mean. Especially with Mom here and Ashlyn missing. Adira was right in that Mom would have a hard time resisting a new couple's lust. But more than that, what would a new fury think about a best friend who illegally hired underage druids?

In my room, I lay on my bed and wondered how I'd deal with this new problem. Outside, the light gradually faded.

A COOL BREEZE caressed my cheek a moment before lips pressed against my skin.

"My sweet girl," Mom said.

"Is it time to go already?" I said, forcing myself to sit up. "What do you want me to wear?"

She made a sound between upset and annoyed at my toneless questions.

"She really has broken your spirit, hasn't she?" Mom asked.

"Who?"

"Adira."

I shrugged.

"She doesn't ever work alone."

Mom took my hand in hers.

"We'll skip New York tonight and wait a few days until you're ready," she said.

"A few days won't change how I feel, Mom. I know how to feed, or are you forgetting the month I spent with you on our way here? Why do you think I wanted to stay here alone with the Quills so badly? I don't like your version of feeding. I was fine before you came here."

"You weren't fine, sweetie. You were dying."

"But I'm not anymore, right?"

"It's hard to say. Yes, you seem a little better, but for how long when you're refusing to eat?"

"I'm not refusing to eat. I am forbidden from eating my way."

"All right then. I propose we meet in the middle. You continue to feed your way, but you give me a chance to show you that my way isn't as evil as you think it is."

I thought of feeding off of Mrs. Quill and knew I couldn't go back to that. But Fenris had brought up a good point. There had to be others.

"Okay," I said.

She kissed my cheek and left me alone, feeling like I'd just made a deal with the devil.

CHAPTER TWENTY

The ringing of my phone interrupted my favorite dream. With a fair amount of longing, I watched my cakes disappear from existence before I opened my eyes.

Burrowing deeper under my covers, I stretched out a hand to snatch my phone and pull it into my warm cocoon with me.

"Hey, Megan," I answered sleepily after a glance at the number.

"Hey. Sorry I didn't call sooner. It's been crazy."

"I heard," I said with a smile. "You ruffled some feathers with your Oanen-is-mine speech."

"Good. They need to stop toying with people."

"Agreed."

"Good news, though. Oanen and I are heading back to Uttira today. Well, as soon as we find his car," she said.

I sat up in bed.

"Um, you might want to rethink that."

"What? Finding his car?"

"No. Coming back to Uttira." It hurt saying the words, but it was the only safe way I could think of for both of us. At least until Ashlyn was found.

"Don't you love me anymore?" Her playful words didn't completely hide the subtle hurt in her tone, and my heart ached for us both.

"Like crazy. And that's why I want you to go somewhere else for a while. Somewhere romantic and amazing where you and Oanen can do all the new couple things you're probably already doing. When you get it out of your system, you can come back."

She was quiet for a moment.

"Are you afraid of being around us?" she asked.

"Yes and no. I'd be fine with one of you at a time. But, wanting you to stay away has more to do with my mom. New couples are too tempting. You give off too much energy."

"You mean sexual energy."

"Yes. That. And with Mom being pregnant, I just don't want to worry about you."

"How long do we need to stay away?" she asked.

"Mom's due in five months, but I don't think it'll take that long for your new, um...attraction to wear off."

The phone changed hands, and Oanen spoke.

"Eliana, Megan needs to see you as much as you need to see her. We'll stay away for two weeks. Then we're coming home."

The phone was passed back to Megan, but I barely registered the rest of the conversation. All I could think of was that I had two weeks. Two weeks to get rid of Mom to protect Megan and Oanen from Mom feeding on them when they came home. Two weeks to find Ashlyn to ensure my best friend wouldn't send me to hell the moment she saw me.

While Megan's return would be dangerous for Megan and bad for me, the imminent threat of her arrival was the best thing that could happen for Ashlyn. Finding Ashlyn, with no help from the missing druids, would be impossible. I didn't have the nose to hunt her scent down or the magic to locate her. However, Adira would do everything within her power to find the missing girl quickly. Even hire a druid.

With Adira working on Ashlyn, I could focus on removing Mom. But how? My first attempt to banish her from Uttira had been a complete botch job, so much so that I wasn't about to try magic again. I saw only two possible remaining options. Well, only one really, because forcing her to leave through physical means would be as pointless an endeavor as using magic. That left appealing to her.

Lost in thought, I got out of bed, closed the window that was somehow open again, and quickly got ready for the day.

Even though talking to Mom had failed miserably yesterday, I needed to try again. Only this time, I would approach her from a different angle. She didn't want me to feel controlled, so perhaps proposing weekly check-ins would work.

Optimistic, I left my room to speak with her. However, her room was empty. As was the entertainment room.

Hoping she hadn't made good on her threat to walk around Uttira to find my car, I went downstairs. The clink of silverware drew me to the dining room.

Despite Mom's earlier assertion that we should drop the pretext of needing human food, she had a plate before her piled with pastries. She noticed me and smiled.

"You're just in time," she said. "Breakfast is almost ready."

I glanced at her plate.

"That's okay," I said. "I'm not really hungry for sweets." They were never as good as my dream sweets.

"Then it's a good thing I made you your favorite," my father said, emerging from the kitchen, carrying two plates laden with French toast.

I couldn't breathe for a moment.

He looked so different from the last time I saw him. Thinner. Dark circles under his eyes. Mostly he looked cleaned up, though. His brown hair was neatly combed, and his white button-up shirt was pressed and stain-free.

The shock of seeing my very human father in Uttira robbed me of any filter.

"Dad? What are you doing here?"

"He's here because I invited him," Mom said.

I turned on her.

"When?"

"Last night. Adira helped me bring him here once he agreed. I wanted you to see that I didn't ruin your father. That he's still who he was before I met him."

"Ruin me?" Dad said with a laugh. "Hardly. You gave me the world when you entered my life."

I didn't look at him. I stayed focused on my mom.

"I forgave you once; I won't forgive you again. Let him go."

"How can you be so selfish, Eliana?" Dad said, his hurt tone demanding my attention.

I met his watery gaze.

"I've waited years for all of us to be together again as a family. Years of fear, wondering if you were both safe. Wondering if you were fed and happy. Years of loneliness. And you want to return me to that?"

"Jason, calm yourself," Mom said. "You know why Eliana said what she did. And you're proving her right."

Dad took a deep, calming breath and set the plates on the table.

"Sit, Eliana," he said, taking his seat. "We can say grace and enjoy the first of many meals together."

I didn't sit; I got angry. Clutching the back of my chair, I faced Mom again.

"Look at him, Mom. Is that how he looked when you met him? Emaciated? Exhausted? Always on the verge of tears? If you want to lie to me, fine. But don't lie to yourself. You did that to him."

"He said he's been deeply involved in a project that caused him to forget meals and work long hours," Mom said.

"Just another reason I belong here," Dad said. "Recuperation. I hear you need the same, Eliana. We'll get well again together, baby girl."

Hearing the endearment broke my heart.

"I can't," I said. "I can't watch you break him again."

Mom gave me a sad look. "That's why he's here. To prove to you that he's not broken. He missed you, Eliana. And I know you missed him, too. Don't make me send him away yet."

I looked at Dad. His head was bowed, and his shoulders were shaking, but he wasn't pleading with me to let him stay. How could Mom not see how wrong this was?

"I gotta go to school."

I hurried from the room. I didn't even stop to consider my car might not be in the garage until I saw it sitting there. At least, Mom had done that one thing right.

I started the car, hit my steering wheel, then took a calming breath. It hurt deeply that she'd brought Dad here. More so that she'd contacted him, a hard boundary I'd set four years ago. She wouldn't have broken my trust lightly when it came to Dad. Doing so showed her level of concern for me, and it also made me realize I'd never be able to talk Mom into leaving, now.

Lost in my own thoughts, I didn't stop to look for the druids when I arrived at the Academy. I went straight to the first session and sat there, wondering what I was going to do.

If I asked Mom to send Dad home again, I knew she would. She'd made that clear. I also knew my dad might not survive it. No matter what his faith said about giving up on life, having to say goodbye to Mom again would push him over the edge.

What was I supposed to do, then? Pretend everything was okay?

The bell rang, and I went to second session. Instead of Ashlyn, Eugene was there.

"Hey, Eliana," he said.

"Hi."

"Do you know what's going on with Ashlyn? No one is telling us anything other than she's not well. Is she in a human hospital?"

Very aware that everyone in the room was listening, I shrugged as if I was as clueless as they were.

"I wish I knew."

He accepted my answer without question and started walking around to help the students with their homework. Eugene was crazy smart. In math and science, anyway. If he were world smart, he would have asked to leave Uttira the moment he arrived.

When the bell rang again, I hurried to third session, needing Fenris's advice about my dad, but he wasn't there. The class was once again back to normal. I wanted to flip one of the desks in my anger. Instead, I walked out and went to the pool.

A mermaid hissed at me, and I hissed back. She dived under in a splash and stayed at the bottom of the pool. The other fish-folk swam to the far side of the pool and gave me the peace I craved.

By the end of the day, I had no real answers. Magic had failed me where Mom was concerned. Adira and the Council obviously wanted her here to "fix" whatever was wrong with me. And talking to Mom seemed to make things worse.

I drove home with a heavy heart.

Maybe it would just be easier to give in and feed. What were a few sex slaves in exchange for my mark and freedom? The ability to get out of Uttira and never come back had a very strong appeal. I'd be free of Adira's meddling and wouldn't need to watch Dad suffer. I sighed, really liking the picture I was painting for myself.

When I walked into the kitchen, Mrs. Quill greeted me cautiously.

"How was school?"

"Messed up. Adira changed classes around again so I didn't bother going to most of them. There's no point anymore, right? It's feed and get my mark so I can leave this hell, or stay here and be tortured forever. Going to school isn't going to change the outcome."

"Eliana, I'm so sorry you feel that way."

I laughed.

"Are you?"

"I truly am."

I shook my head and started to head to my room.

"Wait. Take this with you. Your father needs to eat more. And, see if you can talk him into resting. He might listen to you."

I took the covered plate and headed upstairs.

The loud thumping music from Mom's room ensured that I wouldn't knock. It was bad enough when I saw what she did with strangers. There was no way I wanted to know what she and Dad were doing.

Closing myself in my room, I almost dropped the plate when I turned and saw Dad standing a few feet from me.

"Dad? What are you doing in here?"

"I'm giving your mother some space. She needs to eat." He glanced at the plate. "Is that for me?"

"Yeah."

I handed it over. He ripped the cover off, grabbed a sandwich, and took a huge bite.

"It's good to see you with an appetite," I said. When I'd still lived with him, it'd been hard to get him to eat consistently.

"I need to regain my strength for you and your mother. And I want to set a good example. Your mom says you're not eating like you should, either."

A faint moan penetrated my room, and he looked at the door.

"She'll come for me soon," he said absently before taking another large bite.

"What kind of sandwich are you eating, Dad?"

He looked startled by the question and looked down at what he held.

"I'm not sure."

"What does it taste like?" I asked.

He paused, considering the sandwich.

"Nothing."

"When was the last time food tasted like food?"

He looked at me, his gaze sharpening.

"Before you were born."

"No. Before you met Mom. What does that tell you? She's consumed your life, Dad, and left you nothing. Do you know what else does that? Drugs. Addictions. You know she's not good for you. You need to leave."

"You're wrong. I'm not addicted to her; I'm trying to help her. Your mother has a sex addiction. She's sick and needs our help. We can sneak her out of this place tonight and take her somewhere quiet. Somewhere she won't be tempted by other people."

"Somewhere she'll be tempted by only you?"

"Exactly. We're married, so physical relations with me are okay."

I shook my head, pitying him.

"I wish I could help you, Dad. But I can't even help myself lately. Want to watch a movie with me? The entertainment room is closer to Mom's room."

He quickly agreed, and I spent the next two hours with him, holding his hand like I used to do on the really bad nights. The nights where he cried himself to sleep.

That's how Mom found us.

"Darlings," she said, sweeping into the room. "You better go change for dinner. We'll be late."

Dad stood and took Mom's hand, turning her so he could see her dress. It was a long, tight-fitting number and showed her chest almost to the nipples.

"You look ravishing, my love," he said. "Are you hungry?"

He pulled her into his arms and kissed her neck.

"I'm here for whatever you need," he added.

I quickly fled the room.

Choosing a dress that wouldn't embarrass my father, if he even looked away from my mom long enough to notice, I changed for dinner. I didn't immediately leave, though. I stared at myself in the knee-length A-line dress, seeing the image of the innocent girl I'd tried so hard to hold onto. However, I knew what lurked underneath the harmless wrapping. A monster, just waiting to be born.

My vision flickered, superimposing Dad's fatigued, gaunt look over my features.

Afraid of what I saw, I turned away from the mirror and left my room.

Mom and Dad were already gone from the entertainment space, so I started down the hall, taking my time because I was dreading the meal to come. Now that I knew why Dad was here, I knew what to expect. Mom would try to show me that he was normal and feeding from humans was all peaches and cream. Meanwhile, Dad's delusions would grow stronger.

Male laughter echoed up the stairs. I couldn't tell if it was Mr. Quill or Dad.

Resigned to a long night, I entered the dining room then stopped short. Mr. and Mrs. Quill were at each end of the table. Adira, Mom, and Dad were at one side, and only one of the spots on my side was unoccupied.

Two boys I'd never seen before were sitting on each side of my chair. I noticed they were my age and identically cute as they turned to look at me.

I glanced at Mom then Adira.

"Eliana," Mrs. Quill said. "Allow me to introduce Nico and Nikhil Elestite. They're family from the Mantirum stronghold in Arizona."

"Hey, Eliana," they said at the same time.

The one to the right stood and pulled out my chair for me.

"I'm Nico. That's Nikhil."

"Thanks."

I took my seat and glanced at my dad. His gaze met mine, and I saw a flicker of fear there. For me. For my soul.

As much as Dad tried to deny that Mom was something other than a sex-addicted human, I knew he understood there was more to her. Why else would he wait in my room and say mom was eating when any normal human would say she was having sex? Why else had his sermons consisted of the temptations of the flesh and the devils walking among us? Yes, deep down, he knew what she was, and he knew I was her daughter.

Mom leaned over to whisper something in his ear. His expression changed to one of love and longing.

"This is our first time to Uttira," Nikhil said. "We were glad to receive the invitation. It gets a little boring in Knoxres."

I recognized the name of the Mantirum stronghold in Arizona.

"I'd love a little boring right about now," I said.

Mom kicked me under the table, and I looked up at her, my eyes going black.

"Don't push me, Mother."

She tilted her head, studying me.

"You look like you could use some air," she said.

"I'll escort you," Nico said, already standing.

"Me, too." Nikhil offered his hand and a sheepish smile. "We've never seen snow."

It wasn't their fault they were baited into coming here. I wondered if they knew their intended purpose, though.

"There's a pretty garden off the back of the house. I'll show you," I said, choosing to stand without his offer of help.

The twins followed me through the house, not saying anything. When we reached the door, I opened it and led the way to the snow-covered bench near the back of the garden.

"This is beautiful," Nico said, looking up at the stars in the clear sky. "Our parents said our homeland is like this. Snow all the time. That's why they chose Knoxres. They want the warmth."

He blew a few experimental breaths and grinned at the clouds he created. Nikhil studied all the snow then turned to me expectantly.

"You know why you're here," I said.

"Yeah. Adira told us you're a picky eater. Frost giants only.

We've been around succubi before, but none that ever showed any interest in feeding from us." He shrugged slightly. "We were curious."

"Curious about what?"

"What it would be like, of course."

His bright blue gaze held mine, and I could smell a hint of his and his twin's lust. While they might be fine with their purpose, I wasn't. All the anger and frustration that I'd suppressed at just about every adult in my life surged forward.

"It feels like this," I said. "Get on your knees."

They dropped to their knees before me, their eyes going wide.

"Give me all that you desire. Surrender everything that you are and become mine."

I opened my mouth and pulled. They resisted. I stepped forward and ran a finger along Nico's cheek.

"So handsome. So young. Why resist me?"

He groaned, and his lust flooded the air. I didn't take that, though, I took all his non-sexual energy until a cold blast of air knocked me onto my butt.

I didn't try to get up. Instead, I stared up at the stars and listened to the sound of their feet as they ran away. I could have done things differently. I could have fed from their lust and proved myself to Mom and Adira without fear of creating lovesick fools like my father. Why hadn't I? Would it be so awful to be completely obedient? To make everyone happy? Everyone but me?

Sitting up, I hugged my knees and continued to watch the stars.

It didn't take long for Mom to find me. She sat on the nearby bench and said nothing for several long minutes.

"Adira thinks you're being difficult just to be difficult. How can a woman who's spent years with you know you so little?"

I looked at Mom.

"And you know me better?"

"I think I do. You sent those boys running on purpose because you're feeling cornered, not because you're stubborn." She sighed. "None of us like feeling cornered, Eliana. I would have struck out, too."

"Isn't that why Dad's here?"

"No, baby. Never. He's not a punishment. He's the reason you are the way you are."

"No, Mom, you are. He's human and simple. Give him food and water and shelter, and he'll be fine. Well, he would have been before you fed from him. Now he doesn't even think of the things he needs to live because all he thinks he needs is you.

"I don't even know who I am. How can I be the center of anyone's existence?"

She studied me a moment then looked up at the stars.

"You're a deeper person than I am. I don't always understand you, but it will never diminish my love of you. Nico and Nikhil didn't work out. It's not the end of the world. We'll try again. And next time, it won't be a surprise or forced on you. We'll plan together."

I stood and brushed off the snow.

"I don't want random food, Mom. I want forever. Something I can't have without ruining whomever I choose. My life isn't a blessing; it's a cursed existence with a string of regrets waiting to happen. You want to help me? Please, just leave me to whatever fate I find on my own."

"I can't do that, baby, because you've made it very clear what you would choose."

I walked away from her, taking the path to the outer edges of the garden where it was the quietest. There, I let a few frustrated tears fall.

"It's a little cold out here for that," Fenris said from nearby.

"Nothing is working, Fenris. They won't listen."

I turned and saw he already had his arms open. This time, he wasn't asking for payment; he was offering comfort. I threw myself at him, wrapping my arms around his waist and letting the tears free. He made soothing sounds and smoothed his hand over my hair. I didn't know how long we stayed like that.

It wasn't until the tears finally dried up that I realized how dangerous breaking down like that could have been for him. But as he continued to run his hand over my hair and rested his chin on the top of my head, I knew nothing bad had happened. So, I stayed as I was and didn't let go.

"Want to tell me what happened?" he asked softly.

"Adira brought family over for dinner. My dinner. Two frost giant twins named Nico and Nikhil. I got so mad." I shook my head into his bare chest. "I shouldn't have taken it out on them. I think I scared them."

"You?" Fenris asked with a slight laugh to his voice. "All five feet and one hundred pounds of you?"

I lifted my head to scowl at him. "I'm five four and weigh more than that."

He gave me an appraising look then shook his head.

"Nope. Doesn't matter. Still doesn't make you scary."

I sighed and set my head back on his chest.

"Am I being stupid and stubborn, Fenris? Should I just do what they want and feed on someone?"

"Could you?" he asked. "If I offered myself to you right now, could you feed from me without hating yourself for it?"

"No."

"Then you're not being stubborn. You just have some issues to work through." His hand smoothed over my back, pressing me a little more firmly against his heat. "And you will work through them. I have faith in you."

"Thanks," I said, giving him a slight squeeze before reluctantly pulling away from him. "Things were way less complicated before my mom got here. I know she loves me, but gods, I wish she would just leave. I can't deal with her and Adira at the same time.

"Do you know what my mom did?"

"No. What?"

"She brought my very human and very sick Dad here to prove to me that feeding from a human doesn't hurt the human. You should see him, Fenris. She thinks I'm sick even though I look fine on the outside, but when she looks at Dad, she doesn't even see the hollow cheeks or the dull look in his eyes when her attention isn't on him." I shook my head. "It breaks my heart, seeing him like that. Why can't she understand?"

"I think she does but that she's so desperate she's willing to do whatever is necessary to help you. Even if the choices she's making now will make you angry later."

I sighed and shivered slightly, wishing I'd picked a dress with a longer skirt.

"You ready to go inside?" he asked.

"Not just yet. It'll be a while before the dinner party breaks up."

Fenris walked with me to the nearest bench, and we sat to watch the stars. My legs grew cold then numb, but I didn't say anything. I didn't want to go back inside and see either of those boys, or worse, hear my mom with my dad.

Instead, I leaned against Fenris. He wrapped an arm around my shoulders, sharing his heat. I'd never been more grateful for his quiet company and friendship. Where I'd once seen him as a hopeless flirt, I'd learned he was so much more. He had a vast depth and capacity for understanding.

Closing my eyes, I exhaled slowly and told myself tomorrow would be better. After all, it couldn't possibly get any worse.

THE DELICIOUSLY WARM air wrapped around me as I walked through the barren trees. My dress rode up awkwardly with each step. I frowned, looking down at it. The A-line, short skirt tickled a memory of me sitting with Fenris on a bench in the Quills' snow-covered garden.

The scent of cakes filled my nose and distracted me. Inhaling deeply, I looked at the trees once more. I loved this part of the dream. The anticipation of finding food and eating until I was bloated with no fear of consequence.

"Take what you need."

The words echoed around me a moment before the cakes appeared. The perfectly small circles, no more than four inches wide and equally as high, were covered in dark chocolate shavings. With my mouth watering, I grabbed the nearest one, and I started to eat. I laughed as I danced through the woods filled with my current favorite cake, Death by Chocolate.

"I will always be here for you."

I loved this place, this forest, and wished it wasn't a dream. I never wanted to leave it. I grabbed another cake and stuffed it in my mouth. Then another. The cakes were still warm. Hot even. They warmed my hands and my middle. I started to sweat but didn't stop eating.

The trees squeezed in closer around me.

My inner thighs warmed.

Something was wrong.

I dropped my cake.

"Don't stop."

I backed up a step, turning a slow circle, wishing for the first time ever to escape the cake dream. The trees shook, then the cakes and the forest faded. But the heat didn't. It radiated over me, warming my front, especially my legs. Why my legs?

Disoriented, I opened my eyes and blinked up at Fenris. It took a second for things to click into place: the sight of my bedroom ceiling above him, the way my skirt had ridden up to my waist, how he was braced on his arms to keep his weight from crushing me, the way my bare legs were around his jean-clad hips under the covers, locking him in place.

What had I done?

Before panic could fully take hold, my bedroom door opened.

"Eliana, I had an idea about how—oh!"

I couldn't tear my gaze from Fenris as he winked at me. His eyes weren't clouded with obsessive lust but clear and full of humor.

"Eliana, baby," my mom said. "Why didn't you telling me you were feeding from the wolf boy? This is perfect."

Perfect? In no world was this perfect.

Fenris grinned down at me and wriggled his eyebrows, saying nothing. I wanted to kill him.

"Mom, leave now."

"Of course. You need your privacy and your mother out of your hair. I'm going. Your dad and I will stay somewhere else in town so you can be as loud as you want. Call me tomorrow when you wake up."

The door closed. I didn't move. I couldn't.

"You did this on purpose," I whispered.

"Yep. And now your problems are solved," Fenris said. "Because your mom thinks you're feeding from me, she and Adira will leave you alone. Plus, your mom is moving out. You're welcome."

His smile never wavered, and the future repercussions of his actions grew in my mind.

"Fenris, what have you done?"

THANK you for reading The Howl, the first book in the By Kiss and Claw series. The series continues with The Hunt. Coming soon!

Just how much do you love Fenris?! Have you caught on that his easy-going smile is just a mask for everything going on under that playful exterior? I cannot wait to explore all the feels he'll finally be able to share with Eliana in book 2. Once she's ready, of course.

It was crazy hard to balance their push and pull because she was pushing so hard. The poor girl just wasn't ready for him at the start. How could she be when she's so afraid of herself and what she might do to the people she cares about? Hopefully her complete refusal was making more sense to everyone as the story went on.

And just how loving was her mom, huh? Breakfast in bed, presents, a free pass to skip school any time she wanted. It's everything a teen wishes their mom would do. Yeah, not so much! Ha! It was fun putting myself in a creature's head from a maternal standpoint. I wanted to make her so loving by their standards while showing how "alien" she was to the human standards, which is what Eliana grew up learning. Talk about cultural conflict!

Speaking of conflict...Piepen. There were so many times I interrupted my sprinting crew (authors I Skype with who keep me accountable and working) because of my spontaneous laughing. I'd have to stop and explain what I was doing and completely sidetrack all of us. But it was so worth it. I love Piepen and cannot wait to come up with new ways for him to torture...er, I mean love...Eliana.

Book 2, The Hunt, is going to be a ton of fun! While Eliana may have gotten her wish to have her Mom gone and Adira off her back, her troubles are just getting started.

If you want to hear more about The Hunt, be sure to sign up for my newsletter at melissahaag.com/subscribe.

Happy reading!

**Judgement of the Six Series
(and Companion Books) in order:**
Hope(less)
*Clay's Hope**
(Mis)fortune
*Emmitt's Treasure**
(Un)wise
*Luke's Dream**
(Un)bidden
*Thomas' Treasure**
(Dis)content
*Carlos' Peace**
*(Sur)real***

**optional companion book*

***written in dual point of view*

Of Fates and Furies Series
Fury Frayed

Fury Focused
Fury Freed

Other Titles
Touch
Moved
Warwolf
Nephilim

www.ingramcontent.com/pod-product-compliance
Lightning Source LLC
Chambersburg PA
CBHW030400200726
48286CB00015B/1812